Torque
911 t

911
SCREWDRIVER
An imprint of Torquere Press Publishers
PO Box 2545
Round Rock, TX 78680
Copyright © 2005, Chris Owen
Cover illustration by SA Clements
Published with permission
ISBN: 1-934166-52-9, 978-1-934166-52-9
www.torquerepress.com

Part One
Chapter One

It wasn't that Drew hated hospitals; in fact, he rather liked them. They were busy and bustling, and he spent enough time in them that he understood all the bodies and noises were part of a large, organized mass of effort to make people healthy.

He just wasn't fond of spending time in them as a patient.

He looked around the triage area, not even able to see Dave as a curtain had them separated from each other. "Hey," he said in a voice slightly louder than conversational level.

"Hey, yourself," he got back, Dave sounding surly.

"How much longer, do you think?" Drew asked, knowing full well that Dave wouldn't have any more idea than he did.

"Dunno. The doctor said they just wanted to keep an eye on us for a bit."

Drew sighed and Dave fell silent behind the curtain. That was the rub of it—there wasn't even anything wrong with them. They'd just been in the wrong place at the wrong time, depending on how one looked at it. Drew was looking at it from the perspective of a fireman just doing his job, clearing a warehouse that had gone up in flames, and suddenly being confronted with large barrels with a hazardous material sign on them.

They hadn't known the barrels were there, nor what was in them. They'd evacuated, the chief had gone ballistic on the owners for improperly storing God knows what, and the whole team had been trooped down the hospital to get checked out.

"They didn't even blow," Drew said for the fourth time in three hours.

"Yeah, yeah. And we'll be let go as soon as the doctors confirm we're fine."

Drew snorted. He was fine, and if he wasn't, sitting in an open triage unit wasn't going to help any. "What do you think of that Dr. Campbell?" he asked. "Kind of young, yeah?"

Dave growled. "I'm sure he knows exactly what he's doing. And he's probably your age—not exactly a spring chicken."

"Hey," Drew protested. "I'm not even thirty yet, old man."

"Forty ain't old, and shut up. The doctor is fine. We're fine. And any minute now, that kid of a doctor is going to show up and tell us we can leave."

Drew grumbled a minute or two and let silence reign again. Dave was pissy. Drew was pissy. He thought about Dr. Campbell for a couple of minutes, and aside from deciding the man was really cute, he couldn't come up with anything else. "Call Vicky Lynn?" he asked finally.

"Yeah, soon as they let me have a phone. She's not real happy. Worried, you know?"

"Of course." He didn't have a phone. The fact that he hadn't asked for one didn't really make a difference in his mind. Damn hospitals. He sighed again.

"Will you stop that?" Dave said irritably. "Sound like a dying cow."

"Oh, shut up," Drew said mildly.

"This keeping you from something?" Dave went on, poking at him. "Big date?"

"Right, I always schedule my big dates for two in the afternoon. Easier to get reservations that way."

The curtain was pulled back suddenly revealing the doctor, standing between the two beds, clipboard in hand. "Not a bad plan," the doctor said with a smile. "Have to date someone who works shifts, though."

Drew winked. "That's the only kind of people I know, Doc."

"Shut up and let the man talk, Smyth." Dave glared at him before turning pathetically hopeful eyes on the young doctor. "We sprung?"

"Well, yes and no."

Dave and Drew both groaned.

The doctor held up his hand in what Drew assumed was supposed to be a placating manner. "Now, now. Protocol, gentlemen. I've talked to your chief. The barrels have been confirmed to be empty, and you both check out as fine for that, obviously. We did the standard oxygen tests, too, just because you'd been in a smoke-filled environment, and all is well there, too." He pointed to Dave. "You can go as soon as you get your boots on."

Dave beamed. "Thanks, see ya, and I'm outta here," he said, swinging his legs over the side of the bed. He paused. "What about Drew?"

"Ah, that's the other thing."

Dave looked at him with worried eyes and Drew groaned. He was going to wind up with Vicky Lynn at his house mothering him, he just knew it.

Dr. Campbell shook his head. "Nothing dire; the lab's just taking longer with your blood work. As soon as they call up, you'll be free to go."

Drew rolled his eyes, but Dave looked relieved. "Aw, you care," Drew said with a grin. "Say hi to Vicky Lynn for me."

"Will." Dave pulled on his boots and grabbed his coat. "See you tomorrow, Drew."

"Later, man."

He watched Dave practically run out of the triage area and shook his head. "His wife is going to be pretty happy to have him home," he said to the doctor, just to keep the man there for a couple more minutes.

He was really cute.

Dr. Campbell smiled at him, nodding. "I bet." He glanced around, still holding onto his clipboard, and added, "Do you need to call anyone? Tell your hot date you're still here?" His eyes were teasing, and the smile had become something closer to a grin.

Drew grinned back and shook his head. "No one like that to call," he said, meeting the doctor's eyes. Testing the waters.

But the doctor just nodded and took a step back. "Okay, then. I'll let you know as soon as I hear from the lab."

Drew gave himself a mental whap on the head and nodded back. "Sure thing, Doc."

Dr. Campbell left, and Drew sighed. He really didn't like hospitals all that much. He looked around him and counted the various boxes of things he could see, then he counted the IV stands along the wall by the nurse's station. He looked up at the ceiling tiles and then over at Dave's empty bed.

"Ah, shit," he groaned, catching sight of his coat and shoes. One of the guys had brought his stuff by and taken his equipment back to the station, but he was stuck without his car and, with Dave gone, without a ride home. He closed his eyes and leaned back on his plastic covered pillow, feeling altogether annoyed with the world.

"You okay?" a voice asked, and cool fingers took his wrist, seeking his pulse.

"Yeah, I'm fine," he said, opening his eyes to look at Dr. Campbell again. He didn't take his hand back, choosing instead to just let the man touch him. "I'm pathetic," he said to himself, watching the doctor feel up his wrist.

"Oh, I wouldn't say that," the doctor disagreed, looking at his watch. "You're fine."

Drew smirked and turned it into a grin before the doctor could see. "No, I'm without a way home, is all. Guess I'll have to walk— or find a cab, I suppose." He pulled a face, knowing how hard that would be.

"Yeah?" The doctor gave him a glance and then let go of his wrist. "Where do you live?" he asked, picking up Drew's chart again. "Oh, that's not far. What, about a five-minute drive from here?"

Drew nodded. "Yeah. The walk'll do me good."

"Well, it won't kill you, anyway. But I can give you a lift, if you want. The lab called and my shift is done. Just have to do about five minutes of paperwork—the rest can wait until I get back." Dr. Campbell gave him a quick smile. "It's no trouble."

"Yeah?" Drew hoped he didn't look as surprised as he felt. "That would be great, thanks."

"No trouble," Dr. Campbell repeated. "Get your stuff together; I'll be back in a few."

Drew watched the doctor walking away and shook his head, smiling as he reached for his shoes. He figured it was just a strange day all around.

***

"This is it," Drew said, pointing to his house. "Thanks, Doc."

"Scott."

Drew grinned, waiting until the man had pulled into his driveway before offering his hand. "Drew. Thanks, Scott."

Scott just smiled at him, putting the car in park.

"Want to come in?" Drew asked on impulse. "Think there's some beer."

Scott blinked and then said, "Sure, that'd be nice. Thanks."

Drew smiled and opened his door. "Come on, then." He led the way to the side door in the garage, letting them into the kitchen. "Hey, it's not even a mess, yay me."

Scott laughed, taking off his shoes. "It's nice," he said, looking around the kitchen.

"It's a good house," Drew agreed, tossing his jacket over a chair and going to the fridge. "Let me show you around," he said, passing Scott a beer. He took the man through to the living room, toeing a magazine under the couch. "I bought it a couple of years ago, and it's worked out well. Close to the station, nice quiet neighborhood. Just three bedrooms, but I don't need more than that—no dining room or second family room or anything like that. Just a nice little bungalow, you know?"

"It's great," Scott said. "Are all three bedrooms upstairs?"

"Yep. Come see," Drew invited, walking down the hall. "This one is storage," he said, pushing open a door on his right. "The next one is... well, storage as well. My room's on the left, and the bathroom's at the end. Nice and neat, no muss, no fuss. I was going to rip out all the crap carpeting this spring, but property taxes went up, so instead I get to find a roommate just to cover it."

"You live alone?" Scott seemed impressed as they walked back to the kitchen. "Oh, backyard, too. Wow, that's nice. Like the flowers."

Drew pulled a face. "The flowers are my mom's doing. At least it's just wild flower seed, and easy to maintain. No freaking if a weed winds up in the roses or anything."

"It looks nice," Scott said again. He leaned on the counter and looked around the kitchen, licking his lower lip before he lifted his beer bottle and took a drink. "Um. You serious about needing a roommate?"

Drew gave the doctor a long look. "Yeah. Hadn't really started looking, figured it would be pretty easy—just let the word out at work. Between the firefighters and the EMTs there's a lot of people working shifts, and that's important. Need someone who gets that I sleep at weird hours."

Scott nodded and put his bottle down. "Well, I'm doing my residency. Means long hours at the hospital and lots of studying when I'm home. Right now, I'm going to my parents to sleep and shower, but it's a ways to drive, and it's... well, it's living with my parents. I'm interested."

Drew grinned. "Sounds okay to me. So long as you don't bring every girl you date home or have wild parties."

Scott snorted. "No time for parties, and the girl thing is a non-issue."

"Me, too."

They looked at each other carefully for a long moment and Drew just waited, not sure if they were going to spell it out or not.

"I'm not out at work," Scott finally said.

Drew nodded. "I don't hide it, but I'd be surprised if more than a handful have it figured out. Seeing anyone?"

Scott shook his head. "You?"

"Nope. Still interesting in moving in?" It could change things, both of them single. Drew was willing to admit that he was attracted to Scott, and that could make things weird.

Scott thought about it for a minute. "Yeah. I am."

"All right then." Drew pulled out a chair and sat down. "Let's talk about it, then. Figure out the utilities and stuff and find out what I want for rent." He grinned. "I really hadn't put much thought into this."

Scott came to the table and sat down, grinning as well. "We'll sort it."

Chapter Two

As it worked out, Drew was working at the station when Scott moved in the next weekend. He got home and found the larger of the two spare rooms full of boxes and Scott struggling with the frame of his bed.

"Give you a hand?" Drew offered from the doorway.

Scott looked up at him from the floor and blew hair out of his eyes. Drew thought he looked adorable.

"Yeah, thanks. If you can get past the wall of books."

Drew shifted a couple of the heavy boxes and made his way to the other side of the bed frame, almost knocking the mattress down from where it was leaning on the wall. "All of this is books?" he asked, not quite believing it. It looked like Scott could open his own library.

Scott nodded and handed him a screwdriver. "Yeah, mostly. Was a bitch to get them all packed and moved. Heavy as fuck."

Drew stared at the multitude of boxes. "Shit. You must've really wanted to leave your parents to do this in a day. How the hell did you manage by yourself? Would have helped at least get them in the house."

Scott smiled at him and ducked his head. Yeah. Adorable.

"I did. Let's get this thing set up, yeah? I'd rather sleep on it than the boxes."

Drew grinned at him and they set to work. It only took a few minutes to get the bed set up and Scott started poking through random boxes. "One of these has sheets in it. Actually, one has sheets and towels, one has crap, and the rest are books."

Drew shifted boxes until he found one that wasn't heavy. "Here's one," he said, and Scott handed him the box cutter before shifting more boxes.

Drew cut the box open and peered inside. "Uh. Not the right one, though."

Scott glanced up and looked at him before leaning over to see inside the box. He blushed scarlet and said, "Oops. Right. Not that one." He closed the box and moved it to the closet, still blushing furiously.

Drew tried really hard not to laugh. Not that there was anything inherently funny about a box full of CDs, envelopes of photos, a couple of candles, and a shit load of lube, but Scott was really blushing, and that was funny. Mind you, Drew wasn't sure he'd seen that much lube in one place outside of a drugstore.

Drew was still grinning when he found another light box. He glanced at Scott and said, "You wanna open this one? I promise not to look." He finally laughed as the fading blush came back as strong as ever.

Scott took the box and ripped it open. "There. Sheets. Oh, shut up. Like you've never seen lube before." He was trying not to laugh as well, his eyes bright.

"Not that much, man. You planning a big weekend?" Drew laughed harder as Scott glared at him and finally gave in and laughed as well.

"We'll just have to see." Scott said as he turned away and started making the bed. Drew was just as glad, seeing as how he was pretty sure that his rather sudden hard-on was a little obvious as a testing-the-waters-flirt. He excused himself as gracefully as he could and made his way to the bathroom. Jerking off in the shower was always a fairly discreet way to get calm.

***

By the end of the first week Drew was hopelessly confused. Scott seemed to be interested in him, but he wouldn't say or do anything that left an opening of any kind for a slow come on. Drew figured he could play it two ways—either just walk up and kiss him or do something equally impossible to misread, or play it by ear and see what was what.

Drew decided to go with the slow and easy approach. If they weren't sharing a house he would have been more direct, but if Scott wasn't interested in anything more than a mild flirtation, trying to jump the man would make home life less than pleasant. Drew liked things to be pleasant.

So he waited. They watched TV and movies when they were both home and Scott didn't have his nose in a book, and talked about important things like which brand of beer to buy and whose turn it was to get laundry detergent. They laughed at the same stuff, and didn't talk at all when one of them came home with the stink of their jobs wrapped around them. It wasn't often; Scott worked too much for them to spend a great deal of time together, but Drew liked what he knew. Liked it a hell of a lot.

After a couple of mix-ups about who would be home to take care of getting the garbage out or mow the lawn, they put a big whiteboard calendar up in the kitchen. Drew wrote his schedule in and handed the marker to Scott. After Scott had filled in a week's worth of times when he was going to be at the hospital they wiped it off and he wrote in when he was going to be home. Took up a lot less space.

"How long do you have to work those hours? Christ."

Scott shrugged. "Another three years of residency. If I don't die from overwork first."

Drew just shook his head and put his shifts back on the board.

At some point during the fourth week, Drew decided that Scott was checking him out, for real. He was looking at Drew with frank appreciation when they were together for any length of time, and he was pretty sure that one man didn't need to shower that often, even if he did work at a hospital. So Drew started being more open about his own looking, letting Scott catch him watching when Scott bent to pick up books or when he walked around in his faded jeans and a worn Dalhousie med school sweatshirt.

They took to sleeping with their doors open. Drew didn't know why, other than it was a silent invitation that neither of them took up.

Scott's hours meant that he often slept at odd times and Drew began to checking the chart in the kitchen as soon as he came home to see how quiet he had to be. He got home one evening and saw that Scott was supposed to be home, but the house was dead silent. He was sleeping, most likely. Drew moved through the kitchen to the hall, intending to go to sleep himself. It had been a long day, and if Scott wasn't up for him to look at, he might as well go to bed and dream about him.

Scott's light was on, the door open. Drew glanced in and saw him on the bed, fully clothed, asleep on top of his books. He shook his head and went back to the kitchen. Scott had to be back at the hospital in six hours.

He went back to Scott's room and knocked on the door. "Hey, Doc. Wake up for a couple of minutes and get more comfortable."

Scott stirred a little, then stilled.

Drew sighed and went in, shook him gently by the shoulder. "Doc. At least put the books away. You'll wind up with print on your pretty face."

"M'not pretty."

"Yeah, you are. Now, c'mon, get ready for bed." Drew stood back as Scott levered himself up and shoved the books off the bed.

Scott's eyes were still mostly closed and he moved sluggishly. Drew expected him to just flop down on the bed and go back to full sleep, but Scott managed to stand and started undressing.

Oh, Christ.

"See you in the morning, Doc." Drew turned around and left the room, switching off the light as he left. He went into his own room, setting the alarm. He'd wake up early, just in case Scott hadn't set his alarm before falling asleep.

***

When the alarm went off, Drew lay on his bed for a couple of moments to see if Scott would get up on his own. He didn't hear any movement from across the hall so he got out of bed and turned on the hall light, ready to knock on the doorframe to Scott's room. His hand raised, he paused to look for a moment, stealing a bit of quiet for himself.

Scott was up to his chin in sheets and blankets, head half buried under his pillows, a shock of dark hair sticking out like a rooster tail. Drew sighed, not sure if he was glad or if he would really have preferred the test to his willpower that a little less covering would have caused. He decided not to examine the thought too closely until Scott made a slightly more overt move than just looking at him.

Or until he went insane.

"Scott," he said in a normal tone of voice. "Time to wake up."

Nothing, not even a twitch.

"Hey, Doc," he said a little louder.

Scott rolled over and pulled the blankets with him, treating Drew to a rather stunning view of his back and naked ass. Drew took a deep breath. Christ on a crutch. Insanity seemed possible.

"Scott!"

Scott rolled again and sat up, blinking. "What?"

Drew snorted at him. "Time to get up. You have to be at the hospital in an hour, man. Shift your ass."

Scott blinked again and pulled the blankets up as he fell back on the bed. "Damn. Already?"

"Yup. You awake now, or do I have to pour water on you in ten minutes?"

12

There was pause then Scott muttered something that sounded suspiciously like 'cold shower' before he said, "'M awake. Thanks."

"No problem." Drew went back to his room and fell onto his bed, trying to banish thoughts of Scott in the shower.

The man was going to kill him if he didn't get into the shower soon. Drew stupidly hadn't closed his door and he had a naked butt inspired hard-on to take care of. Scott finally got up and went into the bathroom and Drew took himself in hand, thinking about that ass and hot pounding water from the shower, his effort to banish such thoughts an utter waste of time. He didn't last long, biting his lip to stifle his moans as he came.

When he got himself cleaned up, he spent a few moments reminding himself that the plan was to go slow. Not a good idea to go barging into the bathroom and help Scott wash his back. Nope. Bad idea to go in and tell him that they had to conserve water and they were now sharing shower time.

Bad idea to even think about it, he decided, pulling his sweatpants on over his once again interested cock. He frowned down at himself. Go slow.

The water in the bathroom was turned off and Drew figured he was awake for the day. Best take his shower as soon as Scott was out of the bathroom and avoid lingering looks over breakfast. Get some self-control before he'd see Scott again. He went out to the kitchen and checked the schedule. Scott would be home at eight that evening, which hopefully was enough time to find a bit of the ever elusive restraint.

Drew's resolve to move slow broke as he walked back down the hall at the same time as Scott came out of the bathroom wrapped in a towel. They walked past each other and Drew couldn't help staring, didn't bother trying to hide his erection. The man was hot. More muscle than he had thought, dark nipples and firm abs. His hair was sticking up everywhere from towel drying, and there were still water drops on his shoulder.

And Scott didn't bother hiding the way he eyed Drew's cock, even smiled at him as he walked into his bedroom, his head turning to keep looking as they moved in opposite directions.

Drew swore and headed into the bathroom for his own shower. Eight o'clock. Screw the self-control—he was getting some doctor.

Chapter Three

As it turned out, Scott wound up working late and didn't get home until Drew was asleep in bed. They spent the next two weeks working opposite shifts and barely had time to say hello, let alone get anything started, then a firebug hit and Drew's pager went off more often than Scott's.

Scott had been living in the house almost two months when things finally calmed down and they both had an evening off. Drew was sitting on the couch watching TV, wearing nothing more than his favorite pair of worn-out sweatpants, a cold beer in his hand, when Scott came home.

They called out greetings to each other and Scott went down the hall to his room. Drew heard him toss a load of clothes in the washing machine and come back down the hall into the kitchen.

"Want a beer?"

Drew held his up and considered. "No, got one, thanks."

Scott wandered into the living room, the inevitable book in hand. Drew didn't bother trying to figure out what it was; he was pretty busy trying to remember how to breathe. He'd never been one for paying attention to clothes—he figured you were either naked, dressed, or wearing enough shit to protect you from the heat of hell itself—but he knew that if he were ever to say that he'd seen a look fit to be called 'fuck me now wear' this was it.

Scott sat sideways in the easy chair, one leg hooked over the arm, and opened the book. Drew stared. Bare feet. Jeans faded from wear and too many washes. Low slung with a button fly. Top button gone. That was it. A lot of skin showing, tight and smooth over lean muscles.

Scott glanced at him. "Anything good on TV?"

Drew looked at the TV. It was on. "Uh, maybe?"

Scott raised an eyebrow and went back to his book. Drew knew that the only reason Scott even had the book with him was that he needed to feel like he wasn't wasting his time. The beer, the jeans, the fact that he was in the living room and not his bedroom or the kitchen, meant that he was relaxing. He just couldn't seem to let go entirely.

Drew tried to watch TV, he really did. But he kept looking at Scott, and Scott was looking back most of the time. Drew gave up on the TV after a while and just looked at Scott, not bothering to hide his growing erection. Scott glanced at him often, and more and more frequently the gaze was leveled at Drew's groin.

Drew's cock was starting to ache. He made sure Scott was watching as he dropped a hand to his lap to adjust himself, heard Scott's hiss as his hand moved over the stretched fabric of his sweatpants.

Christ, what was it going to take to get the man to do something?

"Fuck this," Drew said under his breath. It was either jerk off right here in the living room and put on a show, or make a dash for the shower. Or, just maybe, he could try the unexpected.

He glanced at Scott again, taking in the way that Scott's jeans were fitting him now, his erection clearly showing through the soft denim, and reached for the notepad on the side table. He opened the drawer for a pen and wrote two words, then tore the sheet off and folded it in half, standing up.

As he crossed to Scott's chair he said, "Sorry it's not engraved, but here's the written invitation you seem to need." He handed the paper to Scott and returned to the couch.

Scott looked at him for a second and opened the paper, then dropped it on the floor as he stood and moved to the couch. He didn't even sit down next to Drew, just straddled his hips and sat on him, grinding their cocks together. "That's not an invitation," he said as he bent his head to lick Drew's neck from collarbone to ear.

"Thought about writing 'Wanna fuck?', but 'Ride me' had more of a ring to it." Drew hardly knew his own voice, tight and hoarse with need.

"Whatever." Then Scott kissed him, hips moving hard and fast as they rocked together on the couch. Fuck, but the man could kiss. Drew let his tongue slide with Scott's and moaned. Scott moaned as well, and shifted his weight back a little, his hands sweeping up Drew's body in a featherlight touch that had Drew arching forward, needing more.

God, he wanted to be everywhere at once, wanted to lick and suck and touch and kiss and take his time. But not now. Right now was about making up for two months of wanting, about waiting for too long and needing fast and hard and now. Drew broke the kiss and tried to catch his breath, but Scott was too fast. Lips and tongue worked at Drew's neck and Scott lifted up, knees on either side of his hips, hands pushing into Drew's gym pants with determination.

Drew groaned and leaned to the side, pulling Scott with him until they were lying on the couch, Drew on top. Scott's hands slid around his hips to his ass and he pushed down hard, rubbing his cock on the man beneath him.

"'Kay, Doc. Get the edge off and then we'll have some fun," he said, taking another deep kiss.

Scott didn't say anything, just ground up into him and they pushed against each other, dry humping like they were teens doing this for the first time ever. Drew's balls ached and every thrust had him grunting. Fuck, Scott was so hot and willing once he got going. He was going to be real fun when they finally managed to get naked.

Scott sucked on his tongue, every thrust of his cock echoed in the steady, hot suction. Drew could feel Scott's legs tense beneath him and trembles ran up his spine when Scott clutched at his ass and bucked against him. Scott groaned and broke the kiss, his head falling back on the couch as he cried out. Drew felt heat spreading between them, and added his own, coming in shuddering jerks.

His head dropped down and he gasped for breath, finally just laying his head down on Scott's chest. Hands stroked his back for a couple of moments, then traced up and down his sides.

"Stop that, it tickles," he said with a grin, lifting his head up.

"Yeah, I know. Get off me, you big stubborn jerk. Gotta get cleaned up."

Drew chuckled and rolled off him. "I'm stubborn? You're the one who needed an invitation."

Scott just grinned at him and undid his pants. He stood up to peel them off and then Scott was naked in front of him, cock at half-mast. Drew stared and licked his lips. Drew needed to explore him. In detail.

Scott stroked his cock with a loose fist. "Move this to bed?"

"Hell, yes," Drew said and skinned out of his sticky sweatpants, using them to wipe himself off. When he stood up he grabbed Scott's shoulders and kissed him hard, loving the way Scott just moved into him, an arm slinking around his waist, the other one over his shoulder. They stood together kissing for a moment and Drew had an unpleasant thought. "Doc?"

"Hmm?"

"I know you're the king of lube, but please tell me you've got some rubbers somewhere."

Scott frowned a little, then said, "Yeah, somewhere. I think."

Drew kissed him again, one hand dropping to Scott's ass and pulling him closer. "God, I hope so."

Scott laughed and they slowly made their way toward the bedroom, pausing in the hallway when Scott slammed him into the wall and ground against him, teeth scraping at his neck.

"Shit, we gotta get to the bed. Now." Drew's cock was awake again, stiff and insistent. "Need you."

"Oh, God." Scott pressed into him harder, one hand finding Drew's prick and pumping it steadily. "Yeah."

Drew pushed him across the hall and into the other wall, kissing him hard and tugging at his nipples while Scott pulled at his cock. "Shit, Doc. Gonna fucking do you right here if we don't move."

Scott moaned and thrust against him. "Could do that."

"Lube's in the bedroom."

"Don't care."

"You will after." Drew grabbed Scott by the shoulders, pushed him away, and took off down the hall. He veered into Scott's room and threw himself on the bed, rolling over in time to catch Scott as he landed on top of him.

Laughing, they rolled on the bed, hands roaming over each other, using their bodies to press one another into the mattress, the wall, against the pillows. Scott finally produced a tube of lubricant and as Drew pushed two slick fingers into him he arched his back and thrust his hips down.

"God, yes."

Drew worked his fingers into Scott again, and then rolled him onto his back. "Rubbers?"

"Oh, shit. Somewhere... let me think."

Drew groaned. He couldn't remember being so desperate to be in someone. A large part of him was trying to tell him to just go ahead and damn the consequences. That part was whispering things to him about he knew he was clean, and hell, the man was a doctor, he'd be testing as regular as anything. Just ask him.

The logical part of his mind—squished into a tiny but still functional part of his brain—was screaming. Forget the fucking need, just get a condom and nail him. Talk later when the rest of your brain isn't trying to get inside the man. Fuck now, talk later, and be damn smart about it.

Drew was about to snap when Scott pushed his hand away and leaped off the bed. He jumped to his dresser and tore through a couple of drawers, finally tossing a couple of foil packets on the bed. "Jesus. You might want to check the expiry date on those. That's all I've got."

Drew already had one open, and he held Scott's gaze as he rolled it on. As he reached for the lube again he said, "Turn around."

Scott stared at him for a second before turning, hands on the top of the dresser. Drew slicked the rubber and moved behind him, one hand sliding over Scott's hip to grasp his hard shaft. "You ready?"

"Fuck, yes. Just, oh, God—" Scott's words broke into a groan as Drew pressed into him, Drew matching the sound with one of his own.

Drew pushed all the way in, his hands moving to Scott's hips. He stopped, letting them both get used to the feeling, and kissed Scott's shoulder lightly, then started to suck up a mark. He grazed the skin with his teeth and was rewarded with a shudder that moved through Scott and traveled up his own spine, making him gasp. He tightened his grip on Scott's hips and started to move, his thrusts slow and even.

Scott's knuckles were white on the top of the dresser, his head dropping down as Drew fucked him. When Scott started moving back, picking up the tempo, Drew grinned a little and added more force to his next thrust, a little higher, a little harder.

"Oh, shit. There," Scott gasped.

Drew bit down on Scott's shoulder and did it again. When Scott's movements started to get shaky and his legs began to tremble, Drew pulled out altogether and spun him around. "Not yet, Doc. Waited too long for this to let you come now."

He pushed Scott down on the bed and lifted his legs up and back, driving into him again, fast and hard. Scott cried out and arched his back, his hands grasping at the sheets. As Drew's cock slid over his gland again and again he let go of the sheets and clutched at Drew's arms with strong fingers.

Drew could feel his orgasm building, could feel it sharp and tight at the base of his spine, in the pit of his stomach. He grabbed at Scott's hips and pulled the man onto him, getting as deep as he could. Scott was losing it quickly, his eyes rolling back and his body moving on the bed as he tried to pull Drew into him.

"Gonna come, Scott. So close." His voice was tight, hoarse even to his own ears.

Scott just groaned, a deep rumble in his chest that took Drew by surprise, and then Scott was pulling him down, kissing him with a hungry mouth. As Scott's tongue slid over his Drew came, his entire body shaking. He thrust sloppily a couple of times and then just let himself quiver until his climax was over. Scott was still kissing him.

He shifted back, just enough to ease out of Scott's ass, and then up again to lay mostly on him, kisses softening to warm and wet and slow. He brought a hand to Scott's chest, wanting to feel the beat of the man's heart.

Scott rolled him over and licked his neck, then nibbled a path up to his ear. "My turn," he whispered, and Drew heard the crinkle of foil as Scott opened the other condom.

Goddamn. Man hadn't come.

Drew barely had time to shift on the bed and ditch his own rubber before slick fingers were opening him, and Scott was kissing him again, making him breathless and hungry. Drew felt Scott move around on the bed, fingers suddenly leaving him empty, only to be replaced by the blunt head of his cock.

"Look at me," Scott said, and Drew opened his eyes to watch Scott's face as he entered him, filled him.

Oh, shit. He was in so much trouble.

Scott was too close to coming for anything fancy, and Drew was too far along the road to happily blissed out and totally well-fucked to be of any help. Scott fucked him fast and hard, mouth dancing over Drew's chest to suck at one nipple and then the other. Drew clenched his ass around Scott's prick and Scott groaned, so he did it again, working the man's cock all he could.

"Oh, God. Oh, God, oh, God," Scott gasped, and Drew felt the prick inside him throb, and watched Scott's eyes roll back as he came.

Scott collapsed onto him, taking his time to get his breath back. When he eased out of Drew's ass he rolled to the side and said something that may have been English, or it may have been Klingon. Drew wasn't sure.

Drew grinned at him and got up, pulling Scott to his feet. "Clean up. Meet me in my bed."

Scott just rolled his eyes and headed for the bathroom, treating Drew to a lovely view of his ass. Drew figured he should always try to walk behind Scott.

He went into his room and got in the bed, waiting for Scott. It was a nice bed. A big bed. And a fuck of a lot more comfortable than the one in Scott's room. Scott came in and got in the other side, sliding over to meet him in the middle.

"Hey."

"Hey, yourself. C'mere." Drew pulled him in close and wrapped a leg over Scott's. "Go to sleep now."

"Just a nap."

Chapter Four

Over the next few days they fell into a routine as best they could, given their work schedules. They came home, they ate, they fell into bed or onto the couch. And they talked. They talked about their work, they shared gossip about people they knew, they planned the garden for the next summer, including a lot more vegetables than Drew would ever have planted.

Scott more or less just stopped using his own bed. Drew hadn't even thought about it until he woke up with a warm man against his back where there hadn't been one when he fell asleep. He rolled over, wrapped an arm around Scott, and smiled. He could get used to this.

He was getting used to a lot of things, like the way Scott slept curled around him, and the way Scott would wait until Drew either said something inviting or touched him before he would play. It was weird, and a little confusing, but when Scott got a clear sign that Drew wanted him he reacted with a great deal of enthusiasm and passion. Drew didn't know why Scott held back, and he wasn't sure he wanted to ask, but once he figured it out he made sure to let the man know what he wanted.

He was also getting used to strange things happening. Thursday night, Scott had called his mother to see if she had gotten any mail for him from one of the medical societies. When he hung up the phone he turned to Drew, his face pale.

"Christ, what's wrong? Is someone sick?" Drew asked, suddenly worried.

Scott shook his head and bit his lip. "She's coming here. On Saturday. She wants to see my new place."

They looked around the living room at a pile of Scott's books, two pop bottles, three pizza boxes, a dead plant, three beer bottles, and more dust than a desert.

"Oh, hell."

Scott started to gather up the garbage and Drew did the dishes. They checked the calendar and decided that if they worked really hard on Friday night they could get the house in decent shape, but only if they got all the laundry and general picking up done before they went to bed. It was like they had chores again, and Drew felt a little like he was fifteen.

When they finally went to bed Scott melded himself to Drew's back, his arm tight around Drew's waist.

"Your mom freak you out?" Drew asked quietly.

"No. Mom's pretty cool. Why?" Scott's voice was muffled against Drew's back, his breath a warm tickle.

"You're clinging," Drew observed. Scott started to pull away and Drew shook his head. "Doesn't mean stop. Just commenting."

Scott settled against him again, and kissed his neck gently before starting to nibble. Drew raised an eyebrow, glad it was dark and Scott couldn't see the surprise on his face. That was the most overt move the man had made yet. Drew shifted back, pressing his ass into Scott, just to let him know he appreciated it.

Scott murmured something into his hair.

"What was that?" Drew kept his voice low and wiggled again, feeling Scott get hard against him.

"Just said thanks. For helping me clean up for my mom." Scott pushed back a bit and Drew grinned.

"Hey, my house. Gotta make it look pretty for company." He wrapped an arm behind him, stroking Scott's thigh. Scott rubbed against him again, and Drew could feel the wet trail Scott's cock was leaving. He wondered if he could get Scott to really take the initiative, but he figured it would take time and he was feeling kind of impatient. He also thought that if he really wanted to push that particular boundary he should wait a bit. Sometimes walls were there for a reason.

He put one hand on the arm around his waist and traced it with his fingers until he reached Scott's hand. He tangled their fingers together and brought their hands to his own erection, wrapping their fingers around it. He thrust into their fist a little and turned his head. "Want you," he whispered as Scott moved to kiss him.

Scott's kiss started gentle this time, lips featherlight and the tip of his tongue barely tracing Drew's lower lip. As Scott pumped his cock, Drew moaned softly and tried to deepen the kiss, tongue chasing after Scott's. Scott played with him for a couple of moments, keeping the kiss light and shallow, then suddenly he ground against Drew's ass and plunged his tongue into the kiss.

They moved on the bed, getting tangled in the sheets as they twisted and wiggled. Drew tried to roll over to face Scott but he wasn't permitted to move, Scott pinning him with his body. Scott lifted the topmost of Drew's legs, draping it back and over his own, opening him, and Drew hissed as he felt Scott's finger tease at his entrance.

"Lube," Scott said, his voice tight. "Now."

Drew threw out a hand, searching. They had learned quickly that the solution to any lube and condom problem was to scatter as many tubes and jars as possible all over the house; under the couch, in a canister next to the fridge, in the pocket of the easy chair, both nightstands, the bathroom, and under at least one pillow in both beds. Drew's blindly seeking hand found a tube and he managed to get it open, all the while being driving insane by the hand moving over his cock and the soft skin behind his balls.

Drew slicked his fingers and brought them down between his legs, sliding over Scott's fingers. He stifled a gasp as their fingers tangled together, Scott holding his hand tightly and guiding it back. The finger slowly pushing into him was his own.

Behind him, Scott moaned. "So fucking hot, Drew."

Drew pushed back again, feeling Scott's cock throb against him. "Hurry. Please." He thought he might have whimpered, but he didn't particularly care. He wanted Scott in him as soon as possible.

Scott bit down on Drew's shoulder as he finally moved his own slippery hand back to slick his erection, the condom packet retrieved from under the same pillow as the lube. Drew kept moving his fingers, fucking himself slowly, anticipation splintering into need and driving necessity. Scott moved his hand away, and Drew gasped as he felt the blunt head of Scott's cock press against him.

"Yes, want you," he breathed, and Scott pushed into him, one hand holding his leg up and back. He felt the first burning stretch and forced himself to relax, to keep breathing while Scott filled him. When he felt Scott's hips pressed tight against his ass he moaned softly, wrapping a hand around his own cock.

Scott thrust into him, slowly at first, short strokes that made him crazy. He hardly pulled out at all before sliding deep in again and Drew wanted more, wanted faster and harder. Scott was being stubborn, though, and flat out refused to pick up the pace, holding him in place by keeping his leg still. Drew couldn't move, could only take what Scott gave him. He moved his hand faster, slippery fist sliding over his cock from shaft to tip over and over.

Scott moved about a quarter of an inch and stars exploded behind Drew's eyes. "Oh, fuck! There!"

The sound Scott made could have been a laugh, though it was hard to tell between the shuddering breaths and sighs. He was close. Drew tried to work him, tried to get him off, but he was completely off balance; all he could feel was Scott's cock sliding over that one perfect spot again and again and again. He could hear Scott, could feel his own hand pumping his shaft, but everything was secondary to Scott moving in him.

His orgasm crashed over him like a wall tumbling down, everything shaking and pounding as he came, shooting in pulsing bursts that left him gasping for air and feeling boneless. He heard Scott call out when the first wave of shudders ended and felt Scott throb inside him.

It wasn't until Scott eased out of him and let his leg go that Drew was able to turn and kiss him. The kisses were long and slow while they came down and cleaned up a bit, and gradually their breathing evened out. Drew fell asleep, warm and comfortable, his head on Scott's chest.

Chapter Five

Scott rolled over in the bed and poked Drew in the side. "What time is it?"

Drew rubbed at his eyes before checking his watch. "Nine. When's she gonna be here?" His eyes were barely open, dark blond hair stuck to the side of his head. Scott thought he looked edible.

"She said eleven. Which means any time between ten-thirty and two this afternoon." Scott poked him again, then slid a hand over Drew's stomach. "At least the house is clean. Good enough to pass the mother inspection."

"Thank God. I don't think I could take another night like that," Drew said as he captured Scott's hand in his own and pushed it lower. "Touch me," he whispered.

Scott shuddered, need unfurling as he curled his hand around Drew's cock and pumped it slowly. "What, marathon cleaning isn't your idea of a good time? It looked like you were having fun when you were cleaning the tub." He worked his hand slowly up and down Drew's shaft.

"About as much fun as you had scrubbing the stove." Drew tilted his head and kissed Scott gently. "Time to play before we have to get up and shower?"

"Oh, yeah. Could play in the shower, too."

"You're easy," Drew laughed. He slid a hand around Scott, grabbing at his ass. "Want you."

"And you say I'm easy?" Scott moved closer, hand moving down to cup Drew's balls. The man made him hungry for it, made him feel bold. Almost too bold, really, but it was worth it to be like this.

Drew inhaled sharply. "Oh, like that."

"Like this?" Scott murmured as he squeezed gently and rolled them between his fingers. He loved the sounds Drew made, the obvious enjoyment Drew brought to everything they did.

Drew groaned, letting his legs fall open as he pulled Scott in for a deep kiss. Scott made a sound that was mostly a moan, partly a whimper. God, he loved kissing this mouth. His hand worked at Drew for a moment and then he rolled on top of him, knees forcing Drew's legs farther apart as he reached for another condom, rolling it on as fast as he could and smoothing lube over himself.

"Gonna fuck you again," he said, hoping he could get away with the growl in his voice.

"Yeah, Doc." Drew closed his eyes and groaned deep in his chest as Scott pushed into him. "Fuck. Feels good."

Apparently he could. "Yeah. Real good, Drew." Scott pushed all the way in and leaned down, kissing Drew hard as he started to move, long deep strokes that made them both gasp into the kiss.

Scott's hips sped up as he lost himself to the tight heat around his cock. He braced himself on his hands and pushed harder, changing his angle to sink deeper into Drew's ass. When Drew canted his hips Scott moaned and broke the kiss, lowering his head to Drew's chest to bite at one hard nipple.

"Oh, fuck, yes." Drew wrapped a hand around his own cock and started pumping it fast as Scott slid in and out of him. "Shit, Doc, you're so deep."

Scott just moved faster, slamming his hips down to meet Drew's. He leaned back and moved his hands to Drew's shoulders, pulling down hard when he slid in, forcing Drew down onto his cock, harder and faster.

"Oh, Christ. Gonna come, Drew," he said hoarsely.

Drew just gasped and jerked, his hand moving faster. He swept his thumb over the tip of his cock and shuddered, then he did it again. "Oh, God!" Drew came hard, his ass grasping and clenching around Scott, his cock throbbing as he shot onto his stomach.

The smell and the sight sent Scott over as much as the feeling of Drew coming around him. Scott thrust into Drew again and froze, every muscle in his body tense as he came. He fell forward onto Drew and kissed him, mouth soft and warm.

"Fuck. You feel amazing, Doc."

Drew's arms were loose around him and Scott felt warm and sleepy. He slipped out of Drew's body and rolled onto his back with a groan. "Wanna nap," he moaned, stripping off the condom and tying it off.

Drew grinned at him. "No time for that, Doc. Get in the shower or your mom will come in and find you naked in my bed."

Scott snickered. "That'd teach her to wander in. Good thing she doesn't have a key." He got off the bed and was headed to the bathroom when he heard a knock on the door. He groaned and reached for his jeans. "Shit. She's early."

Drew swore and jumped off the bed, grabbing the sheets and trying to make it in a rush. They both froze when a cheery voice

26

called out, "Hello? Anyone home? I let myself in, I hope that's okay!"

"That's not my mom!" Scott hissed.

"No. It's mine." Drew grabbed his jeans and Scott slammed the door shut. "Be right there, Mom!"

"Oh, fuck. Oh, fucking shit." Scott tried to keep from sounding hysterical, but suspected it was leaking through.

Drew finished doing up his jeans and grabbed a sweatshirt. "Get dressed," he whispered. "Calm down. Just...fuck. Get it together, man."

Scott nodded and tried to squash his frantic need to hide. This was so not good.

Drew looked at him steadily and then rolled his eyes before pulling the door open. "Panic is kind of a good look on you," he whispered before vanishing.

Scott waited until he heard voices in the living room and made a dash for the bathroom, taking the bedroom trash with him. He showered quickly and tried to calm down. Christ, he wasn't a teenager anymore. He had no idea if Drew's family knew he was gay, or if they had something that was in the realm of 'Hey Mom, this is my boyfriend.'

Drew and his mom were sitting at the kitchen table with coffee cups in front of them when he wandered into the kitchen. They both looked up at him as he walked in, and he smiled at Drew's mom, ignoring Drew. "Hi," he said politely.

Drew smiled and said, "Mom, this is Scott. Scott, this is my mom, Ellen."

Drew's mom smiled and offered her hand, so Scott took it. She had a nice handshake, firm and warm. She was about sixty-five, round and soft looking, with dark hair turning to gray. She had happy brown eyes, the same color as Drew's. She was nicely dressed in a blue pantsuit, and didn't have any makeup on that Scott could see. Her smile was friendly, if a little speculative, her face falling into the expression with ease, as if she was used to being open and meeting new people.

"Drew just told me last week that he had a roommate," she said. "How long have you been living here, Scott?"

"About two and a half months, Mrs. Smyth," Scott said as he got a coffee cup from the cupboard.

"Call me Ellen, please," she said with another smile. "I was looking at the calendar. What kind of job do you have that lets you work so few hours? I mean, thirteen hours in three days? Nothing for three days at a time?" She waved a hand at the calendar, sounding vaguely disapproving of his slack and lazy ways. "Must be nice, even if it is shifts."

Scott glanced at the board and smiled. "Actually, that's when I'm home. I'm a doctor."

Ellen stared at him. "Oh. Oh, my. That's when you're home?" Scott could almost see her retreat from her previous assumptions. "You poor thing! Do you sleep well? Are you eating all right?"

Drew groaned. "Mom, lay off. His own mother will be here in a bit, let her do that."

Scott laughed and sat down at the table. Ellen blushed and apologized, which made Scott smile more. Drew's mom was cool.

They talked for a while, and Scott told her all about his current schedule, and what his options were when his residency was done. Ellen nagged Drew about his pizza habit, and Drew ran his hands through his hair, making it spike up. He looked about ready to tell her to lay off again when there was another knock on the door.

Scott answered it and was greeted by the whirlwind that was his mother. She burst through the door, hugged him, and passed him bag after bag of things.

"This is the mail that came to our house, this is the mail that the jerk you used to room with forwarded to us, this is leftovers, this is spare towels. Oh, hi, you must be Drew! I'm Kate! And this is some beans from the garden, I know you're not eating enough green things, and this is fresh oranges I got at the market."

Scott set all the packages on the counter and took a breath. "Hi, Mom."

She hugged him again. "Hi, sweetie. I've missed you."

She smelled like baking, just like always. Short, blonde, and full of energy, constantly surrounded by the scent of rising bread or sugar cookies; nothing felt quite as nice and homey as his mom hugging him. Scott smiled. He saw Drew grin at his own mom, and he saw Ellen nod her head.

"Mom, this is Drew. And this is Ellen Smyth, his mom. She dropped by sort of unexpectedly. We would have planned lunch, otherwise." Scott was faintly apologetic about the lack of planned lunch for the moms, even though only one had been expected.

"Parents day!" Kate exclaimed, her voice extra chirpy. "Hello, Ellen, it's nice to meet you. And you, too, Drew. This looks like a lovely home." She beamed at them as they replied to her greetings and exchanged fast handshakes. Drew kept on grinning which Scott thought looked adorable, and was only slightly more welcome than the fact that his mom was being warm and happy instead of over-protective and prying.

He hoped it was a sign of things to come.

Ellen, Kate, and Drew made polite and friendly chatter for a few moments about when Drew had bought the place and the current state of property taxes, while Scott got his mother a cup of coffee. When he handed her the mug, she said, "Show me the house, Scott, and let Drew's mother do her job. I'll bet she hasn't even had a chance to see inside the fridge yet."

Ellen laughed and looked slightly guilty. She was holding the leftovers Kate had brought and was halfway to the fridge. "I'll tell you how bad it is when you get back."

"And I'll check the medicine cabinet."

"Oh, good, I hate looking in there," Ellen replied with a mock shudder.

Both moms laughed when Scott and Drew exchanged a panicked look. "Oh, come on, Scott. I'm not really going to look in there," Kate said as she started down the hall. Scott chased after her.

Just in case.

He showed her the living room and the spare room, pointed to Drew's bedroom and then led her into his own. She closed the door behind them and leaned back on it, like she was guarding it.

"When are you going to tell me?" she asked lightly.

Scott blinked and then eyed her warily. "Tell you what?" he asked slowly.

She rolled her eyes at him. "About you and that young man out there," she said with exaggerated patience.

Scott opened his mouth, but nothing came out.

"Oh, Scott. Think. This house is spotless. You cleaned. He cleaned. Have you ever had a roommate who would clean his own room when I was coming over? And this room...it's very nice, dear, and tidy. Too tidy, and the air is stale. If you've slept in here once in the last week I'll make and deliver your meals for a month."

He bit his lip. "Mom, we're not...it's just—"

"Don't you dare tell me that it's just sex, Scott." She held a hand up to him, followed almost immediately by patented Mom Finger Shaking. "Not him. A nice man with a good job and a house? Don't you dare torture me with the thought that this doesn't mean anything. You want it to be nice and easy, fine. But for God's sake let me have a dream!" Then she gave him the warm, happy mom smile he loved.

Relief washed over him as he looked around the room. "You like him?" he asked shyly.

"Yes, Scott. Do you?"

He nodded and said, "Yeah, Mom. I like him fine."

"Good. Now, let's go visit with your man for a bit, and I'll check out the fridge."

She hugged him hard and Scott smiled. She really did seem fine with it, and it had been a long time since they'd walked down the relationship path. He hoped this time she'd just stand on the side and watch; like Drew was a good first step.

They found the kitchen empty, voices coming from the backyard. They went through the side door and around the corner of the house in time to hear Ellen say, "—a doctor, for pity's sake. You let him go and I'll kill you myself."

Scott groaned, burying his face in his hands, and Kate laughed out loud. Drew spun around, his eyes wide and a little wild. Ellen blushed, but Kate just laughed harder, a hand on Scott's arm. "See, dear? Mothers always know. Never doubt it. Ellen, how was their fridge?"

Ellen tucked her hair behind her ears as her blush faded. "In need. Three pizza boxes and a half-dozen eggs. I made a list."

Scott and Drew moved off to the side while their mothers wandered around the yard, pointing out weeds that Drew had missed in the flower beds. To Scott, it looked like they wanted most of the bed dug up.

"She knew?" Drew asked, watching him out of the corner of his eye.

Scott nodded. "Uh-huh. Clean house and stale air in my room. How did your mom know?"

"Stupid smile on my face, clean house, the fact that I answered the door in the so-called 'afterglow'."

Scott started to laugh. Drew whapped him on the head and he laughed harder, holding onto his stomach. Nerves had totally given way and he felt like everything was leaking out around the edges. He knew he wasn't quite hysterical, but the sheer absurdity of the day had finally taken its toll. He saw their mothers pause and look at them, saw his own mom roll her eyes. He laughed so hard he thought he might be sick, but it also felt like a relief to let all the

30

energy out. Drew swore at him and started laughing, too, leaning on the house. It felt good. When he calmed down again he leaned on the house as well, just watching as their moms started to actually pull up weeds.

"So. Our mothers know. And our fathers will." Scott wiped at his eyes and leaned against Drew's shoulder.

"Yeah. I guess we're official," Drew said, his tone light and still hinting at laughter.

Scott grinned. "Guess so."

"Fast courtship."

"Hey, two months before I let you kiss me," Scott teased, leering obnoxiously.

"Shut up. You would've been all over me the first week if you weren't so damn stubborn about needing an invitation." Drew leaned a little closer so their fingers touched.

"If you weren't so damn stubborn about saying something instead of just walking around hard all the time." Scott moved his hand over, tracing a line on Drew's thigh.

"If you hadn't…oh, hell. Think they'll notice if we go inside for a quick roll?"

"Probably."

They watched the moms for a few moments. "When are they going to leave?" Drew asked.

"When they're done torturing us."

"I gotta work tomorrow."

"Yeah. Me, too. Maybe they'll let us have some unsupervised time tonight."

Kate and Ellen laughed at a shared joke on the other side of the yard.

"Maybe not."

Chapter Six

Drew sat in the passenger seat of Scott's car, fighting an uncharacteristic case of nerves. It was a Saturday in mid-September and they were on their way to Scott's parents' place for dinner which, in and of itself, was a good reason for him to be nervous. In the two months that he and Scott had been together, Drew had spoken with Kate a handful of times but he had never met Scott's dad.

It was also Scott's birthday, a fact that he hadn't even known two days before when Kate had called to invite him to dinner.

"Are you coming with Scott on Saturday?" she had asked.

Drew had given himself a mental pat on the back for not saying 'Repeatedly, I hope', and had replied, "Where? As far as I know we don't have any plans."

There had been a long pause and Kate had finally said, "You do know that it's Scott's birthday, don't you?"

He hadn't, and now he found himself as neatly dressed as he could get without wearing a suit, on his way to meet Dr. Daniel Campbell. He was wearing a new long-sleeved golf shirt so he didn't have to worry about a tie, and his dress pants. The only things that were vaguely uncomfortable were his new shoes. His mother had always had a fit when he wore sneakers with his dress pants. He wondered if maybe he should have worn a dress shirt after all, but then there was the tie thing again.

"Relax," Scott said, giving him a sideways glance. "Just my dad. Nothing scary."

"Your mom scares me," Drew said seriously. "She's psychic. What if she knows what we did last weekend?"

Scott blinked, then his eyes glazed over a little. "Stop that. I'm trying to drive here."

Drew looked out his window and smiled. If he managed to survive this evening maybe they could do it again. Or something else.

Scott took a right hand turn onto a quiet street. "What did you get me for my birthday?" he asked for the eighth time since they had gotten in the car. Drew thought he would have been bouncing if he weren't wearing a seatbelt.

"Nothing. And if you ask me again it really will be nothing."

"You're mean."

Drew thought the man's pout was the most adorable one he'd tried yet. "Let's go home. Wanna fuck you insensible."

Scott gripped the steering wheel tighter, his knuckles white. "Stop that. Again. Supper with my parents—focus, will you?"

Drew's case of nerves came back as they pulled into a driveway. Scott stopped the car and looked at him. "Hey."

"Hey."

"Ready?"

Drew leaned over and kissed the corner of his mouth. "No. Let's go in anyway."

The evening could have been worse. Kate moved between the kitchen, dining room, and living room, as chatty as ever, bustling with energy. Scott's father was polite, and made a point of asking Drew about his job and his family; nothing too personal, just making sure that Drew knew he was interested in his background. Just before they sat down to dinner Daniel pulled Drew aside.

Drew followed him down the hall, part of him so nervous he was sure his hands were shaking, and part of him taking note of how unlike Scott and his father were. Daniel Campbell was tall, taller than Drew, and had dark hair flecked with gray. Drew could see the physical similarities more readily than with Scott's blonde mother, but he could also see the hard planes on Daniel's face, contrasting with the open and easy expression Scott had made for himself. Where Scott's features were fine and almost delicate, Daniel's were sharp and edgy.

"I'm glad you came," Daniel said, leading Drew into the room he evidently used as an office. It was a comfortable space, with an over-stuffed arm chair and more books than even Scott had. The walls were full of diplomas and certificates, the blank spaces filled with family photos.

"Thank you, sir. It's nice to be included."

Daniel didn't sit down, nor did he offer a chair to Drew. It was either going to be a very fast chat, or Daniel was asserting himself. Drew hoped it was going to be quick; he was feeling a little out of his depth. He hadn't had an official talking to by a partner's parent in years, and the last one hadn't gone very well.

Daniel looked at him, his eyes serious. They were blue like Scott's, and now Drew could see warmth in them which helped to soften the angles of his face. "I wanted to talk to you for a moment. Katie and Scott think that I'm over-protective, but I think it's just a matter of setting my own mind at ease. He's my only child, and it's important to me that he's happy." He held up a hand as Drew started to speak. "Now, now. Katie says you're a nice young man, and I trust her to tell me. Can't lie, though; I always hoped I'd be looking over a nice young lady. Been dealing with that for almost ten years, now."

Drew didn't know how to reply to that. He could understand a parent's preference on the matter, but he had no intention of apologizing for what he was, or for what Scott wanted. He assumed something along those lines must have shown on his face, because it was Daniel who looked faintly apologetic.

"That's my issue, not yours." Daniel said. "The only way you and I are going to have an issue is if Scott turns up here because you hurt him. Can you promise not to hurt my son?"

Drew stared at him. "No, sir. I can't promise that any more than he can promise not to hurt me. I can tell you that we'll both try not to."

A slow grin passed over Daniel's face. "You'll do." He put a hand on Drew's shoulder. "Let's go have supper."

Drew didn't think he could eat following that conversation, but Scott later assured him that he'd managed to swallow everything put in front of him, including two pieces of cake.

They left as soon after supper as they could politely manage it. Kate pressed leftovers into their hands and kissed Scott repeatedly. Daniel shook hands with them both and hugged Scott just as they left.

They weren't more than two streets away before Scott started asking about his present again.

"Not telling," Drew said with a grin. "Tell you all about what I'm going to do to you when we get home, though."

Scott shook his head and smiled. "Driving. Behave."

"Drive then. Sooner we're home sooner I can bend you over the arm of the couch. Gonna fuck you, Doc." Drew shifted in his seat, spreading his legs. "Want to be in you, feel you riding my cock. Gonna make you come so fucking hard…" He adjusted his erection, letting Scott see how hard he was.

"Drew," Scott said in a strangled voice. "Shut up. Driving." Scott was trying to watch the road and Drew at the same time. Good thing they were still on quiet suburban streets.

"Sorry, can't help it," Drew apologized, utterly unrepentant. "Just thinking about the way you feel in my mouth when I go down on you makes me hard." Drew shifted again. "Want you, Doc. Pull over somewhere, need to taste you."

Scott pulled over. In less then thirty seconds he had the car parked behind a high school, his seatbelt undone and the seat pushed back.

Drew's hands were already working at Scott's jeans, pulling his zipper down and shoving material out of the way. "Fuck, Doc. So hungry for you."

Scott made a breathless noise and his head fell back on the headrest. "Please, Drew. Hurry."

Drew dropped his head, taking Scott deep into his mouth. Scott was shaking, already desperate, rock hard and smooth as velvet in his throat. Drew licked and sucked, taking long pulls on Scott's cock, tasting pre-come and sweat, his own cock throbbing. He started to hum 'Happy Birthday'.

"Oh, shit." Scott had his hand in Drew's hair, hips pushing his sweet cock into Drew's mouth. "Drew—"

Scott came in great pulsing bursts, pumping into Drew's mouth and throat. Drew jerked, his own cock held tight in his jeans, humping the seat. He came just as hard as Scott, heat spreading up his belly.

"Oh, fuck." Scott gasped. "We gotta get home."

Drew laughed weakly. "Yeah, Doc. Where there's a bed and a couch and more room than this to play."

"And where my present is," Scott said as he did up his pants.

Drew laughed and dropped a kiss on his shoulder. "Yeah. Your present."

They got home without any further incidents of public obscenities by ignoring one another. When they finally pulled into the drive they wasted little time getting into the house.

"Shower," Drew said, pulling Scott behind him. "I've got come all over me."

Scott just laughed, but went willingly enough. They showered quickly; when Drew slid soap-slicked hands over Scott he got a grin and a quick kiss, but that was all.

"Want my present."

Drew rolled his eyes. "Fine. Get dry and meet me in bed, I'll get it."

He didn't think he'd ever seen Scott towel off quite that fast. The man really liked to open gifts, apparently. Drew dried himself off and went into the spare room for the box he'd hidden behind the ironing board. They never used the ironing board, thus it was the perfect hiding spot. Drew was beginning to suspect that Scott was the type to search for his presents. Good thing to know.

What he didn't know was if Scott would like the gift. He'd only had two days warning, and no real clue what to get him. Scott didn't have much spare time for hobbies, and his taste in books ran to textbooks and pulp fiction. Drew had made a halfhearted attempt to locate a rare copy of something that Scott would read, but without having a solid knowledge of what was already on the shelf, he was limited. Maybe for Christmas, when he'd had time to research it a bit, but for now, all he could do was let Scott open the box and find out if Scott would think him an overly sentimental goof.

He went into the bedroom to find Scott sitting the bed, Indian style. Naked.

"I suppose you want to open this before I fuck you senseless?" Drew said mildly, admiring Scott's half-hard cock.

Scott beamed at him. "Yep."

"Figured." Drew put the box on the bed in front of Scott and leaned over it to kiss him. "Happy birthday."

Scott kissed him back, and Drew was rather pleased that he seemed to have gotten at least as much attention as the box, which Scott was already holding on to. He shook his head and chuckled. "Shit. You're hopeless. Open the damn thing so I can have my way with you."

Scott just grinned at him and started to peel the tape off the sides.

"Goddamn. You're one of those save the paper people, aren't you?" Drew tried not to laugh as he moved around the bed to sit behind Scott. He nestled himself against Scott's back, arms around the man's chest and waist as Scott picked at the tape.

Even Scott had a limit to how long he could wait, apparently, and he finally tore the paper off with glee, ripping far more than he actually had to. He looked like he was having a blast. Drew made a mental note to get many small presents at Christmas time and wrap everything individually. Hell, he'd wrap some empty boxes, too.

Scott opened the top of the box and peered in. Drew held his breath.

"This is…wow. This is…" Scott seemed at a loss for words.

"An antique. And dumb, but I thought you might—"

"So not dumb! Where did you get it?" Scott asked, lifting the worn leather bag out of the box. "There's stuff in here, too!"

"There better be, it was full when I got it." Drew knew he was grinning like an idiot. Scott liked it. Better, Scott seemed totally taken with it. He had the bag open and was taking inventory.

"There's pill bottles and glass jars and fuck, there's even powder in this one, and scalpels and Christ, I don't even know what this is, and a stethoscope, and, wow—" Scott paused for breath and spun around to look at Drew, his eyes wide. "Thank you."

Drew smiled, pleased as hell. The look on Scott's face was perfect. His eyes were wide and he looked faintly stunned, all happy and excited.

"I love you." He hadn't meant to say it. He didn't have a sweet clue how Scott felt and he hadn't wanted to push, didn't want to pressure him. Every other time he'd felt the words try to come out he'd been able to force them back, but this…Scott was just so damn right.

"You do?" The blue eyes were even wider, if that was possible, and Drew gave himself a mental kick in the ass. Fuck. A large knot formed in his stomach.

"Yes." What else could he say?

Scott picked up the jars and bottles and put them back in the bag, then carefully put the bag and the box on the floor. He moved next to Drew and looked at him intently. "Say it again."

Drew put a hand on Scott's neck, pulling him in so their foreheads touched. "I love you, Scott."

Wait. Breathe.

"I love you, Drew." The words were quiet, serious.

A sound tore from Drew's chest that might have been a sob if it hadn't been muffled by their kiss. Drew moved over Scott's body, touching and holding him, drawing him as close as he could, kissing him deeply.

Scott pushed up against him, body hard and surging as they loved, movements growing frantic as they kissed and bit, moans turning to cries. Drew reached for the stuff under the pillows and got the condom on fast, his fingers opening Scott quickly. He slid into Scott's heat with a sigh.

He moved in his lover, held tight by his body, his arms and his eyes. They moved together, eyes locked, kisses at times soft, then turning more aggressive as need and hunger peaked.

"Love you," Drew said once more and Scott came for him, spilling over Drew's hand. Drew followed, unable to fight his climax any longer, the pleasure on Scott's face driving him as much as Scott's echoing words.

"Love you, too."

***

Two days later, Drew stopped in at the hospital on his way to the station house and let Scott stick him with a needle. One of the nice things about playing with a doctor was that you could get a rush done on blood work. Not that either of them was worried; it was just nice to know that they wouldn't have to wait long for the results to be back.

On his way home from work that night, he stopped at the drug store and bought more condoms. No need to stop playing while they waited for the lab work, after all.

The afternoon Scott arrived home waving their test results fresh from the lab Drew let him know in very certain terms what he wanted and they used the washing machine for something other than its intended purpose. It was the first time Scott had gone down on him, and Drew came so hard he thought he may have gotten close to passing out. Scott assured him that normal, healthy people didn't actually pass out during sex, so Drew went on to prove that some things are better experienced than discussed.

Chapter Seven

Scott got home at six in the morning, dead tired. He headed straight for the bed, skipping his shower and hating the need to even undress. All he wanted to do was fall onto the bed and sleep for a week. He only had ten hours, though, and he wanted to make the most of them; sleep for nine, take a shower and drink a pot of coffee to get him through his next shift.

When he got into the bedroom Drew was sprawled over their bed, sound asleep with one leg tossed over the covers and an arm wrapped around two pillows. Scott stripped and made himself pull the blinds down and close the curtains before he got in bed; nothing worse then noon sun when all he needed was sleep.

He got into bed, trying not to disturb Drew. He hadn't checked the schedule, but he was pretty sure Drew had to work soon and he wanted his lover to have as much sleep as he needed, too. The last thought he had as sleep fell over him was that Drew would do the same for him.

When he woke up he was alone. If the light sneaking in around the edges of the blinds was anything to go by, it was about mid-afternoon. Perfect. He stretched and rolled over, hoping to sneak in some more sleep before he had to get up. He couldn't remember if he'd set the alarm, though, so he forced himself to look at the clock. Two-thirty. He had half an hour to spare.

The next time he woke up the phone was ringing. He reached for it blindly, arm flailing in the general direction of the sound. It rang four times before he managed to snag the receiver and pull it under the covers with him, not wanting any body heat to escape yet. It was warm in bed, and friendly. The world out there would just have to wait.

"Hello?"

"It's three. I love you. Get up and go to work."

The alarm went off.

"Drew?"

"Doc, wake up. I love you. Go to work."

"'Kay."

"Are you sitting up?"

"Yeah."

"Liar. Get up."

Scott sat up. "I'm up." He could smell coffee.

"Coffee's on. Take a shower, drink it. I love you. I'll see you later."

"Drew?"

"Yeah?"

"I love you, too."

"I know. Go to work."

Chapter Eight

Their first Christmas was a horrible tangle of work schedules, limited downtime and the phone ringing off the hook as their families tried to decide where Scott and Drew would be at any given time. Scott had to work Christmas Day, and Drew was on call throughout the week, so they finally told their moms that if they could both turn up at once they would, but not to count on it.

Their mothers didn't take it well.

"God," Scott said as he hung after another stressful phone call with his mother. "What is with them? Mom's never been this worked up about Christmas dinner before. If I was there on Christmas Day, there was a turkey. If I could only make it on Christmas Eve, there was a turkey. Now she's freaked that you'll starve or something."

Drew grinned up at him from where he was sprawled on the couch. "She likes me, is all."

Scott snorted. "And your mother has been calling three times a week, why?"

"To make sure we'll both there for Christmas dinner." He held up his hands. "Yeah, I know. Last year I didn't even get any, and this year there'll be tears if I don't get two. Wanna run away?"

Scott smiled. "With you? Always."

Drew pulled Scott down into his lap just as his pager went off. He took a quick look at it and said, "Shit. See you later, Doc."

Scott grabbed hold of his arm even as he was dumped onto the couch. "Be careful."

Drew looked at him. "Always," he said softly.

Then he was gone.

He got back home six hours later, tired, sore, and thoughtful. He went to toss in a load of laundry and found the washing machine full of scrubs and the dryer full of his own T-shirts and jeans. He moved laundry from machine to machine to basket, then took a shower and went out to the kitchen to re-check the whiteboard. Scott should have been home, but he wasn't. Disappointed, Drew made himself something to eat and sat in front of the TV, watching Christmas specials for an hour and a half before the kitchen door opened and Scott came in, arms full of bags. He grinned at Drew before giving him the official stay the hell out of the bags warning.

Cool. Presents.

Scott came back from hiding the bags and fell onto the couch beside him. "You okay?" He slid cold hands along Drew's neck.

"Hey!" Drew shivered and grabbed for Scott's hands, pulling him down for a kiss. "Yeah. Just a kitchen fire that went a little nuts. No one hurt, but a real mess to clean up."

Scott kissed him again and curled into his body, just right. He always felt just right after a hard day. Always felt just right. They watched a couple more specials, finally turning off the TV after Charlie Brown got his tree. Drew held Scott to him, wanting to talk about something but not sure how to bring it up.

"What's wrong?" Scott asked quietly, and Drew grinned to himself. Man always knew.

"Nothing really. Just something that happened at the fire." Scott looked up at him, eyes troubled until Drew shook his head. "Nothing bad, just interesting. We get there and everyone is out of the house, standing around watching the fire, right? A man and two women, a couple of dogs. Turns out that the three of them all live there."

Scott nodded his head and Drew figured he hadn't explained it very well. "Together, Doc. This guy, his wife, and their girlfriend."

Scott blinked up at him. "The guy moved his girlfriend in?"

"No, she's their girlfriend. The three of them are together." Drew watched as the idea sank in, Scott's eyes getting wide. "It was kind of strange at first, when we figured it out. They're off to the side, watching us soak down their place, and the three of them were all sort of..." he paused, trying to find a way to explain what he'd seen. "They're all comforting each other. They're touching each other, or holding hands, and it really didn't seem like it mattered who they were holding. They all love each other; they all got what they needed. The women, as well; I could see how much they needed each other. It was kind of cool."

Scott sat up and looked at him. "The three of them? I mean, I can see three people getting together for fun and games, but for a relationship?"

Drew nodded. "Yeah, that's why I thought it was cool. I mean, I only saw them for a couple of hours, I don't know how it works. But, shit, Scott. You and me, we see people when their lives are falling apart. It was good to see them drawing from each other, see how much they could rely on one another. That can't be a bad thing."

Scott settled against him again and was quiet for a bit. When he spoke again his voice was speculative. "Three. That'd be hard to do. I mean, I'm sure it would work for the right people, but how do you find the right people? I mean, do you go looking? Do you just find someone and say, 'Hey, my partner and I were wondering if you want to be a part of us?' or do these things just happen?"

Drew shrugged. "Don't know. Probably both. I expect that there are people looking to only be a part of a group, and other people who just sort of wind up in a relationship with a couple. Happens all the time for sex, right?"

Scott nodded slowly. "Well, yeah, I guess. But sex is different. Isn't it? I mean, two people in a relationship can go to a bar and pick someone up for a night, right? How often do you think that turns into something real?"

"Sometimes it does, maybe." Drew kissed the top of Scott's head. "Just thought it was neat to see something like that working, you know? I'm going to bed, you coming?"

"Yeah." Scott sounded distracted. "I'm going to get another load of scrubs in, I'll be right there." He looked up at Drew and smiled. "Get my side of the bed warm."

Drew grinned and went to bed, listening to Scott lock up and get the laundry shifted and the machines going. He made sure to warm up the middle of the bed.

When Scott got in the bed they curled around each other, legs and arms twisting together until they were comfortable. At least, Drew was comfortable. Scott kept moving restlessly, shifting a little every few minutes.

"What's wrong?" Drew finally asked.

Scott sat up, and Drew looked up at him the dark, not quite able to make out his features.

"Just thinking about it, I guess. Could you ever see us with someone else?"

Drew rolled onto his back and thought about it. He'd had the occasion fantasy about being with two guys at once, but he figured that was normal. He pictured himself with Scott and another body in their bed. That was...okay. He tried to picture Scott, laid out on the bed with him inside him and someone else kissing them, another set of hands touching them. That was more than okay. "Umm. Not sure what you want to hear."

"The truth." Scott's reply was sure and immediate.

Drew sighed. "Honestly? With you and me I think it would have to be all or nothing, you know? Some hot guy we're both into, fuck all night and send him home, never see him again and get on with our lives."

"Or?"

Drew sat up as well, looking toward Scott in the dark. "Or the real deal. Everything. Someone who loves you, loves me. Someone we both love."

Scott's hand touched his face, tracing his jaw. "You think there's someone like that out there?" he asked quietly.

Drew reached up, capturing Scott's hand in his own. "Don't know. But I'm sure as fuck not going looking. Got what I need."

Scott responded with a searing kiss that said more than words could. Eventually, they slept.

Chapter Nine

New Year's Eve and Scott would be working. Drew wasn't sure why that surprised him, but it did. Scott was always working; he thought he'd have gotten used to that by now. Six months of spending most of his free time without Scott and he was still disappointed when he looked at the whiteboard in the kitchen.

He glanced at his watch. Less than an hour and a half before Scott had to leave, and then he wouldn't be home for twelve hours. At which point they would both be home for about two hours, but Scott would be in bed asleep and Drew would be getting ready for his shift at the station house.

Drew pushed a hand through his hair as he studied the chart. Goddamn. Something had to be wrong with it, it just didn't make sense. He picked up the sheet of paper he'd tossed on the table and looked at it, checking that he'd written his shifts in correctly. He'd just been put on a permanent rotating shift, effective January first, and he could have made a mistake writing it on the calendar.

For the first two weeks he was scheduled from eight until four in the afternoon, third and fourth weeks midnight to eight, then two weeks of four to midnight. It wasn't going to change no matter how long he looked at the paper, and he'd put it up on the wall right.

"Scott?" he called out, still staring at the board.

He heard a muffled reply from the bedroom, then Scott came down the hall to the kitchen, dressed in his jeans and sweatshirt, not rushing to get ready for work.

"Still got the sheet with your shifts on it?" Drew asked, still looking at the board.

Scott raised an eyebrow and said, "Yeah, over here, I think," He crossed to the cupboards by the back door and dug around for a moment. He held out four sheets of paper.

"Uh, this is the last four months." He grinned sheepishly. "Suppose I should put them in the recycling, huh?"

Drew smiled and winked at him. "Why start now?" He turned his attention to the sheet for January and spent a few moments making some calculations. "Pass me a pencil," he finally said.

Scott snickered and handed one out to him.

A couple of minutes later he checked Scott's off hours with the ones on the wall. He nodded to himself. "Right. That fucking sucks." He looked at Scott and shook his head. "Do we have a calculator around here?"

Scott crossed to the cupboard again and searched through a couple of drawers, finally producing one. He handed it to Drew wordlessly and waited while Drew sat at the table, pushing a pile of books out of the way.

Drew wrote numbers on the back of one of the shift sheets, looking back and forth between his calculations and the calendar. "We have," he said, still looking at the paper, "an average of thirteen hours a week when we're both home and not asleep. Thirteen. One week there's fifteen, and the week after next we've got ten."

He sat back on the chair with a sigh and looked up at Scott, who was staring at the chart and biting his lower lip, forehead drawn. After a couple of moments he nodded and glanced at Drew.

"Yeah, that sounds right. Plus, we share about two days off in the month." He didn't sound surprised. Or upset.

"You knew it was that little? I mean, I know we don't get to just hang out much, but I guess I thought I saw you more than that." Drew was a little taken aback by Scott's matter-of-factness. He really had thought they spent more time together than that.

Scott shrugged. "Well, I'm the one working the hours, you know? I know how much I'm not here. But when we're both here, it's good. Even if we're asleep, it's better than when we're apart, you know?"

Drew smiled at him. "Yeah, it's good. Just thought it was more." He reached over and tugged at Scott's belt until he could maneuver him into his lap. He wrapped his arm around Scott's waist, resting his head on his back. "Miss you when you're not here."

"Hmm. Miss you, too. But again, I'm working. You're just sitting here being bored."

"No, I'm not," Drew said absently. Scott smelled good, like fabric softener and soap and the light smell of just Scott.

He felt Scott chuckle. "Not bored? That's good. Although you really do watch too much TV, then."

"No, I mean I don't stay here." Drew rubbed a hand across Scott's flat stomach and wondered if they had time to play before Scott had to go to work.

Scott stiffened in his arms. "Where do you go?" he asked, far too casually.

Drew froze, not sure what to say all of a sudden and wondered why he was feeling defensive. He hadn't done anything wrong.

"Uh, sometimes I go play pool with Dave," he said cautiously. He didn't loosen his hold on Scott. "And sometimes I go see a movie with someone. Once in a while I'll go to Shots with the guys from work."

"Oh." Scott didn't sound mad, or upset, or even overly casual anymore. He just sounded flat, like he didn't have anything to give to the conversation anymore.

Drew wished he could see Scott's face. "What?" he finally asked.

Scott moved Drew's arms from his waist and stood up. "Nothing. Really. I'm glad you have stuff to do and...stuff."

He didn't look glad. He was chewing his lip again and he couldn't seem to decide what to do with his hands. He moved around the kitchen, like he wanted to sit but he wanted to lean on the counter, too.

"Yeah, I have stuff I can do," Drew said, his eyes not leaving Scott. "And it's not like you sit here when I'm working nights and you're home."

Scott stared at him and he knew. "You do," Drew said quietly. "You just stay here."

Scott shook his head. "Not like that. Not the way you think." He growled a little, deep in his chest. "Look, I don't think you quite understand this. The time I spend with you is time I take away from the other stuff. When I'm home alone, I work." He gestured with his hand, waving to the pile of books on the table. "I catch up on charts, I study, I go over procedures. That's the way it is for me. I work, I work some more, and I'm with you."

Drew shook his head, not understanding. "But you've got to have a life, Scott. Shit, are you telling me that for the last six months you haven't gone anywhere that I haven't?"

Scott crossed his arms in front of him and frowned. "This is my life, Drew. When I don't study 'cause I'd rather be with you, I have to make up the time when you're not home. When I go back to that hospital I have to face attending physicians, patients, supervisors, the head of the program...I may not be having exams, but I'm sure getting tested. You knew what I did before we ever started up, so don't give me your 'poor Scott' shit now. This is the way it is for me."

Drew shook his head. "There has to be more, Doc. That's just not…not healthy, you know? I can't be everythi—"

"You're not." Scott was standing straight, his back rigid, arms still crossed in front of him. "It's not like I don't have a life at all. You think I was completely alone before I moved in here?"

"No, that's not—" Drew tried to interrupt, but Scott's voice was rising. Drew'd never seen him like this, and it was unsettling, to say the least.

"I have friends. I talk to people—all day long, I talk to people who do the same thing I do. You aren't my world, Drew. I love you, but you aren't my world."

Drew knew he flinched and hated that Scott would see how much that stung. He watched as Scott's eyes widened with regret, his shoulders slumping, making the angry posture one simply of pain. Drew stared, unable to respond. He took a deep breath and went over the conversation in his mind, unable to see where this had all started.

"Help me out here, Scott. Are you pissed 'cause I go out, because you didn't know, or 'cause I didn't know that you stay home?"

Scott closed his eyes and leaned on the counter, his hands falling to his sides. "I…I'm not mad that you go out. I wish I'd known; would have been nice to know what movies have sucked lately, if nothing else."

Drew tried to smile at the attempted joke, but didn't manage very well. Scott didn't even try. "So, what then?"

Scott looked around the kitchen for a moment and then looked at Drew. "I don't know," he said softly. "Guess maybe I feel like I'm the outside of reality sometimes. When it hits, it gets me twisted."

Drew nodded slowly. "And you and me, we've been living in our own little world."

"Yeah, maybe." Scott sighed and pushed himself away from the counter. "I gotta go get ready for work."

He walked toward the hall and Drew reached out a hand to grab his arm as he passed. "Scott."

Scott stopped and looked down at him.

"You can't keep doing this."

Scott looked away. "Yeah. I can. I have to."

Drew watched Scott stalk down the hall to the bathroom and swore. Then he reached for the phone.

Chapter Ten

Scott stayed in the shower a long time, berating himself for what he'd said. He'd had no idea that Drew spent his time going out, being with other people...having a life. He hadn't looked, and maybe he'd made sure not to look. Once more, he'd managed to fool himself into thinking that the way he lived his life was normal, that others lived by the same sort of structure and strict schedule.

His head hurt. He knew that he was being stupid. He knew that he couldn't—and shouldn't—be everything for Drew. It wasn't healthy for two people to be that wrapped up in each other. But he'd been mostly convinced that they were all they needed. He'd made that mistake before.

His stomach was churning. He felt his skin flush and knew that he was red, not from the hot water, but from humiliation. He felt a wave of nausea pass over him, and shuddered at the memory it brought with it. Everything came back to that, everything was tied to another man, another time.

He'd been so sure that Jeremy was happy, that the separation of three provinces during the school year wouldn't matter. Jeremy had been there for him all through his BSc, why wouldn't he be there through med school? For two years in Nova Scotia, all was well. He studied, worked, went home for the holidays. Phoned Jeremy as often as possible, saw him when he could, loved him as often as they could manage it. He spent the entire time completely unaware of what Jeremy was doing, wrapped up the warmth of his own perceptions.

And then he found out how wrong he had been, and how little Jeremy had shared with him. He'd spent a long night in the dark, wandering around in woods away from their tent, rethinking everything and finally seeing how willingly blind he had been, how stunningly overeager he always was. What a fool he'd been.

Scott had learned most of the lessons well. He wasn't pushy anymore, never made the first move or any move at all unless he was dead sure it was wanted. He didn't make demands and he didn't expect to be treated like royalty. But he'd missed the lesson about paying attention to what his partner was doing in his free time, intent on not becoming a suspicious person. He had thought that even asking was evidence of a suspicious nature, and he had never wanted to be nosy. He'd never asked, and Drew had never offered.

Scott shook his head, spraying water out of his hair. Stupid. Stupid. Stupid. He turned off the water and got himself ready for work, trying with only moderate success to shove his anger at himself and the idiocy of his past away once more. He still had to apologize to Drew and try to make this right again, then get to the hospital. He didn't have time to linger over his weakness.

He could see the past repeating and knew the outcome would be inevitable. Drew would tire of being alone so often, miss him in bed too many times, resent waking up alone, and go to one movie too many without him. And then it would be over.

Scott looked at himself in the mirror as he shaved and frowned.

"Fuck, you're sick," he whispered to himself. "Are you going to just give it all up, throw him away before he chucks you?"

His reflection stared back, not giving any indication of the right way to go with this…this…whatever the hell it was. Crisis? Breakdown? Moment of intense selfishness and wallowing?

Scott dried off and looked away from the mirror while he dressed, and then back again. "No goddamn way. Give him more credit than that. And no running."

He went back to the kitchen to find Drew still sitting at the table, his eyes tired and sad. Scott stood in the doorway, taking in the slumped shoulders that straightened as soon as Drew knew he was there. They looked at each other for a moment before Scott stepped forward and sat down at the table.

"I'm sorry," he said quietly. "I have a screwed up view of how life is supposed to be lived, I suppose."

Drew was already shaking his head, brown eyes serious. "Not really. But sort of. Look, you've got yourself into this mind-set, right? It's like you know that there is an end to having to work so hard, so you just block out everything else, knowing that it'll be different when you're done your residency."

Scott nodded. "Yeah, I guess."

Drew was looking at him carefully, and Scott got the impression that he was being assessed.

"You play poker," Drew said suddenly. It wasn't a question. "Pardon?"

"You. You play poker." Drew was insistent.

"Uh, yes?" Scott said, confused by the sudden change of topic.

Drew shook his head and took a breath. "You're going to get out of your shell. You're now playing poker on Wednesday nights if you're not working. Dave's place, and if he's working it moves to

Jim's. If I'm off, too, we both go. You can study when I'm home if you have to."

Scott stared. "Excuse me? You're ordering me to play cards with your friends? Isn't that taking guilt a little far?"

Drew stood up suddenly, his eyes flashing. "I don't feel guilty, Scott. I have nothing to feel guilty for. But you are going to start playing real life now if it kills me. I won't let you live like this."

Scott looked at the table and stood up carefully, going to the closet for his coat. "I'm going to work now. I'll not be told what to do, or how to live my life, Drew. Not by anyone." His heart was beating loudly in his ears and he felt a little faint. He pulled on his shoes and opened the door before looking at Drew again.

Drew was standing by the counter, watching him, his mouth a thin line, hands clenched. "I'm not trying to give you orders, Scott. Trying to help you."

"Did I ask?" Scott's voice sounded harsh to even his own ears. He stepped out into the cold December evening. "I'll see you later," he tossed over his shoulder.

He was next to useless at work that night, barely making it through his rounds on the cardio ward without screwing up. He kept thinking about Drew and hating himself for being such a jerk. Everyone around him still seemed to be caught up in the holiday spirit, the halls still decorated with garlands and bows. The nurses were smiling and chatty, and he finally escaped to the doctors' lounge just before midnight.

The room was empty, everyone else gathering around the few available phones; most wanted to call their loved ones right on the stroke of twelve. Scott didn't think Drew would expect him to call.

He looked up when one of the nurses came in and gave her a half-wave when she greeted him with a bouncy hello.

She stopped and looked closely at him, then sat down. He didn't know her really well, but her eyes were all concern anyway as she asked him what was wrong.

"Not much," he said mildly. "My roommate's decided that I have no life and he's gotten me into a regular poker game."

She blinked at him. "That's nice."

Scott snorted. "He didn't ask first."

"Well, no," she said as if speaking to a child. "You would have said no. And then he wouldn't have been able to help you, right? C'mon. I watch you guys all the time. You wanna know something I've noticed?" Scott shrugged and she went on, "The ones who burn out, drop out, and give up? They're the ones who work the hardest, study the most, kick ass at the job. Until they can't do it anymore."

Scott stared at her, not sure what to say.

"The good doctors?" she continued, looking him in the eye, "The ones who give and work and do their jobs the best they can? The one's who last, who care the most? They're the ones with balance. This roommate of yours, he's trying to help. If you don't want to play 'cause you hate cards, fine. But take it from me, you need something like this. Tell yourself it'll make you a better doctor, if that what it takes to get you interested in something; don't be stubborn just 'cause you don't want to give in to this guy."

He sat and thought for almost ten minutes after she left. He thought about it some more as he went back to work. At one in the morning, he called Drew.

Chapter Eleven

In March, Scott attended a residents' meeting designed to organize a Christmas charity event to raise money for the pediatrics ward. At the end of the meeting he was somewhat startled to find himself co-chair.

Drew was doubtful. "Yeah, 'cause you have so much free time. How did you get suckered into this?"

"It's a good cause," Scott said defensively. "Besides, I have eight months to get this thing together and a bunch of people helping."

Drew just shook his head and made Scott promise not to ditch any Wednesday night meetings. Poker night was not to be missed for anything other than work or serious injury. Scott nodded, surprised at his own lack of reluctance to the agreement.

He'd agreed to the poker games as a way to apologize to Drew for being an utter shit on New Year's Eve, intending to go as often as he could, play a few hands, and have a miserable time. It had been the middle of January before he'd had a free Wednesday and he'd thought very briefly of trying to get out of it, but things between him and Drew were still tense and he didn't want to make anything worse.

He'd spent the night before the game going over charts in the living room, his feet in Drew's lap. Drew had rubbed his feet and watched TV with the sound down really low and had made every effort to let Scott get as much work done as he wanted to. When they'd gone to bed, Drew had told him that an evening like that wasn't any different than just sitting watching TV with him.

"Don't care what we do, Doc. Just want to be with you."

Drew had made love to him carefully that night, underscoring his statement with the way he moved, with every touch. He'd loved with his hands and mouth, touching and whispering, making Scott believe for the first time that it would be okay to sit with paperwork during their time together. The key was that they were together.

He'd gone to that first card game with Drew and had been thankful. He'd met a couple of the guys before, but not in a social setting, and he'd been unsure about just arriving into a group of people who were easy and relaxed with each other. What he'd found had set his mind to rest quickly.

There were about ten regular players and on any given Wednesday only five or six could show up. The other players were all firemen or EMTs, so shift work ensured that the table would always have different faces. That particular night, Scott was the sixth, so he sat out the first couple of hands, just observing.

Drew introduced him around and the others all settled around the table, drinking beer and chatting about who was working and who would be there next week, and what the hell happened at some fire. Scott helped himself to a beer and sat on the couch, answering questions tossed his way, happy enough to be on the outskirts for the moment.

They had a twenty-dollar limit, in that everyone showed up with twenty and when it was gone you were out, end of story. They had settled on a dollar to ante and you could bet or raise as much as you wanted, but when your money ran out, you were done.

Drew was sitting with his back to him and Scott could see his cards. He had a shit hand and was trying to bluff his way into the next round, but dropped out when Dave wouldn't back down. Scott smiled to himself as he watched them play. He may not have wanted to really be there, but it looked like it could be a profitable night, at least. He kept quiet until one of the guys opted out of the third hand, leaving a chair free, then settled himself.

Drew looked to be having a good time. He was laughing and joking with the others, complaining about his mother of all things, and wishing the weather would warm up. He'd been out a lot on flue fire calls and was starting to get tired of the stupidity. The others agreed that it would be good for someone to teach people who owned fireplaces how to inspect their chimneys. Scott followed the conversation casually, drawing two more cards when asked how many he wanted, raising the bet a little each time it came around to him.

By the time the others started to really pay attention, he had the pot up to twelve dollars. One by one they dropped out, watching him with sharper eyes, until it was just him and Drew, eighteen dollars on the table between them.

Drew glanced at his cards again and looked at Scott. "Fuck."

Dave laughed. "You've lived with him for eight months and you can't read him?"

Scott glanced at him and grinned and then back at Drew, waiting. Drew sighed and raised again, another dollar. Scott didn't hesitate to up it once more.

Drew stared at him. "Fold." He tossed his cards on the table and endured the heckling from the others for a few moments before reaching across and grabbing Scott's cards. He looked at them and swore again. "Bastard."

Scott leaned back in his chair and smiled as sweetly as he could as he gathered his winnings and started to organize it for the next hand. "You asked it I played poker. You didn't ask how well."

The others watched Scott fairly closely after that, but didn't manage to win much money back from him. Scott didn't clean up the table, but he certainly left with more money than he had arrived with; he was feeling pretty good by the time they went home.

He was honest enough with himself to admit that only part of the good feeling was the money. He'd enjoyed being out with Drew, had found himself enjoying the joking and the chatter, the relaxed atmosphere.

He had enjoyed watching Drew, as well. Drew came alive with the other guys around. His laugh was louder, his wit fast and sharp. He was in his element, trading insults and jokes, teasing Dave about his attempt at growing a moustache and the red-headed guy—Tyler? Tyren?—about his upcoming wedding. He smiled almost nonstop. When they wound up in the kitchen together, alone for a brief moment, he kissed Scott hard, sharing the taste of chips and beer and whispered a quick thank you.

Scott didn't think about books or patients or anything medical all night. He laughed and drank and watched Drew, wondering about what he'd been missing the last few years.

He wondered for the first time if there was something beyond loving Drew and trying to be the best doctor he could. He wondered if there was something more for him, something open and friendly, that would be okay for him to get used to.

Chapter Twelve

Sometimes, Scott woke up from his dreams still smelling antiseptic and blood, shaking as Drew held onto him and kissed his hair. He'd let Drew calm him, let Drew talk him down, and then he could lose himself to the heat that Drew built around him. Usually it worked and he would sleep again, but some nights he would lie still and listen to the even breath coming from the warm body beside him, in him, and he would still be awake when it was time to get out of bed and go back to work.

When Drew dreamed it was harsh and unforgiving. He'd cry out in his sleep, his voice broken with pain and fear, and Scott would gather him into his arms and wait until Drew woke up. He would try to soothe the fear away, try to be something warm and alive that Drew could take and feel safe in. Most times it was enough. When it wasn't, he would get out of bed and make sweet tea, and they would watch TV, legs tangled on the couch until they were exhausted.

This time, Scott woke up when Drew started to thrash and he reached out for him, half-formed words and phrases already spilling from his lips.

"Drew. Shh, baby. Wake up, it's okay. Just me here; it's okay."

Drew sat up in bed and shuddered, then threw back the sheets. "Be right back."

Scott lay on the bed as Drew left the room, confusion overriding the sleepy fear that always happened when they woke like this. As Drew began turning on the lights all over the house Scott got out of bed and pulled on a pair of shorts, following him to the kitchen.

Drew was testing all the smoke detectors in the house. When he had checked the one in the basement and the shrill beeping had died away, he got the fire extinguisher off the kitchen counter and tested that, too.

"We need another one." Drew's voice was steady, but it was clear that he wouldn't stand for an argument. His shoulders were tight, his entire body so tense he was trembling.

"Isn't that one working?" Scott asked carefully.

Drew looked at him, his eyes dark and serious. "It's fine. We need more, though. There should be one in the basement, and we could put one behind the bedroom door."

Scott just nodded and said, "If you want. Yes, if you think so. Can you get them tomorrow?"

Drew's eyes were still on him and Scott realized that Drew was ready to go get them now, that he couldn't take another minute in the house without more fire extinguishers.

"Drew. Come to bed. We'll be fine until tomorrow."

Drew looked at the floor, and then back up at him, but he didn't move. Scott turned off the lights and took his hand, pulling him, rather than leading him, back to bed.

When they were back under the warm blankets, Scott held onto him and stroked his back, holding them chest to chest. "Want to talk about it? The dream?"

"No."

Scott kissed him gently. "Okay. Are you going to be able to sleep?"

"No."

Scott rubbed at Drew's back for long minutes. Gradually Drew relaxed in Scott's arms, and just when Scott began to think that he might actually be able to sleep, despite his saying otherwise, Drew sighed.

"Scary, you know?" he whispered.

"Fire? Yeah." Scott did know. He didn't fight the fires, didn't know the heat and hunger of it, but he dealt with the aftermath, the people who came in with burns, their eyes blank with shock. People who would look at him and whisper, 'It chased me'. He knew because Drew sometimes had dreams, and occasionally smelled like smoke and burned wood, melted tar and chemicals. Scott knew that fire was scary.

Drew shook his head. "Fire. But not that. Dreaming…not being able to do anything. Not having control as homes burn, not being able to get in and save you." Drew's voice wavered at the end.

Scott's hands stuttered over Drew's back, his rhythm faltering in his surprise. "Me?"

Drew kissed his chest. "You. First time I've dreamed about you and fire and I didn't save you."

Scott looked down at him. "I'm here. I'm okay."

Drew kissed him, not gently. "Here," he said hoarsely. "Make sure you're here." A dam had broken somewhere and Drew surged up Scott's body, hands roaming over him, hard and searching. Scott took in a sharp breath as Drew's fingers dug into his arms, his legs, his ass. He was rolled onto his back as Drew moved above him, hands and mouth moving restlessly over his skin.

"Drew," he said, his voice tight with want, though he wasn't sure if he wanted Drew to slow down or just take what he needed. Drew captured his mouth in a fierce kiss, teeth and tongue claiming his breath.

Drew was hard against him, layers of muscle and smooth skin on his own hard cock pushing at his hip. Drew groaned and moved to bite at his neck, taking skin in his teeth almost hard enough to draw blood. Scott moved with him, hunger building under the assault of raw need. He thrust up into Drew, drawing harsh sounds from Drew's throat.

Drew pulled himself up farther, knees spreading Scott's legs. Scott gasped and wrapped his legs around Drew's hips, fumbling only long enough to find the lube and stroke Drew quickly with a slick hand before pulling the man down and in. Drew pushed into him, stretching and filling him, hard cock moving into him slowly until Drew was in as deep as he could possibly be.

Scott stared up into dark eyes and saw something powerful that hadn't been there before. Drew stared back, not looking away as he began to move within Scott, thick cock sliding until he was almost out and then sinking in again. Drew held his gaze even as his breathing become moans and sighs, words that meant nothing and everything.

Scott's hands were on Drew's back again, fingernails drawing lines as he pulled Drew into him, clutching and feeling muscles work as he tried to stop Drew from pulling out of him and relaxing again as Drew pushed in.

It went on for ages, the sounds they were making growing more intense as they looked at each other. Scott cried out as the head of Drew's cock slid across his gland and Drew did it again.

Scott began to shudder. He arched his back as Drew pushed deep, need spiraling out of control, his hips snapping up to meet Drew's as the pace increased. He slid a hand around Drew's body, from his back down his side, across the planes of his belly until he could touch himself, pulling himself as Drew brought him closer and closer to the edge.

Drew was still looking at him, meeting his eyes. Scott stroked himself and felt his balls draw up, knew he was going to come. He saw something flare in Drew's eyes and then Drew was kissing him, tongue matching the thrust of his cock as Scott came, heat splashing between them. Drew groaned and Scott shuddered, muscles twitching as his orgasm passed over him. He was flying, had no control left at all, his body riding out its pleasure as he moved on Drew's cock.

Drew broke the kiss and pulled away from his mouth far enough to say, "You're here," and then he was coming, filling Scott with his heat.

"Here," Scott answered. "Right here."

Chapter Thirteen

By May, Scott and the committee had a venue for the gala event and had tentatively lined up entertainment. Scott was particularly pleased that he had nothing to do with the entertainment: that sounded stressful. All he had to coordinate was the food, the decorations, and the venue. Within budget, of course.

Scott came home from work one night later than he had expected. He'd been hauled into one more conference about the event, which was now known as the Resident's Gala for Kids, and had been held up for an hour. When he went into the living room he stopped dead.

"Uh, Drew?"

"Yeah, Doc." Drew didn't look up from where he was sorting metal rods amid a huge mess of canvas and netting.

"What are you doing?" Scott looked around the room. Canvas, netting, lots of metal bits, a gas lamp…oh, God. Camping crap.

"Sorting the tent pegs from the support poles." Drew glanced up and grinned at him, happier than a dog with a new bone, his eyes dancing.

"Why?" Scott asked faintly.

"Because I checked the calendar and you and I both have two days off. And I checked the weather, which is going to be stunning. And you, dear doctor, and I, fine firefighter, are going camping." Drew beamed up at him and Scott's stomach knotted.

"Oh," he said as he backed into the kitchen. "That's…gotta be a mistake."

But a quick glance at the whiteboard said no, in fact, it wasn't. Not only did they have the coveted two days off together, but someone other than himself had taken the red marker and written 'Drew's Birthday Camping Trip' across the blank squares.

Oh, fuck. Fate sealed.

Arms looped around his waist. "Scott?"

"Yeah. Uh…okay. Camping. Cool."

Drew turned him around. "You hate camping, don't you?"

"Not so much. I'm sure it will be fine. And…and…fun, even." He tried out a smile.

Drew frowned at him. "Why don't you like camping?"

Scott searched his mind for something true that wouldn't drag his insecurities and neurosis out into the open.

"I got poison ivy in Algonquin Park when I was eight," he finally said.

"So stay away from poison ivy. Don't give me that shit, either. You looked sick when I said camping, and I doubt very much if a case of poison ivy would do that to a doctor. Why don't you want to go?" Drew's voice was quiet, full of concern.

Guilt washed over Scott. He didn't want Drew to worry about this; it was too stupid for that. "I'll go with you. Really, I will. It's what you want for your birthday, and how did it get to be May twenty-fourth so damn soon anyway?"

Drew kissed the tip of his nose. "The endless rise and fall of the sun, and don't change the subject. I'm not going to drag you off into the woods unless you're cool with it, and you aren't. We can talk about it or we can drop it. But I don't like it when you keep shit from me."

Scott leaned his head on Drew's shoulder and sighed. "And I don't like it when you spring shit on me. But I want to go camping. It makes you happy."

"So tell me why you're so freaked about it. And I'm sorry; I thought it would be a nice surprise, not something that would bother you." His hand was rubbing circles on Scott's back. It felt nice.

Scott took a breath. "Went camping with Jeremy and got dumped. I hadn't seen him in about two months, and I came home early just as he was leaving, and he said for me to go with him so I did, and it turns out that he'd met someone and being alone with me proved he didn't want to be, and I spent most of the night in the woods crying and then I had to hitch a ride back to the city in the morning, and I know you're not going to do that, but it really sorta bothers me."

Drew's hand stilled. "Excuse me?"

"You really want to hear about this?" Scott wasn't sure if this was the sort of thing you share with your current lover or not. And he was damn sure he wasn't going to tell all of it, but he was resigned to at least easing Drew's worry.

"Umm, maybe just in a more coherent sentence or three. I'm pretty sure you forgot to breathe." Drew let him go and went to the fridge. "Beer or juice?"

"Beer." Drew handed him one and he sat at the kitchen table. "Okay, it went like this. I was away at school, hadn't seen Jeremy in about two months. I got back to the city a couple of days early and turned up on his doorstep just as he was loading the Jeep. He said 'C'mon', so I hopped in and we were off."

Drew nodded and drank from his beer, leaning against the kitchen counter. "Yeah, that's cool. Get out of town, see your man. Got that part. But what's with the dumping and the crying?"

Scott looked at the table. "He wasn't expecting me, right? He was taking off for a couple of days to think. He'd met someone and didn't know how he felt, thought he owed it to me to really get his head on right."

"How long had you been together?" Drew sounded curious and Scott suddenly realized he knew nothing about Drew's past lovers. He didn't think he wanted to know.

He looked up. "Over six years."

"Shit," Drew said matter-of-factly. "Long time."

Scott nodded. "Yeah. And I was completely oblivious. All I knew was that I hadn't seen him in two months and we were alone." He shrugged. "He didn't want me. He told me he'd met this guy and I took off. Spent some time wandering the trails and hitched back in the morning."

Scott thought that a little selective retelling was justified. He didn't see any point in telling Drew the details, about how he had waited and waited while they set up the tent. He hadn't even so much as been kissed, and he was desperate to be with Jeremy. He'd spent two months alone and missing him and needing him and there he was. So he'd waited until the sleeping bags were laid out and he'd wrapped his arms around his lover and kissed him. He'd pushed him back onto the air mattress and moved against him, wanting him so much.

Jeremy had pushed him off and wiped his mouth, staring at him with dark and angry eyes. "Wait for an invitation, asshole," he'd said.

The complete and utter humiliation Scott had felt had only doubled and trebled when Jeremy started to tell him just how little he really knew about the last six months of their relationship. How little he was cared about.

And somewhere in the back of his mind he could hear his mother. "Oh, baby, I'm sorry. But you were never there. You were at school for so long, and then you left for two years…he needed to be happy, too." Never there, too busy, leave your man alone too much. His mom had worked herself into being gay positive, but she wasn't quite on the positive side of long-term relationships, then.

That conversation had made him feel worse. Jeremy had hurt him, and the humiliation lingered like smoke around him, his own mother helping the stench to cling even though she hadn't meant to.

"He really hurt you."

Scott blinked at the sound of Drew's voice, coming back to the kitchen and reality with a start. He looked at Drew and nodded. "Yeah." Not much point in mentioning his mom's role. "But that was five years ago, and I know you're not going to do that. I just…I was surprised."

Drew finished his beer. "I get that. C'mon, give me a hand." He went to the living room and started to bundle the canvas.

Scott sighed, hating that it was his fault Drew wouldn't get a simple camping trip for his birthday. "Drew, don't put it away. We can go camping. I want to go with you."

Drew looked at him and smiled. "Not putting it away, Doc. Grab some of this shit, will you?"

Confused, Scott gathered the poles and the lantern and waited while Drew stuffed the netting into a bag. When they had everything, Drew said, "Follow me," and led him through the kitchen to the back door.

Scott followed along, a grin starting to form. The man was a nut. A sexy, brilliant, crazy nut.

"Voila!" Drew said when they were outside, dropping the canvas. "Our first camping site." He spread his arms and gestured at the backyard. "We even have access to cold beer and a toilet that flushes."

Scott shook his head and grinned. "You're insane."

Drew dropped a quick kiss on his mouth. "Yeah. Help me put the damn tent up, will you?"

Chapter Fourteen

Drew had predicted—to himself, if not Scott—that the charity event would be a huge time suck. He was right. By late September Scott was hopelessly bogged down. He was constantly fielding phone calls from committee members, vendors, volunteers, and the man Drew often referred to as 'The Savior'. He tried not to let Scott know how much the lack of time together bothered him; there really wasn't anything Scott could do about it, and he'd already promised not to get involved with anything else until his residency was finished. Drew was pleased, however, that Scott always made it a point to go to every poker night that he wasn't working. Mind you, in Scott's case that could have been just for the profit.

In the beginning Scott hadn't had much trouble with the gala planning. Surprisingly, he wasn't having any difficulty getting volunteers to help out; time was in short supply for all the residents and a sense of camaraderie kept the offers flowing. The trouble, as Drew had expected, was money. The venue—a large hotel with a good reputation—had stuck to their quoted price, but they were the only ones. The first caterer Scott had hired had gone out of business in early June, and Scott hired the second company in what even he admitted was a fit of blind panic. He'd fired them when they kept adding fees for every little thing, including plate warmers.

Drew had spent a couple of July afternoons rubbing Scott's back and shoulders while he was on the phone, working his way through the yellow pages trying to get a new caterer. When the back rubs didn't have any noticeable effect at calming Scott down, Drew'd switched to his preferred method of relaxation. On the second day it had taken rimming and two blow jobs to reduce Scott to a boneless heap.

Finally, near the end of July, one of the nurses from the maternity ward had come to the rescue by way of a phone call to the house. Scott and Drew had been curled up on the couch watching a movie when the phone rang. Scott leaned over Drew to answer it, leaving Drew with little choice but to start trying to distract him. He'd just managed to get his hand down the back of Scott's jeans when he heard Scott agreeing to meet and possibly marry some guy named Tom.

He left his hand where it was and waited until Scott had hung up before calmly asking what the fuck that meant.

"It means that this Tom guy is going to save my ass from the budget-bastards-who-won't-give-me-any-more-money." Scott looked over his shoulder, his blue eyes wide and far too innocent. "Uh, are you intending to do anything with that hand, or just leave it there?"

Drew moved his fingers lower a fraction. "Depends on who this Tom is and how he's gonna save your ass. 'Cause this ass is mine."

Something flared in Scott's eyes and he wiggled a little. Drew filed that for later; a bit of possessiveness was apparently a good thing. Okay. He waited for Scott to come back to the conversation, though the way Scott's cock was poking against his thigh was starting to be a pretty big distraction, which was sort of contrary to the original plan.

Scott wiggled some more and rocked a bit, rubbing his erection on Drew's lap. Drew didn't respond, so Scott finally gave in with a sigh and told him that Tom was a professional event coordinator from Toronto who was offering to help get the Christmas gala back under budget.

"What, he just called you up out of the blue?" Drew was skeptical. Plus he was having trouble thinking, what with his cock trying to get out of his pants and Scott pushing all his own boundaries of what the first move was. Drew's hand down his pants was usually a good opening, but this was the first time Drew had started then stopped. It was kind of fun, really, although he wasn't too sure how much initiative Scott would take. Drew forced his mind back to the conversation with an effort. "He just trolling for charities to help out?"

Scott rolled his eyes. "No," he said patiently. "That was Fiona from Labor and Delivery; he's her brother. She heard about the catering crap and called him up to see if he'd help out. She was just letting me know that he's gonna call to see what he's got to..." he paused as Drew pushed his hand further into Scott's pants, tracing the line of his crease with one finger. "...to salvage. Are you going to do anything with that hand or are you just going to torture me?" Scott rocked his hips as he spoke, looking at Drew with hungry eyes.

Drew pretended to think about it for a moment, but by teasing Scott he wasn't getting off either and that just wasn't right. He pulled his hand out of Scott's jeans and reached for the remote control. "Did you want to watch this movie?"

Scott shook his head and wiggled his ass again.

"Up you get, Doc." Drew pushed Scott off his lap onto to the floor and waited until Scott stood up before grabbing him by the hips. "Going somewhere?" he asked as he pulled Scott's button fly open and admired Scott's prick.

"Uh, no?" Scott squeaked as Drew took him into his mouth.

Drew hummed happily as he sucked, playing over the hard flesh with the flat of his tongue as he used his hands to push Scott's jeans lower. He felt Scott clutch at his shoulders and heard the gasps and moans start up. He loved it when Scott got noisy.

He loved the way Scott tasted, the way his skin smelled. He nibbled his way along Scott's shaft and licked again and again at the head of Scott's prick, drawing out the flavor gathering there. He cupped Scott's balls in one hand and tugged gently as he ran his tongue around the base of Scott's cock, making needy little sounds that Scott echoed. His own cock was throbbing, but he was lost in the heat of Scott, the feel of this hard as fuck dick in his mouth and hands.

He used his hands and mouth to get Scott babbling and damn near crying out, then looked up. Scott was watching him with wide eyes, still making soft needy noises. "Wanna come, Scott?"

"God, yes. Please, I need to, I'm so close, please, Drew—" He certainly sounded desperate.

Drew fastened his lips on the left side of Scott's belly, sucking up a mark on the soft skin just above his pelvis, scraping with his teeth. Scott gasped and rocked against him, moaning softly. When he'd made a dark mark he studied it for a moment and made a twin for it on the other side, avoiding any contact with Scott's leaking erection. Scott was beyond words, just moaning and gasping when Drew used his teeth. When the second mark was as dark as the first, Drew looked up again.

"Now, Scott? You still want to come for me?"

Scott moaned. "Please—"

Drew reached under the couch and found the lube, snapping the bottle open as he started to suck Scott's cock again. He slicked his fingers fast as Scott tangled his fingers in Drew's hair, his hips swaying and picking up the pace. Scott was fucking his mouth, harsh sounds filling the room; they turned to a sharp cry as Drew slid his fingers into Scott's ass and brushed against his prostate.

Scott came hard, his whole body shuddering with the release, and Drew felt his own balls tighten in response. He let Scott slide from his mouth and stood up, holding Scott in place until he was behind him. He bit down on Scott's neck for a second and then growled in his ear.

"Ready?"

Not waiting for a response he pushed Scott down, draping him over the couch as he shoved his own gym pants out of the way, slicking his cock. He slid into Scott with a long, smooth thrust and groaned. "Fuck, so good." He thrust slowly, getting as deep as he could. Scott pushed back, hands braced on the couch somehow, forcing Drew even deeper. "Oh, God, Scott, so hot. So fucking tight."

Drew's breath was coming in short gasps as he moved, the pace picking up a notch as they found a rhythm. "Oh, God, oh, God, oh, God—" He was close, could feel it building in his back and in his balls, fire threading its way through his body, heat reaching to match Scott's around him. "Scott, gonna come, oh, fuck, love you—"

He threw back his head and cried out as his body was wracked with pleasure, spasms rolling through him like waves. When it was over he collapsed on Scott's back and stayed there for a minute, catching his breath. "Love you."

"Love you, too."

Drew kissed Scott's neck again and smiled when Scott shivered. He bit down a little and moved to his shoulder blade, scraping his teeth across the skin there, tasting salt. Scott moaned softly and he started to suck up another mark.

Scott gasped and shifted his body, letting Drew's softening cock slip out of him. Drew made his mark and moved over to the other side, starting to do it again as Scott took himself in hand, pulling at his cock with long strokes.

"God, don't stop," Scott whispered.

Drew made mark after mark, some light, some dark, scattering them all over Scott's back as Scott jerked off. He flipped him over and settled between spread thighs, moving to the softest skin he could find. As he closed his mouth over the skin next to Scott's balls, right at the top of his leg, Scott shuddered and sped up his hand, shooting as Drew made the last mark.

Drew licked at the mark, pressing his tongue on it. Scott hissed and Drew relented, finally standing up. "C'mon. Shower. Then bed, yeah?"

Scott smiled at him, happy and satiated. "Yeah. Sleep."

Drew raised an eyebrow at him. "Sleep?"

Chapter Fifteen

Scott was reaching his breaking point. It was mid-November, only three weeks before the Resident's Gala for Kids, and his personal stress level was higher than it had ever been. He was eating antacids like they were candy. He had dreams about a wall of phones, each one ringing incessantly. His mother was beginning to revert to behaviors he hadn't seen in years, which was worrisome. She was saying odd things, her voice always bright and happy, but her attitude was all about pushing Scott and Drew apart. He made a quick note to call his father to check up on her. He hadn't had a Wednesday night free for poker in five weeks, and here it was, Thursday. He'd missed poker by a day again. And he missed Drew. He missed everyone.

He sat on the couch and listened to the silence of the empty house. The quiet was nice, even necessary this time, but Scott would have given just about anything to have Drew there. He'd have liked to lean against something warm and spill out his anxiety to someone. He wanted to talk, to be soothed and held.

He was lonely.

He had taken the phone off the hook, allotting himself an hour with no chance of a phone call from anyone on the committee. He didn't want to talk to anyone about the gala—he was due at a meeting for that in a couple of hours, they could wait. He didn't even want to talk to Tom until then.

Tom. Drew called him 'The Savior', and Scott always laughed, 'cause it was pretty much true. He had connections and charm, and he'd managed to get everything on track within a few weeks, working by phone from Toronto. He'd found a caterer who would work easily with the hotel, thus cutting several costs. He'd talked a colleague into doing the decorating at cost plus twenty percent. He'd even managed to get the hotel to drop their rate on the banquet hall and donate three guestrooms and a suite to the committee members.

Scott and Tom had spoken on the phone frequently and met once when Tom was in town on other business and had dropped by the hospital to say hello. Scott found himself looking forward to their conversations, which were increasingly long and less about the gala. They never just chatted, nor did they share any more than the most innocent of personal stories, but Scott was beginning to feel a need for contact. He thought that perhaps it was not specifically Tom he was reaching for, but simply that he was welcoming a relationship, no matter how casual, with someone who was outside of the hospital, someone who wasn't tied to him through Drew or work or family. He also thought that he might be thinking about it too much.

He was becoming more and more dependent upon the poker nights, as well, and not just because he routinely came home with more money than he started with. He liked the freedom those nights gave him, the chance to just be Scott, not someone's doctor/student/co-worker. He wasn't expected to do anything other than play cards and have a few laughs. He sat around the table with the others, got to know them a bit, and just enjoyed himself. They didn't talk about anything serious, no one asked big questions or pressed him for information about anything other than if he wanted another beer or if he preferred chips or popcorn.

He liked the guys, too. Dave was crude and gruff, always the first with a dirty joke. He was also completely smitten with his tiny wife, Vicky Lynn. If she happened to be home at the start of the evening, swearing was not permitted, and if you slipped up you were expected to apologize to the little blonde. She would roll her eyes and kiss the cheek of the offender before leaving the house, calling out the number of the nearest pizza place that would deliver in less than half an hour. Scott adored her.

Ben was quiet and shy, never saying anything until at least the second hand—which coincided with his second beer. He was completely incapable of bluffing and Scott paid as close attention to how much Ben was losing as to how much he himself was winning, dropping out if Ben was down more than fifteen dollars early on. No fun to play if someone got cut out too soon.

Jim had a crush on Ben, Scott was sure of it. Drew insisted that neither of them was gay, so Scott just kept his mouth shut and tried not to gloat when Drew came out of Jim's kitchen one night with wide eyes. Drew glared at him, but when Ben and Jim came out sporting matching blushes, Scott knew he was right.

There were others who dropped in and out of the games, depending on their work schedules, and Scott liked them all to varying degrees. He liked that he fit in. He liked that no one looked at him funny if he showed up without Drew, or if Drew touched him more often than was necessary. He still didn't have a clue who knew about him and Drew, if any of them did, but it didn't matter. He was accepted for who he was.

He hadn't been there in too long, and now he was hiding from the rest of the world on a Thursday night with the phone off the hook. He stood up and went to the bedroom to change for the meeting, jumping nearly out of his skin when his pager went off in the silence. He snatched it up off the dresser and frowned when he saw the station house's number.

Picking up the portable phone, he called in as he started to change. When Drew finally came on the line he relaxed slightly and realized he'd been chewing his lip. He was going to have it bleeding before this damn charity event was over with.

"Hey, Doc. Who the hell have you been talking to? I've been trying to call for over half an hour." Drew sounded more worried than pissed and Scott shook his head.

"Sorry, I had it off the hook. Didn't want to deal, you know?"

There was a short silence. "Three more weeks, babe. And you better fucking promise me right now that you're not doing this again."

Scott laughed. "No. Not a chance in hell I'm doing this again."

"Better not." There was a pause. "You going out?"

Scott moved the phone to his other ear as he pulled his shirt on. "Yeah, just getting dressed. Meeting at the hospital in a while, gonna get this shit finished."

"Cool. You'll be home later?"

"Yeah, shouldn't be too late. I'll be asleep by the time you roll in, though."

Drew sighed. "Yeah. Listen, I should tell you now, then. I got another call from your mom this morning."

Scott sat on the edge of the bed. "Fuck," he said quietly. "What was it this time?"

"Just the same stuff. I didn't even realize it until I was off the line, you know?" Drew sighed again. "I'm sorry, Doc. Don't want to hurt you."

Scott shook his head. "You gotta tell me when she does this, you know that. What did she say?"

"She was just very concerned about me. Worried that I'm lonely, that I'm spending too much time on my own. 'You're such a nice man, Drew, and I worry that you're not getting everything you need.' That sort of stuff. She just sounds so sincere, I wind up reassuring her that I'm fine."

"That's the problem, she is sincere, and she really does like you. She doesn't see what she's doing."

"Yeah. But if she's doing it 'cause she cares maybe we should just ignore it, live our lives. She wants us to be happy."

"Drew, she wants you happy. She wants me happy. But in her heart she can't see us being happy together. She's still, deep down, hoping I'm going through some sort of phase. Some part of her is hoping that you'll wake up and see I'm not here and then you'll go find someone else."

"Leave you."

"Leave me so I can find just the right girl."

"So how come she waited until we've been together for this long? Why not a year ago, or fifteen months, or hell, why not at the start?"

"'Cause she was busy being all Supportive Mom. And she still thinks she's being like that. Look, I'll talk to her. Tell her we're together, staying together, and she may as well be happy with it. Dad…well, Dad's taken longer to come around, but he's really worked it out. He knows how strong this is."

"He does?" Drew sounded startled.

"Yeah. He does. Mom says the right things, but Dad—he believes them."

There was another short pause and then Drew said, "Cool." He sounded pleased.

Scott glanced at the clock. "I gotta go. I'll talk to Mom, promise. Not tonight, though."

"Don't worry about it. I'll see you when I get home. Love you."

"Love you, too." Scott was about to hang up when he suddenly said, "Drew? Can I ask you something?"

"Shoot."

"Are you lonely?"

"Is this your mom?" Drew asked carefully.

"No. Me." Scott looked around him at the silent house, suddenly itching to get out of it or he'd go crazy. It was always so empty these days. He thought about it for a moment and realized Drew hadn't answered.

"Drew?"

"Yeah, Doc. I'm here."

"Are you?"

"Not so much lonely as…I don't know. I miss you. Wish you were home more. That's all, really."

"I get that. I'll be here when you get home tonight."

"And that's making me want to ditch the last of my shift, so go to your meeting, see The Savior, and get your ass back where it belongs."

Scott smiled. "Yes, sir."

He was still grinning when he got to the hospital. He always liked it when Drew made it clear where he was wanted, where he was supposed to be. The smile grew wider for another reason when he saw Tom in the conference room. Tom looked up and grinned back, standing to shake Scott's hand. He was dressed casually, in jeans and a golf shirt, his brown hair slightly damp from the chilly rain outside.

"Scott, nice to see you again." His voice was low and smooth, cultured. It made Scott's toes curl.

Scott took the offered hand with a warm smile. "You, too. How was the drive up?"

They talked quietly for a couple of minutes while other people filed in, their comments and questions flowing easily, comfortably. When the room was full, Scott started the meeting with a quick recap of what still needed to be done and who was taking care of assorted last minute details. He handed things over to his co-chair who happily stunned the room by announcing that ticket sales were going better than projected and they were already at seventy-five percent of their fund-raising goal.

Scott sat back in his chair, unable to think clearly. They had all worked so hard—were still working—and all of a sudden the objective was brought back to him in all its glory. They were going to actually do it. New equipment. New toys. New ways to ease a child's stay. They were going to make it happen.

When Tom stood up to list off everything that he was assured of, either by the people doing them or the things that he had arranged for, Scott barely listened. He knew it by heart. Tom had come out of nowhere and had done most of this by himself, had used his time and resources to smooth the committee's way and to save them money. Tom was as much—if not more—a part of what the residents were trying to accomplish as the rest of them.

Scott came back to himself long enough to answer a few questions and make a new list of things that had to be done, then he offered everyone a quick smile and closed the meeting. He and Tom walked out together.

"I'll be back up the day before the bash," Tom said as they left the building.

Scott nodded. "Thanks." He stopped and looked at Tom. "I mean—really. Thank you. Your help has been...invaluable, actually."

Tom laughed, a deep rumbling sound, his head tipping back. "No, it's not. If it were, I'd never get my clients to pay. Just tell me I can come see the ward when you get it all spiffed up."

"You bet." Scott grinned. "Listen, call me when you hit town. If I'm not working, I'll treat you supper somewhere, say thanks again."

They stopped walking next to Scott's car. "I'd like that," Tom said. He shook Scott's hand again. "I'll talk to you soon." He looked like he was going to say something else, but he just smiled and shook his head. "See you, Scott," he said over his shoulder as he walked away.

Scott waved then drove home to wait in the empty house for Drew to come home and love him.

Chapter Sixteen

Drew thought he really should have seen this coming. Scott had spent eight months planning this bash so of course he was going. Naturally enough, he wanted Drew there. Drew didn't really mind that part—gala party, lots of food, Scott all dressed up—that was fine. Problem was, Scott expected him to get dressed up, too.

Scott actually owned three suits that were pretty nice. Drew didn't own a single one; he lived his life in sweatpants and T-shirts. He had one pair of dress pants, two golf shirts, and one button-down. No tie. Nothing remotely suitable for this party. He'd called the one person he could think of who would help out in a fashion disaster.

"Mom, I need help."

She'd been thrilled. After she'd stopped giggling and pointing out that it had been fifteen years since he'd let her near his clothes, she took him shopping and sat happily as he tried on suit after suit before finally nodding in approval.

Drew hadn't even had a chance to show it off to Scott yet; for the last two weeks Scott had been home to sleep and that was about it. He'd been working at the hospital, driving all over hell and back seeing about last minute shit for this party, and when he did have a night off he'd gone and taken Tom out to dinner. Not that Drew had even been home, but still…Scott had only about twenty minutes a day to spare lately, and Drew tried to make those minutes pretty fucking memorable. Showing off his new suit was not on the list of things to do when he had Scott home and awake.

He finished getting dressed and looked in the mirror, making sure his tie was straight. He couldn't remember the last time he'd actually had to tie one. He heard the door open and grabbed his keys, heading to the kitchen as Scott called out to him.

"Ready." He grabbed his overcoat from the hall closet. "Everything set at the hotel?"

Scott's voice came from the doorway. "Yeah, looks good. Tom's making sure nothing blows up while I'm away."

Drew walked into the kitchen, pulling the overcoat on, looking over his shoulder at the living room. He was trying to decide if they should leave both table lamps on, or if one would be enough.

"Stop," Scott said in a strangled voice.

Drew looked at him sharply, one arm in his coat, the other still in the air as he held it by the collar. "What? What's wrong?"

Scott was staring at him, eyes wide. Drew stared back, wondering what the fuck was the matter. He looked down. Pants still had their crease. Shirt was still starched and pristine white. Tie was fine. Jacket was buttoned. Shoes were polished. He looked fine. Matter of fact, he looked pretty hot.

Oh.

He looked back at Scott, who was frozen in place by the door. He looked pretty good himself, dressed in a dark suit, his jacket unbuttoned, and a hand in the pocket of his slacks. Sort of an unconscious pose. Yummy.

Drew lowered his arm and carefully draped his overcoat over a chair, still watching Scott, who only moved enough to lean on the wall behind him. Scott's tongue darted out to lick at his lower lip, but he didn't say anything, just watched.

"Got a new suit, Doc," Drew said casually. His cock was mostly stiff already; he could feel it fill and push against his boxer shorts. He walked a step or two closer to Scott and turned around slowly, showing off. "I like the color. Was going to get just dark blue, or charcoal, but the guy at the store talked me into this. Sort of greeny slate gray thing goin' on; what do you think?" He faced Scott again and waited.

Scott gurgled.

Drew smiled and unbuttoned his jacket. "We debated single and double-breasted jackets for a long time but I still don't know why. I figured pick a color, grab something that fits but, you know. Salesmen." He undid the last button and looked carefully at Scott, letting his eyes wander up and down, letting Scott know that he was perfectly aware of how hard Scott was, that he knew how hungry he was.

"Oh," he said, as if it was an afterthought. "He talked me into suspenders as well." Drew took the jacket off and draped it on another chair, not looking at Scott. He knew what he looked like—the shirt crisp and white, the suspenders bright red stripes down his body. Scott made a noise that Drew could only assume was a moan, though there was a hint of a word in there as well. He grinned to himself and walked to the fridge, then turned and leaned on it.

"Scott? You okay?" he asked, raising an eyebrow. Scott was flushed and sort of staring, biting at his lower lip. "You, uh…you look sort of bothered."

Scott nodded and cleared his throat. "It's a nice suit. Really."

Drew beamed at him. "Thank you. Know what else is new?" he asked, unbuttoning his pants.

Scott shook his head, his eyes glued to Drew's fly and, presumably, Drew's hard-on.

Drew teased his zipper down and showed Scott a hint of red. "New silk boxers. They match the suspenders." This time the sound was more of a groan and Scott took a half step forward. Drew looked down at himself and glanced back at Scott through his eyelashes. "Oh, oh. They seem to be getting wet." Reaching into his boxers Drew pumped his cock a couple of times, letting the suspenders slip on one side so he could shove the fabric down, freeing his erection entirely.

Scott was vibrating.

"Doc? We got time to play?" Drew asked casually, still stroking himself.

"Uh-huh." Scott was licking his lips.

"Oh, good. Come here. Want your mouth."

Scott moved, knees hitting the floor hard as he practically skidded into Drew. Tight wet heat surrounded him and Scott started making his whimpery, needy porno noises right away, the vibrations traveling through Drew's body and making him shudder.

"Oh, God." He dropped his hands to Scott's head, tangling fingers in Scott's hair. He let his own head fall back, resting against the fridge as he listened to the wet sounds Scott was making on his shaft, felt lips and tongue working him, then fingers as well. He wasn't sure if it was the unexpectedness of the entire situation or if Scott's hunger was driving him as well, but all too soon he felt himself draw close.

"Scott. Oh, fuck, Scott, gonna...oh, yes, Christ, yeah, oh, God, now!" His hips were snapping as he thrust into Scott's mouth, Scott's fingers digging in as he sucked hard and swallowed around Drew. Scott kept sucking for a few moments after Drew came, then rested his head against Drew's thigh, nuzzling his balls. Drew just tried to stay upright and catch his breath.

Scott finally stood and tucked Drew back into his boxers and did his pants up for him. He kissed the tip of Drew's nose and grinned at him, then headed down the hall.

"Where are you going?" Drew called out, reaching for his suit jacket.

"Gotta change. Came in my pants."

Chapter Seventeen

Scott had good reason to be pleased, Drew decided as they made their way through the crowd in the ballroom. The room looked amazing, and everything seemed to be going smoothly, if the well coordinated delivery of food to the banquet tables and the continuous circuit of waiters with drink trays was any indication. People were chatting and moving in groups and everyone seemed to be enjoying the music.

Over and over, Drew heard people marvel about what a great event it was. He looked at Scott, who was leading him to a table near the front, and smiled. Scott had worked hard for this; Drew was proud. His man had done this. He knew that Scott hadn't done it alone, but still...this was fabulous. He hurried to catch up to Scott, who had stopped a few feet ahead and was talking to someone in a tux.

Scott turned to him just as he reached his side. "Hey." He smiled, putting a hand on Drew's elbow. "This is Tom. Tom, this is Drew."

Drew grinned at the dark haired man and held out his hand. "The Savior. Glad to finally meet you."

Tom laughed and shook his hand. "Not a savior, really. Just a helping hand. Scott and the committee did the work; I just made people lower their asking prices, that's all."

Scott grinned at them both. "Trust me, Tom. You saved my ass. If you hadn't have gotten the budget under control Drew would have killed me just to get some rest from the whining."

The three of them continued to chat about the bash as they made their way to the bar. They all agreed that the string quartet was a nice touch, the classical music setting a tone that worked well for the event. They were going for elegance and refinement; people tended to donate more if they thought they were having a very special night out.

Drew stood next to Scott at the bar and looked around, half-listening to the other two talk. He was glad to finally meet Tom, and he took advantage of the man's obvious interest in Scott to check him out undetected. Tom was handsome, he decided, though not in a conventional way. He was tall and broad, but he held himself lightly, like he could really move gracefully and easily. He had a pleasant face and the crinkles at his eyes were, frankly, sexy.

Tom turned to speak with someone else for a moment and Drew cursed the length of suit jackets. He really wanted to see the man's ass. Scott noticed and rolled his eyes at him, then winked. Drew just grinned at him and winked back.

Drew ordered another drink when his glass was empty and excused himself to go get some food when his second drink was gone. He was feeling relaxed and happy and proud of Scott; sort of floaty and half-drunk, just pleased that life was going to return to normal in the morning. He walked back to the bar and spied Tom, but Scott was nowhere to be seen.

"He's got to go make the check presentation," Tom said, leaning in to be heard above the crowd. The later it got, the more vocal the good charitable people got. Drew suspected that it had to do with the amount of alcohol people were drinking, but he wasn't sure; he was on his third double and his thinking was getting a little fuzzy.

He and Tom watched Scott get introduced on the small stage and applauded loudly when he and his co-chair presented one of those big fake checks to a rep from the hospital's board. The residents had managed to raise a fuck of a lot of money, and Scott looked happy as he shook hands with everyone around him. Drew himself was grinning madly, and he turned to smile at Tom.

"Thanks. You really helped a lot," he said.

Tom smiled at him and looked like he was about to say something, then shook his head.

"What?" Drew asked. Tom was looking at Scott with appreciation and Drew wanted to know what was on the man's mind.

"You live with him, yeah? Know him pretty well?" Tom finally asked.

Drew smiled a little. "Yeah, I know him."

Tom glanced at him and then away, then back again. "Scott into guys?" he asked.

Drew's grin grew wider. "Yeah."

"He into you?" Tom asked, looking him in the eye.

Drew flashed on Scott's mouth around his cock, sucking him off not four hours before, needy sounds coming from him as he took Drew in. "Yeah. He's into me."

Tom nodded and set his drink down, then smiled at him. "Good to know," he said, then he walked away.

Drew waited for Scott to make his way back to him and then steered him into the coat check room. Thinking about Scott's mouth had him hard and horny and it was time to go home.

"You done here, Doc?" he said, moving around Scott, brushing up against him. He leaned in and whispered in his ear, tongue flicking out to lick at Scott's neck. "See everyone you have to, shake hands with all the big wigs?" He slipped a hand into Scott's jacket, around to the small of his back and pulled him closer, rubbing up against him. Scott just nodded and moaned softly, pushing back into his hand and forward into his groin. Drew could feel him getting hard.

"Want you, Scott," he murmured into his neck, pushing him between some coats and up into the wall. "Want to take you right here and make you scream for me. Want to taste you and fuck you and—"

"Scott?" a voice said behind them. Tom.

Scott gasped and buried his head in Drew's shoulder. "Tell me we didn't just get caught making out behind some coats like we're seventeen," he said quietly.

Drew chuckled. "No, we just got caught making out like we're horny and can't wait to get home. Which is dumb 'cause we're in a hotel and hey, could get a room." He pushed himself away from Scott reluctantly and made a show of straightening his clothes before turning to Tom. "Good timing," he deadpanned.

"Sorry," Tom said, looking only a little apologetic. "Wanted to talk to you both, and I figured if you kept going like that I wouldn't get the chance."

Scott was still looking embarrassed and the three of them eyed each other for a moment before Tom finally rolled his eyes. "Look, here's the thing. I'm going back to Toronto in the morning. It's not far, but it's not here, and I want to…well, I want to know if you play. If you'll come up to my room for the night." He looked at Scott and just stood there, waiting.

Drew blinked. He looked at Tom and then at Scott, who was staring at Tom, and blinked again. He opened his mouth to say something and closed it again, deciding somewhere in the non-drunk parts of his brain, if there were any, that this was Scott's choice. And as soon as he realized that he knew he wanted to take them both upstairs to Tom's room and do anything he could. He wanted to fuck, ride, suck, come, watch, taste, jerk off, anything.

He wanted to kiss them and feel them and hear them and just be in the same room if Scott said yes.

"No." Scott didn't even look at him.

"No?" he said, then remembered that it was Scott choice. That made Scott look at him though.

"Uh, maybe?" Scott offered, then shook his head. "No, what I mean is, yeah, maybe we play, but no, I don't want to play with you, 'cause I really like you and I can see it getting really fucking complicated, and I can't deal with that right now. Drew…he's my lover, right? He's mine and I'm his, and if you were just some guy we'd be upstairs with you in a heartbeat. But you're not, you're Tom, and I like you and you're not going to be here tomorrow night, and I can't deal with that." Scott took a deep breath and then took Drew's hand in his. "I'm sorry."

Tom smiled a little and put a hand on the back of Scott's neck, kissing him gently. "You know, that's the nicest rejection I've ever gotten." He turned to Drew and said, "Thank you." Then he turned and walked away.

Drew just stared at Scott for a moment. "Love you. Fucking glad you're the smart one. But…Christ. I love you."

Scott squeezed his hand. "Take me home, Drew."

Chapter Eighteen

Scott felt like he spent December doing damage control for his personal life, having conversation after conversation to set things right again. The first conversation was with Drew, about Tom.

"You thought about it," Drew said as they lay in bed, exhausted and sweaty and barely recovered from their lovemaking. "Before he asked, I mean. You'd been thinking about sleeping with him."

Scott rolled off him and moved into the curl of Drew's arm before answering. "Yeah. Sort of. It wasn't like I had consciously thought about it, or had fantasies or anything, though. It's more like…like I just acknowledged that I'm attracted to him, and that the potential existed. But I was serious when I said no. I'm not willing to start up with him and pretend that it's just fucking, 'cause it wouldn't be."

Drew took a breath and then let it out slowly. "You want more with him?" he finally asked, and Scott didn't know what he was hearing in Drew's voice other than curiosity and a careful distance.

He snuggled in closer. "Not really. Just like him enough to know that he falls into the middle of the spectrum. Don't love him, and don't really want to. Can't just fuck him and let him go. So he's off-limits."

"You didn't say anything to me," Drew said and now Scott could hear the hurt and it made his stomach clench.

He moved up a few inches so he could touch Drew's face, trace his jaw with a finger as he looked at him. "What was I supposed to do? I've hardly seen you lately; didn't want to say anything like 'Hey, love you, going to work now, and by the way if Tom says he wants to fuck me I'm going to say no, 'cause he's really nice'. I mean, really, Drew. There wasn't anything to say and it wouldn't even have come up if he didn't say anything tonight. You know me—not real big on making the first move, yeah?"

Drew relaxed a little and kissed him, then pulled him closer and kissed him again. "Yeah. I get it. Just…if you find yourself wanting someone I wanna know, okay? Not gonna do the big macho jealousy shit, I just…goddamn. I want to know what's in your head, Scott."

Scott nodded and snuggled in again. "Yeah. I get it." He licked Drew's neck, tasted the salt and sweat and musk of him. "And, hey, you wanted to play with him, so maybe we should talk about that."

He was teasing, he didn't really want Drew to tell him about what he wanted to do with Tom, just wanted to let the man know that he hadn't forgotten that little detail.

Drew rolled him onto his back and lay on top of him, hips pushing the evidence of his reawakening arousal into Scott's belly as he bent his head to take a deep kiss. "How 'bout we just drop it and I try to make you scream again, Doc? Fuck, you make me hard."

Scott just gasped and took yet another kiss, letting the heat build again. Nothing got to him like Drew talking.

The next conversation was with his father, about his mother.

"She's worried, is all," his dad said, his voice tired and weary over the phone line.

Scott paced the length of the living room. "Yeah, I get that, I do. But she can't be telling Drew that he deserves someone who's going to be around more. He knows all about my hours, and he doesn't feel neglected." A lie, Scott knew, but for this conversation he was going to let it go. "We know that she wants us happy, but come on, Dad. She's pretty much telling him that he deserves better than I can give him, and it makes us uncomfortable. I need her to stop, and I need you to help me."

His dad sighed, and Scott felt a pang of sympathy. His father hadn't asked for this, any of it. "I'm sorry, Dad. Sorry that I'm pulling you into this, but you have to be there after I talk to her. She doesn't see what she's doing and she's going to be upset with me."

"Yes. She will be. Do you really have to talk to her about this?" He didn't sound very hopeful.

"Yeah, I do. She's not…she's not as happy about this as she thinks she is, and honestly, Dad? Me and Drew, we're going to be together for a long time. She's got to see that I'm not going to find a girl and get married. She has to face that."

"She did. Ten years ago when you told us about Jeremy."

"She didn't," Scott said quietly. "She thinks she has, but she did the same thing to him, when I went away to med school. And when Jeremy and I split up she told me that it was my fault, for not being there. She still tells people that she wants grandchildren."

"She does. We both do. We have the right to want them." He could hear the pain in his father's voice and forced himself to keep his voice down. Getting defensive would take this nowhere.

"Yes, but she doesn't have the right to make me feel guilty for what I am."

84

Daniel didn't say anything for a time, then he sighed. "I know. We don't want you to feel guilty; we want you to be happy. But it's still hard, Scott. We don't have anyone else, and it's not an easy thing to give up."

"I know. Look, can we revisit this one some other time? Right now, I just want to deal with Mom and getting her to stop trying to make everyone happier by pushing me and Drew apart."

Daniel sighed again and Scott figured he'd just aged the man about three years. "I'll be here when you talk to her. Go easy, will you? She doesn't see it as sabotage."

"I know she doesn't. I don't want to hurt her, Dad. Just want her to let me and Drew have our relationship our way."

His father had agreed and wished him luck, which Scott was grateful for. He really wasn't looking forward to talking to his mom.

When he did talk to her, he took what he thought might be the coward's way out. He took them out for lunch and just kind of slipped it into the conversation, figuring that the public setting would keep everyone on their best behavior.

"How's Drew these days?" she asked when they had placed their order.

"Good. He's working today, but he said to say hi."

"It must be hard, both of you working shifts."

"It can be, but he's on a regular schedule now, so we can plan around it. Be nice to see him more, but it's only another year and a half until my time frees up."

She looked at him closely. "That's a long time, Scott."

He met her eyes steadily. "Not really, if you figure in that it's only eighteen months of the next forty or fifty years."

She put down her glass of water carefully. "So he's the one?"

"Yes, Mom."

She looked thoughtful for a moment. "Is there some sort of way that you can…show that? You could get married."

"Uh, yeah, I guess. But we don't want to, haven't even talked about it. We just know that we're together and we're staying that way."

"But I want a wedding, Scott."

"Mom, I'm not out at work, you know that."

She sighed. "This is never going to be easy, is it?"

"I'm not trying to make it hard."

"I know, honey. I do. It's just…every time I think I have a handle on it, it goes off somewhere. But I don't want you to think I don't like him, because I do. He's…kind and polite and he loves you. If you're happy, then that's what I want."

He tried to reply, but she turned to his father and changed the subject. His father had just given him the 'let it go, I'll deal with it' look, and Scott had let it drop.

She still called once a week and talked to Drew if he was home, but she stopped asking if he was getting out enough. She did mention, twice, that she was glad he was with Scott and that Scott seemed to be happier than he had ever been.

Scott figured that that was as good as they could get for the time being.

The fourth conversation actually took place in January, though several phone calls in December led up to it. Tom called him twice, and he had called Tom once, and then Christmas had happened and Scott found himself reaching for the phone on New Year's Eve day. Drew was at the station house and he really didn't have a reason to call Tom, but then, he hadn't had one before, either.

Scott sat for almost half an hour looking at the phone and thinking about it, waiting for it to either leap into his hand or…he had no idea. When Drew came home Scott sat with him on the couch, wrapped up in his warmth, and waited for the New Year to arrive. When the year was less than twelve hours old he sat in the same spot again, with Drew's arms around him, and called Tom.

Tom understood what he was saying, or at least told Scott he did. Scott wouldn't call him. He wouldn't call Scott. It wasn't that Scott didn't want to be friends, or that Drew didn't want them to be friends; it was just too hard, and it wasn't working, and it wouldn't work. So Scott apologized and Tom apologized and Drew got on the phone and tried to smooth it all over. In the end Scott just hung up the phone and went to the kitchen to cook. Drew let him.

Chapter Nineteen

January saw things more or less back on an even keel. Scott's free time was actually free and he was managing to get to about every second poker game. At the first game in January, he won over fifty dollars. When he and Drew were getting ready to leave, Jim cleared his throat and announced that his transfer to Napean had come through and after February first his place wouldn't be available as a second site for the games. Drew and Scott exchanged a glance and promptly offered their house.

Drew and Dave sat down for a few minutes with a calendar and marked out their shifts. With both of them on permanent rotation it was easy enough to see when the games would have to be at Drew and Scott's and which nights it could be at either place. They divided up those nights and Dave said he'd make photocopies for the regulars, with directions to the house.

Scott and Jim had been talking in the kitchen while Drew and Dave got themselves sorted. "Hey, we're going to need more players too, then," Scott said when Drew met him by the door. "The numbers have been falling off, and with Jim moving..."

Dave nodded. "Yeah. There's a couple of guys we could mention it to at work, and I'll ask around with the EMTs too."

The first game in February was at Drew and Scott's and thankfully they were both there; it was also the first night the new faces started to show up, and they had six people at the table, which was what they liked.

Scott was sitting out the first few hands like he usually did, watching Drew win the first hand. Dave was there, munching potato chips like they were going to run out, and next to him was one of the new guys, Tony Mancusso, another firefighter. He worked with Drew sometimes, though he wasn't on permanent rotation, and he seemed nice enough. He was big and broad, looking every inch like the Italian he was, with dark hair and eyes, and a big, booming voice.

Next to him was Ben, looking distracted and vaguely upset. Scott wondered what was going on with him and Jim, now that Jim was out of the immediate area. He was losing badly right off the bat, and Scott made a mental note to watch his playing.

The last guy was new, too, and Scott had assumed he was a fireman as well, due to his size. He was well over six feet tall, and broad enough to make Tony look like a regular guy. But Eric was an EMT, and had been on the catching end of a birth earlier in the day. Scott looked at the size of the blond man's hands and winced. Good Lord, the baby must have just about disappeared.

"So, let me get this right," Drew said as he dealt the cards. "She's in labor, husband's driving her to the hospital and gets in an accident." Eric nodded and both Tony and Ben said something about being surprised that it didn't happen more often. Eric was picking up his cards and tilting them so Scott could see over his shoulder. A queen and a ten of diamonds.

"Then she goes into active labor as soon as we roll up on it," Eric said, adding another ten to his hand. "Nelson gets the gurney out and I'm helping her walk to the bus—" Jack of clubs— "and she screams. I ease her down and get her ready, she pushes once and I have a handful of beautiful baby girl." Another ten.

Scott noted that Eric's face didn't even twitch as he threw down the queen and jack and asked for two.

"What did they name her?" Ben asked with a grin. "Erica?"

Eric laughed. "No, Laurie. For my last name, St Laurent. They called her Laurie Rose. Pretty, isn't it?"

Scott watched as the betting went on, one by one people dropping out. Eric had looked at his two cards but hadn't shown them to Scott, which was damn smart, as far as Scott was concerned. They hadn't played together and he didn't know what Scott's poker face was like yet. He'd learn, like all the others.

Finally, it was Eric and Tony, ten dollars on the table. Tony called it and swore a blue streak when Eric showed off his four tens and collected the pot. Eric tossed Scott a smile and a nod, which made Drew raise an eyebrow. "You don't want to be giving him any favors," Drew said in a warning voice. "He's about to win all that back from you."

Eric looked at Scott carefully. "We'll see," was all he said.

Scott won it all, but it took him three hands longer than usual to do it, he could barely keep Ben in the game, and Eric left with more money than he'd brought. Scott did manage to clean Drew out, though, and he figured he'd have to make it up to him later.

Scott thought Eric was going to fit right in, and said as much to Drew later that night when they were alone and cleaning up.

"Tony, he's all right. I think I'll like winning his money. Now, Eric, he's just hot."

Drew stared at him and blinked, then grinned slowly. "You think?"

"Were we in the same room?" Scott asked, feeling a little nervous about mentioning any sort of interest in anyone after what had happened with Tom.

"Hell, yeah. Just didn't figure you would say anything." Drew was looking at him in a faintly predatory way that made Scott want to run to the bedroom. He inched his way around to the hallway, nonchalantly.

"Not saying we should seduce him," he said, speeding up as he headed for the bedroom with Drew right behind him, already unbuttoning his shirt. "Just saying that the man is attractive, is all."

"Uh-huh." Drew caught him and pushed him into the doorframe, pressing close and sliding his hands into Scott's shirt. "Can I fuck you now?"

"Please."

It was ages before they even made it to the bed.

Chapter Twenty

Scott thought very hard about what to do for Valentine's Day, once he realized that it was February the fourteenth, which was on his way home from work at eight-thirty that night. He made a quick right instead of a left and hit the mall.

He went straight to the grocery store. Nothing said love like strawberries and chocolate. Except it was February. In Canada. No strawberries. He went down the aisles until he found the Hershey's chocolate and went back to the produce section. He rejected vegetables right away, thus narrowing the choices dramatically. He was rather proud of himself for that.

He looked over the fruit. The only fresh berries were some cherries from California at almost five dollars a kilo, so he put them on the 'maybe' list. Sunkist oranges were a good choice; chocolate would go well with them and they split into sections easily enough. Pears, also good. Apples got passed over, as did bananas. Actually the bananas got a second glance, then were dismissed again as being too phallic and hokey. He weighed his options and then pretty much decided he was screwed anyway and got two oranges, a pear and a bunch of bananas. Drew didn't mind hokey.

When he got home, Drew was asleep on the couch so he took a shower and put on a pair of boxer shorts, then went to the kitchen. He heated the chocolate for a few seconds in the microwave to get it nice and warm, while he peeled the oranges and split the sections. The pear he sliced into eight crescents, and the bananas he left alone. He still thought that maybe the bananas were too much.

When he had everything arranged on a big plate he went to the living room and sat on the floor, the plate beside him. He turned off the TV, found something nice on the radio that didn't have a DJ breaking in every few minutes, and looked at Drew. Still sleeping.

He dipped a pear into the chocolate and bit into it, chewing thoughtfully. Could drip chocolate on him and lick it off. Could just shake him, but that wasn't the most pleasant way to wake up. Finally he picked up a segment of orange and dipped it in the chocolate. He leaned over and painted Drew's lips with it and waited.

Drew's tongue flicked out and swept some of the chocolate away, then disappeared. Drew shifted a little and stretched, his tongue coming back out to get the rest of the chocolate. One eyelid opened and Drew smiled at him.

"Hey. Chocolate."

Scott grinned back. "You awake?"

"Nope. But I will be soon. How was your day?" Drew stretched some more and rubbed at his eyes while Scott rambled about the patients he'd seen and how many times he'd had to redo one chart.

Scott kept dipping fruit in chocolate as he talked. Each piece was dipped, then licked clean with featherlight touches of his tongue before being eaten. Just for fun, he occasionally threw in a soft moan and used the flat of his tongue to clean a section of orange or pear. Drew was starting to pay attention.

When Scott finally started peeling a banana, Drew sat up. "Are you going to...?"

Scott gave him a look of utter confusion. "Eat this? Uh, yeah. You want one?"

Drew shook his head. "Not right now, thanks."

Scott shrugged. "Okay. Anyway, so I told Dr. Knickerson that the guy had every indication of making a full recovery—" Drew nodded absently, watching as Scott completely removed the skin from the banana and dipped it in the chocolate. Scott kept talking while he made sure that the chocolate was nice and even over the end of the banana, and then brought it to his mouth. He licked at it with a long stroke of his tongue, lapping the chocolate off one side before sweeping over the end and carefully licking the chocolate from the other side.

When he was done he looked at Drew through his eyelashes as he coated the banana a second time. He was paying close attention, but he wasn't anywhere near ready to pounce yet. Scott had been half-hard when he started this game and he was getting harder by the moment. So was Drew.

He repeated the performance, chatting all the while. He had run out of actual things to say and started making things up in between licking the banana. He kept everything as natural as he could, not being obscene, just...playing. Drew started to shift around on the couch, nodding whenever the chatter paused, apparently trying to look like he was paying attention. It was cute.

After Scott had cleaned the banana for the second time, he dipped his fingers in the remaining chocolate and painted the banana. Then he licked his fingers and sucked on them. Drew moaned. Almost time.

Scott looked at him with wide eyes. "It's good. Sure you don't want some?" Before Drew could answer Scott closed his eyes and tipped his head back, wrapping his mouth around the banana. He sucked at the chocolate, groaning as he pulled the banana out of his mouth and licked his lips. He did it again and dropped a hand to his lap to adjust himself, groaning again as he pressed the palm of one sticky hand against his cock.

Drew snapped.

He didn't even hear Drew leave the couch; one moment he was happily sucking on a banana, the next he was being kissed and pushed flat on the floor.

"Christ, you're gonna kill me," Drew said as he ground into him.

"Huh?" Scott was still trying for bewildered.

"Suck me, Doc." Drew was almost growling. "Gonna drive me insane."

Scott grinned at him and rolled them over. He sat up and helped Drew get his jeans open and down then bent and started to lick at Drew's balls.

"Oh, fuck, yes," Drew groaned, letting his legs fall open.

Scott hummed happily as he licked and sucked, drawing first one and then the other of Drew's balls into his mouth. He wrapped a hand around Drew's cock and pumped it lightly, teasing with a too-light touch.

"Scott, please," Drew moaned.

Scott grinned and licked his way up Drew's cock and swirled his tongue around the tip before taking the head into his mouth and suckling at it. Drew bucked up into his mouth and Scott opened up, brought him in deep. He licked and sucked as he traveled up and down the hard length, loving the feeling and the taste. Drew was addictive.

He moaned and reached into his own boxer shorts, stroking himself firmly as he bobbed his head and sucked at Drew. Felt so good.

Drew gasped and thrust into his mouth, his movements ragged and desperate. Scott sped up his hand and let Drew as far into his mouth as he could, sucking hard. He moved up Drew's cock and sucked at the head, fucking the tip with his tongue until Drew swore and grabbed his shoulders. "Gonna come soon, oh, fuck, so good."

Scott moaned and took him deep again and swallowed. His own balls were tight and he pulled his cock hard.

"Oh, fuck, oh, fuck, oh, fuck—"

Drew arched his back and came, pumping into Scott's mouth. At the first taste of Drew's come, Scott groaned and shuddered, shooting his load as well, soaking his shorts and Drew's jeans.

He swallowed around Drew's cock, licking and sucking and kissing until Drew pulled him up and kissed him, fucking his mouth with his tongue.

"You did that on purpose," Drew finally said.

Scott looked at him with wide eyes. "Did what? Sucked you off? Yeah, that was on purpose."

"You shit. I mean that bit with the chocolate and the fucking banana."

"I have never fucked a banana," Scott said seriously.

Drew rolled his eyes and kissed him again. "Love you."

"Love you, too. Happy Valentine's Day."

Chapter Twenty-one

Eric was in a foul mood. He should probably have skipped the poker game, but he'd been going to them for just over two months and he really liked it and didn't see why his personal troubles should spread out so far that they ruined his weekly night out. But when he looked at his cards and couldn't remember if he was betting high this hand or even if he'd discarded yet, he sighed and folded. He got a surprised look from Dave, but Drew just grinned and said that maybe now he'd stand a chance at winning a hand. He returned the grin and stood up, going into Dave's kitchen to get a beer.

When he turned around Scott was leaning on the kitchen table looking at him. He had a brief thought that the cards must really have been crap for Scott to fold, too, then he remembered that the doctor had been sitting out that hand.

"Bad night?" Scott asked.

Eric passed him a beer and shook his head. "Bad cards, I guess."

Scott snorted. "You folded with two pair, jack high. I've seen you bluff your way through with way worse."

Eric blinked. "You were looking at my cards again?" He meant to sound playfully accusing, but he thought he just sounded tired.

"You showed them to me," Scott said carefully. "You okay?"

Eric leaned against the counter and looked at the floor. He usually didn't talk to anyone about the stuff going on in his life, but this was pretty dull and impersonal. "Just having an annoying time with my current situation. I've got two roommates and one of them eloped last weekend, so now I have three. And we only have two bedrooms, and I'm the only one who works shifts."

Scott winced. "That sucks. You're moving, then?"

"Hell, yeah." Eric drank from his bottle and put it on the counter beside him. "Trouble is, I can't afford to live by myself, at least not anywhere that's close to work. Loans and shit, you know? But I can't find a place with anyone I can live with. I looked at four places today and between people with rock bands that practice at weird hours, and the guy who had a fucking wall of beer cans in the living room, I'm getting stressed out about it." He shook his head and picked his bottle up again, gesturing with it. "I asked at work, but no one needs a roommate, and I'm starting to think I'll wind up with an hour long commute."

"From where?" Drew asked, coming into the kitchen "And, hey, thanks for folding. I won three bucks that hand."

Scott laughed. "I'm just gonna win it off you, you know that, right?"

"Not right now, Doc," Drew said with a grin. "Not right now. Eric, it's your deal. And hey, where are you moving to?"

He opened his mouth but Scott interrupted. "He's looking for a cheap place, close to work, that's shift work friendly."

Drew opened the fridge door and reached for a beer. "What? Like Chez Drew and Scott?"

"That's what I was thinking."

Eric stared. They couldn't be serious. "Hey, I didn't mean to—"

Drew was nodding. "Be nice to have someone else to help mow the damn lawn."

"And be nice to have someone in the house who doesn't have a strictly pizza-fuelled diet." Scott put in.

"But, I didn't mean—"

They ignored him.

Drew drank from his bottle. "Be nice to have someone in the house when you're at work—kind of kill the empty house feel, you know?"

"Main reason I thought of it."

"But—"

Drew grinned at him. "Stop by tomorrow night after five and I'll show you the place properly. You've only seen the front part, right? We can talk about rent and shit." Then he left the room.

Scott just grinned at him and followed Drew to the table.

Well, damn. That wasn't what he was expecting at all. And it was certainly going to put a crimp in his 'find out if either of them is seeing anyone' plan. Or not, if he was going to move in, which would give him the information and slam any door shut on maybe dating one of them. Kinda hard to do that when you're sleeping down the hall. Plus, there was the whole not even knowing if Scott was gay thing; everyone knew Drew was, but no one knew that Eric was, and no one was saying if Scott was.

On the other hand, it was a cheap place and close to work.

"Ah, fuck," he muttered. "Not like I'd make any kind of move anyway. Might as well go for the cheap rent."

With all designs on the fireman and the doctor firmly locked away in a box he went into the living room and dealt the next hand.

***

"Tell me that wasn't a huge mistake." Scott gripped the steering wheel and glanced at the passenger seat, seeking reassurance.

"I don't think it was," Drew said promptly. "He's a nice guy, he understands the whole shift work thing, and you're right. We need someone else in the house, someone we both like, so we don't get so goddamn lonely."

Scott nodded. "Yeah, I get that. But what about that other thing?"

Drew grinned at him. "You mean that thing where you want to lick him from head to toe? That thing?"

"Shut up. Yeah, that thing."

"Up to you, Scott," he said with a shrug. "I think he's hot, yeah. But honestly, I'd really just like to have him around, get to know him, you know?"

"It doesn't bother you?"

"Does it bother you?" Drew sounded serious all of a sudden. "I thought you had it sorted, that's why you offered."

"No, I do have it sorted," Scott reassured him. "Just want to make sure you're cool with it."

"Tell me what you've got on your mind then. Make sure we're clear."

Scott took a breath. "Well, we're back into the same territory we were with Tom, honestly. I like Eric. I think we can be really good friends, and that's what we need, right? So, yeah, I think he's hot. But he's off-limits, 'cause I'd rather get to know him than fuck him at this point. If you know that I'm attracted to him, and are okay with it, I don't think there's a problem. Plus, you know me— not big with making the first move, yeah? Besides, he's probably straight and in three weeks I'll be bitching about his skanky girlfriend."

Chapter Twenty-two

The next evening, Eric was greeted with a friendly smile and a little bit of small talk before Drew offered to show him the house. They made quick work of the basics—kitchen, living room, laundry—because Eric had been there before, and then moved back. Drew pointed to the big calendar on the wall of the kitchen as they passed it, and Eric nodded in approval. Good idea to keep track of who was home and who was sleeping. Saved grumpiness from taking over due to interrupted sleep.

They walked down the hall and Drew pointed to the far end. "Only one bathroom, as you know, but it hasn't been much of an issue with only two here. We'll see how it works out with three."

Eric forced away a mental image of three in the shower and just nodded. "So which room is available?" he asked.

"Well, you've got a choice," Drew said, opening a door to the right. "This here is the bigger one, and this one," he pointed to the room right next to it, "has bigger windows."

Eric blinked. "But where does Scott sleep?" he asked. His brain caught up with his mouth at the same time Drew swung the door open on the last bedroom.

King-size bed, poster of an antique fire truck, and a pile of hospital scrubs on the floor. "With me." Drew looked at him, eyes serious. "This a problem? Thought you knew."

Eric shook his head. "No, didn't have a clue, and no, it's not a problem." Except that meant that they were both on the 'don't touch' list. Just the way his life seemed to go. Here Eric, two hot gay men to live with. Enjoy the view.

Drew led the way back to the kitchen and they sat down. They talked about rent for a bit, and how much the utilities cost. When the doorbell rang Drew leaped up with a grin. "Supper! Hope you like pizza, I live on the stuff. Grab a beer from the fridge while I pay for this, will you?"

Eric got two and rummaged around until he found the plates. He pulled some more pizza from the fridge as well and zapped it in the microwave, wondering if they could actually eat that much. Between the two of them they managed to finish it all, talking about people they knew in common and reliving past calls they'd been on. Eric relaxed, and when Drew offered him another beer he accepted, following along as they moved to the living room.

They sat down and Drew looked thoughtful for a moment. "Listen, about me and Scott…" He paused, and Eric raised an eyebrow, waiting. "I know you said it doesn't bother you, I just want to let you know that we won't…we aren't…oh, hell."

Eric blinked. "Um, not making much sense there. It doesn't bother me. Really."

"Yeah, it's not that. Well, it is sort of. Just want you to know that we're not gonna be all over each other or anything. We're not going to do anything that'll make you uncomfortable, or like you're not welcome here."

Eric tried to reassure him. "Listen, it's cool. I mean, thanks, not sure if I really want to walk in on you doing it in the kitchen, but the whole guy thing doesn't phase me. At all."

Drew just looked at him and Eric felt himself flush. He sighed and kicked himself, then figured what the hell, going to share a house, might as well be open about it. "I'm gay, too."

Now it was Drew's turn to blink. There was silence for a moment and Drew blinked again before cautiously saying, "But not out."

"But not out."

Drew bit his lower lip and looked thoughtful. "Okay. I'll be honest and say that I think Scott should know. But that's all. Your secret to tell."

Eric sat back and smiled again. "Fair enough."

"You with anyone?" Drew asked casually.

"Not right now." Eric kept his voice just as casual. Not much point in letting on how long the now had been going on for.

Drew just grinned and shook his head. "Wanna watch TV?"

"Sure? Cops is on in ten."

They were still sitting there when Scott got home at midnight, half-drunk and laughing their asses off at Saturday Night Live. That's how Eric knew he was half-drunk; SNL hadn't been that funny in years.

Chapter Twenty-three

Eric's partner managed to hold off asking about Drew for almost three weeks, which was at least two weeks longer than Eric had given him credit for. Nelson could be a crude bastard, and when Eric had told him he was moving, he'd seen something in Nelson's eyes that told him better be careful about what he said.

The feeling was confirmed when Nelson said, "Moving into Smyth's house? Better watch yourself around that one. Take care when you bend over, if you know what I mean." Then Nelson had laughed like he was the funniest thing in the world, eyebrows waggling and a sneer on his mouth.

Eric had just stared at him. This was why he wasn't out at work. He pretended not to understand and just did his job.

Living with Scott and Drew, though…that was working out. It was sort of like having only one roommate, however; in the three weeks he'd lived there they had all been home and awake at the same time precisely twice. The rest of the time it was one or the other, or he had the place to himself. Usually it was Drew who was home, and they would hang out in the backyard or in front of the TV. Eric had talked him into putting a basketball hoop up in the driveway, but they hadn't had a chance to use it much yet.

Nelson had waited until they were restocking the ambulance, getting ready for their shift, before saying anything. Eric was double-checking the security straps on the stretcher when Nelson slapped him on the back and said, "So, Smyth doing the doctor?"

Eric felt every muscle in his body tense. "Not that I've seen," he said, trying to keep his voice neutral.

"Oh, come on. You've been there for almost a month now. You can tell me. What's the deal on the doctor?"

Eric turned to face him. "What's it to you?"

Nelson smirked and shrugged. "Just want to know. Everyone knows Smyth takes it up the ass, but no one knows what the deal is with the pretty boy Doc. People are asking."

"Maybe people should mind their own business. No one's business but Drew's what he does, and it certainly isn't anyone's business what they do together, if anything."

"So, they're together then?"

"Jesus. No, not that I've seen." The lie didn't hurt one bit. "And I won't talk about them like this. I live with them, and if I can mind my own fucking business, you can. Got that?"

Nelson stared at him. "Christ. What's gotten into you? You into Smyth yourself? That what's got your panties in a twist?"

Eric rolled his eyes. He wanted to punch the son of a bitch, but he liked his job. "Yeah, that's it. I want to fuck Smyth. God, you're just looking for something to tell the world, aren't you? Look, talk all you want. Just not to me. Not about them."

Nelson had laughed, a mean, nasty sound Eric hated, but he had let it drop. It was another month before Eric found a way to switch partners.

***

The day Eric came home from delivering body after body to the morgue after a huge car accident, Scott was at work. Eric came in through the back door and almost walked right into Drew, who was on his way out to the yard.

"Hey, how was your day?" Drew asked with a grin. The grin vanished as Drew looked at him and Eric figured he must have looked as bad as he felt. Drew turned around and went to the fridge, grabbing a couple of water bottles. "Driveway, man. Work this out."

They played one-on-one basketball for over an hour before Eric felt like slowing down. They didn't talk, other than Eric telling him how many bodies he'd had to take. Drew just played. Eric was pleased that Drew played as well as he did; they were pretty evenly matched and Drew made sure that he was too busy sweating and running to think. When they were both about ready to collapse they lay down on the grass and drank water until the bottles were empty, then they went in and got more.

Drew went to take a shower and Eric looked at the calendar. Drew had to work in four hours, he should have been asleep. Eric felt guilty, but he was glad that Drew had played.

***

Scott was lying on the couch watching something on TV when Eric got home one night after work. He'd actually finished his shift at four, but had gone out for supper with a couple of guys he knew and intended to go play pool with them; he'd wound up with a killer headache and headed home instead.

Scott wasn't expecting him, and Drew was at work.

So, when Scott flew off the couch and turned off the TV and then hit the stop button on the VCR Eric grinned at him.

"Porn?"

Scott turned red. "No. Would actually be less embarrassing if it were, I think."

Eric raised an eyebrow. That sounded intriguing. If it had been porn he'd have teased the doctor without mercy and then gone to his room to let the man have at it—all the while thinking how unfair it was that the man got actual real sex on a regular basis, plus porn—but this was something else. A secret. An embarrassing secret.

Scott and Eric lunged for the video tape box at the same time. When Scott got to it first Eric changed direction and skidded across the floor to the VCR, stabbing the eject button.

He looked at the tape and blinked. "This is...not so bad," he offered.

Scott snorted.

"I've never seen it," Eric said, looking at Scott from under his eyelashes.

Scott perked up. "Really? It's great, you'll love it. It's got everything. But I swear to God, you tell anyone I watch this and I'll kick your ass at the next five poker games."

"Like you could. Please." Eric handed him the tape and said, "Rewind it, I'll go make popcorn."

Scott grinned at him and in a few minutes they were happily lost in the world of Florin, watching Buttercup test the path of true love.

Eric added The Princess Bride to his list of favorite movies.

Chapter Twenty-four

It would have been easy to forget that Scott and Drew were a couple. They weren't all together in the house very often, as Scott was on nights when they were on days, but when they were all there the two men didn't do anything with each other that they wouldn't do with Eric. There was no kissing, no touching; nothing more personal than a swat on the back of the head.

When they were apart and Eric was home with one of them it was just…normal. He talked to them both, he ate and cooked and watched TV with them. He played ball and catch with Drew, touch football with Scott, and he liked them both. A lot.

Scott was easy to talk to about anything. They talked about work, the news, what color they should paint the living room. Scott was funny and intense, and Eric took an abnormal amount of pleasure in pulling him away from his books and charts to go play stupid games in the backyard. Scott needed to relax more and Eric made it his mission to get him out of the house as often as he could.

Drew was relaxed and laid-back. They laughed at the same stupid stuff on TV, and Eric thought he might be getting Drew addicted to Cops, which was a good thing. They read the paper in sections together, claiming the same ones each time and trading at the same time, like they were running on the same timer. Eric was a little worried about the amount of take-out he was eating though, and started making sure to play ball as often as he could, and he picked up extra reps on the free weights. He was a big guy, and he didn't want to get soft.

Eric thought he might be a little vain, but then he figured that was okay. He was living with two beautiful men; he didn't want to shatter the mirror by accident.

There were some problems, though. Sometimes at night he would hear them. Not often, and never if they knew he was home, but it was hard to miss. Drew was vocal, letting Scott know what felt good, and telling him he loved him. Scott was quieter mostly, but when he got loud it was intense and enduring, words of love and need and completion.

Eric spent those nights with his head under his pillow, trying very hard not to hear. He tried even harder not to let them know he'd ever heard anything; he didn't think it would be fair to them. They would try to restrain themselves and he didn't want them to act any differently with each other than they already were. This was their home before it was his, and they were kind enough to keep it at least in the bedroom. If they knew he was home he never heard anything, and he figured that was enough sacrifice on their part.

It didn't stop him from wanting, however.

He came home once when the shower was going, was in his room changing when he realized they were both in there. Maybe it was because he was tired, or maybe because he was lonely…in any event he stood in his room listening, sort of bemused. He felt like he was outside of his body, an observer in his own room as he felt himself get hard. He wondered idly who was doing what.

He lay back on his bed and listened, still not feeling much of anything other than arousal. He wrapped a hand around himself, stroking almost absently as he listened to the water run and the occasional words he could hear. When he heard Drew cry out, "Harder, there, oh, fuck, there!" he came with a shudder and a moan.

He felt sick. Awash with guilt and remorse and complete disgust with himself, he got dressed and left. He went to a bar he knew and found someone to spend some time with, just long enough to make himself feel worse. When he got home Drew was asleep on the couch and Scott was at work.

It was something he did more than once. Sometimes he would pretend that they weren't together, but that was awful, too. They were right together, and apart they were confusing.

Eric was starting to hurt.

***

Eric had lived there for almost four months when Drew began hiding from Kate, Scott's mom. He told Eric that Kate was great, a cool lady who loved her boy, and that she was really sweet. But she was calling Drew, checking up on Scott.

Drew had told Scott, of course, and Scott had told his mom to knock it off, that there wasn't any need to call Drew. If she wanted to know if he was eating well then she should ask. If she wanted to know if he was working too much, the answer was yes. If she wanted to know if he was happy, the answer was yes. But stop asking Drew.

Kate didn't call for a bit, then one night she called out of the blue, about eleven o'clock. Drew checked the number ID window on the phone and cast pleading eyes on Eric. "His mom. You take it, please? She'll talk my ear off for ages—won't do it to you."

Eric grinned and answered the phone.

"Hello, Eric. Is Scott home?"

"No, ma'am. He's at the hospital. Want me to leave a note for him?"

"No, that's okay. Is Drew home?"

"No, ma'am."

"Oh. Is he at work, too?"

"Ah, no, I don't think so. He said something about going out with the guys to shoot pool." Eric glanced at Drew who was sitting on the couch with a shit-eating grin on.

"Out with the… Does Scott know?"

"Oh, I think so. He picked the guys." Eric turned away from Drew as he heard a choking sound from the couch. "Drew likes it that way."

"Excuse me?"

"Well, if Drew's going to play when Scott's not home, Scott likes to know who he's with. So he picks out the—oh, dear, I really have to go now. My pager is flashing at me." He hung up the phone and took off at a dead run, Drew cursing a blue streak as he chased him down the hall. Eric misjudged the turn into his room and Drew tackled him, both of them landing hard on the floor. Drew was wrapped around his legs and Eric found that Drew was stronger than he had thought.

They were laughing as they wrestled on the floor, Eric trying to get his legs free and not kick Drew in the head, and Drew trying to crawl up his body to get him in a headlock. Eric flipped them over and found himself pinning Drew down, both of them gasping for breath and wiggling like mad to get the upper hand.

"That wasn't funny," Drew said, trying to get an arm free.

"Yes, it was." Eric leaned on Drew's arms and tried to dig an elbow into Drew's side at the same time. He had only marginal success as Drew got one arm free and tried to flip them over again.

"Okay, it was funny. Scott's gonna fucking kill us." Drew gave up on trying to flip them, apparently realizing that Eric really did outweigh him by forty pounds. Instead he started to tickle him.

"Oh, shit, stop that!" Eric twisted, trying to get away from Drew's fingers but still keep his rightful place as the superior force in hallway wrestling. He looked at Drew, and froze. Smiling face, smiling eyes, and oh, fuck, he was so goddamn sexy. He rolled off fast, but not before he felt Drew shifting under him. Oh, fuck. He wasn't the only one getting hard. Scott really would kill them.

Drew didn't say anything. They went back to the living room and watched the news over a beer, and Eric went to bed as soon as he could without it looking like he was hiding.

Chapter Twenty-five

Scott was browning ground beef when Eric came home. They said hello and Eric went to get changed out of his uniform. Scott figured he'd had a bad day; it wasn't often that Eric looked so worn-out.

He was washing vegetables at the sink when Eric came back into the kitchen, wearing jeans and a sweatshirt.

"Bad day?" he asked as he dried his hands.

"Had better. What're you making?"

"Just spaghetti. Want some?"

Eric grinned at him. "Real food? Hell, yes. Better not let Drew know, though. He still thinks it doesn't count as a meal if it's not take-out."

Scott laughed as he grabbed an onion. "Yeah. You'd never know his mom is a gourmet chef by the crap he eats."

Eric picked up a knife and started slicing peppers. "She is? Really?"

"Damn close to it. Some of the best meals I've ever had came out of her kitchen. Nice thing about Ellen is that I can count on one good meal a month." He finished chopping the onion and smiled at Eric. "If I miss the once a month dinner with his parents, she sends the leftovers. And you know she's a mother the way she makes sure I get to eat it and Drew doesn't steal it all. Calls me the next day and gets me to recite the menu to make sure I got it all."

Eric laughed. "That is so cool."

"Wait until she meets you. I guarantee the food drop offs will double. She's a real softy." Scott went to the fridge and got the garlic and tomatoes while Eric finished with the peppers.

"How 'bout your parents?" Eric asked. "They seem pretty cool about you and Drew."

Scott snorted. "Fuck, my mom would have set us up if we weren't already living together. She knew as soon as she met him. We'd just started up, weren't even sure that was more than playing, you know?" Eric nodded. "My mom, she's all 'He's got a job! He's got a house! Keep him!'. It was scary. His mom was even worse, though—'He's a doctor!'. The two of them pretty much paired us off right then. Mind you, my mom's kind of weird about things—she thinks she's cool with it, but she has her moments of regressing to wishing I was straight. It's… odd and a little annoying."

Eric shook his head. "Weird. Peppers are done. Mushrooms?"

Scott passed them over and added the garlic and onions to the meat. He was getting the big pot for the noodles when Eric said, "It's cool, you know? That your families are so good about it, even if your mom has her moments."

Scott could hear the longing in Eric's voice and watched Eric as he studied each mushroom before he sliced them. He wasn't sure if this was a soft spot Eric was willing to let him touch, but it was obvious that his relationship with his family was far different than Scott's own. He didn't like to pry, but he also didn't like to see Eric hurting.

"Yours not so cool, huh?" he asked, trying to sound casual. If the man wanted to talk about it, he'd listen, at least. "Maybe they'll come around. My parents had a hard time with it when I first came out, but they talked to some other parents and stuff. Took them ages to work it through, but they did it." Mostly, he added to himself.

Eric glanced at him, then back to the mushrooms. "My parents threw me out. The night they found out."

Scott shook his head sympathetically. "Fuck."

"Gets better." Eric put the knife down and went to the fridge for a beer. He handed one to Scott and sat down at the table. "I was out one night with a bunch of friends, just going to some bars, sort of doing the circuit of the places we liked. I was nineteen, barely legal, and we were having a pretty good time."

Scott leaned on the counter and drank his beer, listening quietly.

"We were at this dance club and a guy came up, sort of cut me away from the crowd. He seemed nice enough, was funny and good looking. Can't remember what his name was. Anyway, we left, went to another club, one he knew, where we could dance without people staring. So we danced and drank and found a dark corner to make out in. He gave me his number when he left and I went home feeling pretty good."

Eric blinked and looked at Scott, who suddenly felt like an intruder, like he was reading someone's diary. He pushed the feeling away; Eric wouldn't be talking if he didn't want to let Scott know about it.

Eric drank from his bottle. "So, I walk in and there's my mom and dad and my brother, all in a nice little row on the couch. I just nod and say 'Hey, goodnight, I'm going to bed,' and my father..."

Eric stopped and cleared his throat. Scott moved to the table and sat down in the chair next to him. "My father tells me I have an hour to get my things and get out."

"Jesus." Scott hadn't meant to say anything, but that was just too far out of his realm of experience. His own parents had cried when he told them he was gay, but they had also said that they loved him.

"I asked why. Turns out my brother had heard something, or seen something, thought I might be queer. So he set me up. The guy I'd just been kissing and feeling up was a plant. My fucking brother paid him fifty bucks to find out if I was gay or not, give me his number as proof, and then report back. My parents…well, they didn't want a hell-bound fag in the family and they just threw me out. Gave me thirty bucks to get a room for the night and that was that." He met Scott's eyes. "They haven't spoken to me since."

"God. Why would your brother do that? What did it matter to him?"

Eric shook his head. "You'll love this. We had three cars. Four drivers. It was just a case of eliminating the competition. I went, he got the car to himself."

"You're serious? Man, that is fucked."

Eric nodded. "Yeah. Completely fucked." He finished his beer with three quick swallows. "Now I'm real careful about who knows my shit, you know?"

Eric was looking at him and Scott met his eyes. The fact that Eric trusted him, trusted both him and Drew, meant a lot. More than Scott had really known before that exact moment. He couldn't think of anything to say so he just nodded and handed Eric another beer.

They finished making supper in silence and ate in front of the TV. When Drew came home they all drank too much and watched a stupid movie, laughing in all the wrong places.

Scott kept thinking about Eric.

Chapter Twenty-six

Usually Eric was more than happy to get home and find one or both of them there, but this time he was dreading seeing Drew. They had both been on the same call that afternoon and it hadn't been good.

Eric and his partner had rolled up on the address and gotten the back doors open in time for Drew to hand him a little girl. She was seven years old and had been home sick from school when the fire started. Her mother hadn't been able to get up the stairs to her room, the hall blocked by fire. Drew had gone in to get her, had carried her out in his arms and had given her to Eric.

She died on the way to the hospital.

Eric had done everything he knew how to do and had kept doing it until the ER doctors could take over. They had worked on her for another twenty minutes or two hours or for however long Eric had been allowed to stand there watching before they had called the time of death.

Now Eric had to face Drew. He went into the house and headed straight to his room, but he heard Drew turn off the TV and come after him. "Shit," he said under his breath as he unbuttoned his shirt. He'd do just about anything to avoid doing this.

Drew stood in the doorway, eyes intent and piercing. "She make it?"

Eric looked at him and shook his head slowly. "I'm sorry, Drew. I tried, I swear—"

Drew was gone, footsteps going down the hall to the kitchen. Eric sighed and changed his clothes as fast as he could. When he got to the kitchen Drew was sitting at the table with a bottle of beer in front of him and a bottle of Jack Daniels in his hand. Eric glanced at the calendar. Scott was due home in three hours and Drew was off for thirty-six. Long enough.

"Glass? Or are you just gonna drink from the bottle?"

Drew just looked at him, brown eyes full of pain and anger.

"Look, it makes no difference to me. I'll be here to drag you into the bathroom when it's time to puke it all up."

Drew took a deep breath and put the bottle on the table, unopened. He looked at the far wall for a moment, then at Eric. "Just pisses me off beyond all reason, you know?"

Eric knew. He knew because he'd worked on that little girl. He'd felt her slipping further away and hadn't been able to stop it. He'd heard her last breath and felt her last heartbeat. He knew how unfair it was.

Drew had walked through fire to save her. Drew had done his job. Eric had done what he was trained to do, and it wasn't enough. Eric told himself that he and Drew saved lives every day, that usually it was enough. But this time it wasn't, and the other times didn't matter so much in the face of that child dying.

Someone was to blame; for the fire, for calling 911 too late, for driving too slow, for something. Drew wasn't to blame any more than Eric was, and Eric knew it. He didn't think Drew did, right then.

Eric got a beer from the fridge. "C'mon," he said and waited for Drew to follow. He led him to the backyard and they bypassed the lawn chairs to sit on the grass in the sunshine.

"Not your fault," Eric said, looking at the flower beds. Perennials. Had to be, or maybe Drew's mom was sneaking in and planting stuff. Or maybe they just had pretty weeds.

Drew nodded and drank from his beer bottle. "I know. But I still feel like shit."

"Yeah. I know." Eric lay back on the grass. "It's okay to feel bad; hell, it's probably good to feel bad. You're still feeling, still doing the job for the right reasons, right? But keep telling yourself it's not your fault."

Drew finished his beer in a couple of quick swallows and lay down as well. He stared up at the sky and said, "So how come it feels like my fault?"

"Don't know. Did you do your best?"

"Yes."

"Not your fault. You got her out alive. You did your part."

They were silent for a while and Eric watched the clouds wander across the sky.

"Was it...when the doctors were working on her, did they hurt her?" Drew's voice was so quiet Eric almost didn't hear him.

He turned his head slowly. "No. The doctors didn't hurt her."

"That's good."

Eric couldn't reply. He looked to the sky again and when he had to he looked away from Drew to mask the tears he barely managed to blink away.

A few minutes later Drew asked, "You know what I need?"

Eric grinned despite himself, thinking, 'Yeah, another beer. And a good hard fuck to make you forget this goddamn day'. What he said, however, was, "Scott."

Drew rolled over and stared at him. "Was thinking about a beer, but hey, wouldn't say no to the Doc if he turned up early."

Neither would Eric. He laughed, and was pleased to see Drew smile back with a real smile, one that actually hit his eyes.

They lay on the grass and looked at the sky, not saying anything for a long time. Eric was getting sleepy, feeling the sun soaking in, making his clothes warm. It had been the worst day he had in months, and it was nice to just be outside with Drew, not doing anything at all.

"'Ric? Can I ask you something?"

"Hmm?" Eric didn't bother opening his eyes. The sun was too bright and he was too relaxed.

"Tell me to fuck off if I'm prying."

That got his attention. He looked over at Drew, but the man was staring at the sky. "Go ahead," he said.

"How come you're not with someone?"

Eric closed his eyes again and prayed Drew wouldn't even so much as glance in his direction. "Lack of opportunity," he offered.

"Bullshit. You go out. You meet people. How come you're not seeing someone?"

Eric though about the appropriate way to phrase his answer. "What I want isn't available to me," he finally said.

"You sure?"

"Yeah."

He heard Drew roll over. "Relationship? Guy taken?"

Jesus. "Yeah."

Drew didn't say anything for a long time and Eric was just starting to relax again when Drew quietly said, "So maybe there's room for one more."

Eric couldn't help himself, he opened his eyes and stared. "What?"

Drew bit his lower lip. "Maybe there's room for one more. You know these guys well?"

"Well enough to know that they have a good thing. There's no way in hell I'm going to do anything to mess that up for them."

Drew looked like he was going to say something else, but Eric kept going. "Let's say I did say something. What if one was into it and the other one not? Instant destruction. I won't do that. No matter how I feel, I'm not going to push my way into something that's working."

Drew bit his lip again. "Okay. I get that. Sorry, I didn't mean to…well, I didn't mean to upset you."

Eric tried to smile at him, but gave up. His stomach felt like lead and he was getting a headache trying to figure this out. Drew didn't have a clue what he was doing, and Eric was positive that if Drew had any idea who Eric was talking about, the conversation would have been entirely different. Easy enough to talk in theories when you don't know who the people are.

Different thing all together when you find out that your roommate is pretty sure he's in love with both you and your lover.

Eric went inside for more beer. Drew stayed on the lawn until Scott got home.

Chapter Twenty-seven

Scott had two days off and he should have been relaxing on the couch with Drew, waiting for Eric to get home for supper. He should have been happy and content, ready to spend a quiet couple of days with his lover and the man he now considered their closest friend.

But he was tight and tense and alone, staring at the TV. The local news had broken into the broadcast of the Jay's game to show a burning apartment building. Fifteen stories of fire and smoke, and Drew was in there somewhere.

Scott didn't get freaked about Drew's job often; mostly he didn't think about it unless Drew came home with wild eyes and nightmares. This was different. This was more fire trucks than he could count, people everywhere, flames and smoke and sirens. He was alone and more than anything he wanted Drew home. He needed to see him.

He watched. He leaned back on the couch and turned his head to say something—anything—to Eric, to connect with someone and feel less alone. But Eric wasn't home. His gut tightened at a sudden thought. He needed Eric. Right now.

The TV mesmerized him. It was a local channel and the coverage went on and on. He tried to see Drew every time they showed a fireman, but he didn't. At some point he moved to sit on the floor, as if he could see Drew if he sat closer to the set and willed the camera to shoot just the right angle.

A big hand settled on the back of his neck and he jumped.

"Easy, Doc." Eric settled on the couch behind him and rubbed his shoulders. "You're wound up tight. Stiff as a board."

"Yeah." Scott's voice sounded hoarse to his own ears, tight and ready to cry. He leaned back into Eric's hands, welcoming the touch. Eric started to knead the muscles.

"Drew in there?" he asked in a low voice.

"Yeah."

Eric didn't say anything else, just rubbed and massaged him for an age. They watched the fire as the sky behind the building darkened to black, night falling fast.

Scott leaned back and rested his head on Eric's knee. Eric let him.

He woke up when Drew touched his cheek. "You're home," he said softly.

"Yeah. Gonna take a shower." Drew was hunched down next to him, reeking of smoke, looking tired and worn-out.

Scott lifted his head and sat up, reaching out for him. "You came home."

Drew stood and pulled Scott to his feet. "Yeah." Then he kissed him, long and deep. Scott wrapped an arm around his neck, the other reaching back for…something. He broke the kiss when he realized he'd been reaching for Eric. Who was sitting on the couch. Being forced to watch them kiss. Shit.

He turned to look at him. "Hey. Drew's home."

Eric was smiling. "Noticed. Cool." He stood up and ran a hand through his hair. "Good to see you, man."

Drew grinned at him and let Scott go. "Good to be here. I'm going for that shower. I smell like hell."

Scott looked at Eric, took in how drawn and tired he was. "Thanks."

Eric looked at the floor, then around the room. "No problem, Doc. Look, I'm going to go out for a bit. Let you two…I'm just gonna go." He started to leave the room, but Drew stopped him with a hand on his arm.

"You don't have to leave, 'ric."

Scott watched Eric meet Drew's eyes. "Yeah. I do. Take care of him, Drew. Man was worried sick."

Scott figured he wasn't the only one who'd been scared.

"You seemed to be doing a good job," Drew said with no hint of malice.

Eric looked at the floor again. "Gonna go out. Be back late." He went to his room and closed the door.

Drew gave Scott a speculative look, then took his hand and led him to the bathroom. "Shower first. Talk later."

Scott just nodded. He could put off this talk as long as Drew would let him.

Drew started the water in the tub as they stripped. Scott stared at the floor, the wall tiles, the water; anything but Drew. He had no idea what was going on in his own head, let alone Drew's.

"Hey. Doc."

Scott looked up slowly.

"Talk later. C'mon, get wet. Need you."

Scott smiled weakly and got in the shower. He let Drew wash himself off and grabbed the shampoo. The lather turned gray in his hands so he rinsed it out and washed Drew's hair again.

The room filled with steam. He watched the soap bubbles slide down Drew's chest and wash down the drain. Drew had his head tipped back, rinsing the last of the shampoo out and Scott reached out a hand to trace the paths the bubbles made.

Drew opened his eyes and smiled at him, a wide, open smile that made Scott catch his breath. Then Scott was pressed against the back wall of the shower and Drew was giving him a mind melting kiss.

He could almost feel his brain shut off. All that mattered was that Drew was there. Scott returned the kiss as best he could, drawing out a low moan. Drew slid a hand down his side and around his leg, pulling it up so Scott could wrap it around Drew's waist.

"Worried about me, were you?"

"Yeah." Scott pushed against him, arms pulling them tight together as his cock slid along Drew's hip and belly.

"I'm here."

"Prove it."

Drew kissed him again, fumbling for the hair conditioner and bending his knees. When he straightened his legs his cock rubbed along Scott's ass, hard and thick and just so right. One quick move and he was pushing in, making Scott know with every fiber of his body that Drew was home, that Drew was with him.

"Love you, Scott."

"Know it. Love you."

Drew slammed into him and Scott groaned. So good. He wanted this forever. Nothing could make him give this up.

He bit down on Drew's shoulder as he rode. Drew moved into him relentlessly, fucking him hard. Scott let his head fall back and held onto Drew's shoulders, trying to pull him in deeper.

"Hold on," Drew said. Then he was lifting the other leg, and Scott clung to him, held in strong arms as he was fucked into the wall. His cock was caught in the friction between them, and he felt his balls draw up, hot and hard.

"Drew, coming."

"Yeah, come on my cock, Doc. Shoot for me."

Nothing could send Scott over faster than Drew talking. He didn't know if it was the words or the way Drew's voice sounded when he was this turned on, and he didn't care. He was slammed into the wall again and Drew said it one more time. "Come on me."

Scott screamed out Drew's name as he came, ass grinding down on Drew, arms tight across his shoulders. When he stopped shaking, Drew kissed him, slow and gentle and sweet. He didn't think he could move.

Drew eased out of his body and lowered his legs gently, letting them both sink down into the tub. He put the plug in the drain and they sat in the shower, letting the tub fill.

Scott was holding Drew, tracing patterns on his chest. When the tub was mostly full Drew turned off the shower and topped it up with hot water. He leaned back on Scott's chest and they soaked, letting the tension and stress drift away.

Scott thought he might fall asleep. Drew took his hand and kissed his fingers, one by one. "You wanna tell me what the deal is with Eric?"

Tension flooded back into Scott. "He…it's nothing. Really. I just…oh, hell."

Drew sighed. "We ever not talked about shit, Scott? Have we ever held back on the important stuff?"

Scott felt miserable. "No."

Drew tilted his head and looked up at him. "Love you. That's not going to change. Tell me."

Scott shook his head. "If we talk about this, we can't un-talk about it. Everything changes whether we want it to or not." He looked into serious brown eyes. "I don't want to fuck up."

Drew sat up. "We should have been talking about this for months, I think. Shouldn't have stopped. C'mon, let's take this to bed. Take a minute to get your head sorted."

They dried off and went into their room, leaving the lights on in the living room for Eric.

Drew got into bed, sitting up against the headboard. "You know where he is, don't you?"

Scott nodded. "Some bar where no one knows him. He's been doing it for a while now, about four months."

"He only goes when you and I get intense."

Scott stood at the end of the bed, just looking at Drew. He was just sitting there, eyes serious, waiting.

"Scott, how do you feel about him? And don't shake your head at me. Tell me."

"Shit." Scott got under the covers, lying still on his side of the bed. "I love you."

"I know that. Look, you want me to do the talking?" Drew barely waited for Scott's nod. "He's smart, he's funny, he trusts us, he's fucking hot, he makes you smile, he worries about us. It makes me feel sick to know what he's doing right now with some creep he doesn't even know. He should be at home. He should be right here. With us."

Scott stared.

Drew looked back at him, eyes serious. "Are you going to tell me that you don't think the same thing? That you're not already half in love with him? 'Cause that'll be the first time you've lied to me."

"I have no fucking clue what to say here, Drew."

"Shit, Scott. He's hot. I've wanted him for ages now, almost as long as you. I know he's into you, and I'm pretty sure he's into me. I just want you to figure out what's going on in your own head."

Scott felt like his world was imploding. Drew was talking about Eric like there was even a slight chance that they could all be happy together, and all Scott could see was Eric running away.

"Don't want to lose him, Drew. Don't want him to move out if we're wrong."

"I know. I get that, I really do. But Scott, you're still hedging your bets here. I really need to know how you feel about him. 'Cause if we're not on the same page here things could get messy. It's all gotta balance if we're going to do anything about this."

Scott took a deep breath. "I know what we said, after Tom. I know that I made it an all-or-nothing deal. Do you seriously think that he could be the all? You actually think we can say anything to him about…about a relationship and he won't run?"

Drew moved across the bed and curled around him. "Yeah. I think we can. He needs us. I think we need him."

Scott ran a hand down Drew's arm. "You love him."

"Almost. I could so easily."

Scott sighed and kissed Drew's forehead. "Yeah. How the hell are we going to tell him?"

Drew shrugged. "No idea. We'll figure it out."

Chapter Twenty-eight

Eric closed his bedroom door and sat on the edge of the bed, shaking. He heard Drew and Scott go down the hall and he waited until the shower started before he changed his shirt and jeans and headed out.

He had intended to do what he always did; find a bar, sit and have a few drinks, try not to think. It didn't work out that way and he knew as soon as he started driving that he was going to have to stop as soon as he could and walk.

He pulled into a parking lot and locked the car, setting out on foot. It was a cool night, and for a while he tried to convince himself that he was cold and that's why he was still shaking. He walked a couple more blocks and headed into the first bar he saw, a dark pool hall with beer. Good enough. He bought a draft at the bar and went to a booth at the back, hoping everyone would just ignore him.

When he had come home and seen Scott fucking glued to the TV he had been sure that Drew was hurt. He'd sat there with him for hours watching, knowing that Drew was damn good at his job, that he'd be careful, but still getting more and more freaked as the time passed. The thought of anything happening to Drew made him feel like he couldn't breathe, like every time he moved he was walking on sand.

He'd wanted to pull Scott up onto the couch and hold him, try to soothe away the man's fear, or at the very least let him know that he wasn't alone. That there was someone else who was just as scared. He couldn't do it. He couldn't offer comfort to him because then Scott would know how he felt about them both, how closely he had managed to tie himself up into them.

If Scott and Drew knew how he felt they would be kind to him. He knew that. They would look at him with sympathy in their eyes and turn him away as gently as they could and everything would change. He would lose them.

They were his best friends; they were his line into what was good in the world. They were always so careful to make sure that he wasn't left out of anything around the house, that he didn't see them being physical with each other. They didn't want him to feel like he wasn't welcome.

They didn't know that the men he picked up always had either dark hair and blue eyes or light brown hair. They didn't know how many times he'd woken up from dreams of them together. How many times he'd lain in bed hearing them as they tried to keep their loving quiet. He knew that they were making the effort; he'd heard them be as vocal as they wanted to be when they didn't know he was home.

They didn't know how ashamed he was, how impossible it was for him to stop himself from falling in love with them.

He'd seen Scott when Drew came home. He'd seen them kiss and it had taken every ounce of self-control he'd had not to get up and go to Drew himself. And then Scott had reached back and Eric had thought it had been for him. The man had let Eric touch him, work the kinks out of his shoulders, and had fallen asleep on his leg. Eric had watched him for an hour. When Scott reached back he'd almost taken his hand, but then it was gone and Scott had looked at him like…like he'd woken up and realized what he was doing.

Drew had seen Scott curled into Eric's leg. He didn't seem to mind, but there was no way Eric could stay there, not when they were going to reassure each other that Drew was alive and well.

Drew was alive and well. Drew was where he belonged; at home, in the arms of the man who loved him.

One of them.

Eric went out, drank cheap beer, and hated himself for getting so twisted up. He left the bar and walked some more, found another bar. This one had dancing and expensive beer. He sat at a table and waited until the right guy came along and left. He was almost to the guy's car when he decided he was done.

"Sorry," he said, stopping. The man turned to look at him. "This is a bad idea. I'm doing this for the wrong reasons."

The guy smiled at him, a little sadly. "There's no right reasons for a quick blow job with a stranger, friend."

Eric nodded. "Yeah. But I'm going home. Sorry."

"S'cool. Hope things work out for you."

"Me, too."

Eric walked back to his car and drove home. He started looking for a new place to live the next morning.

Chapter Twenty-nine

Scott closed the last file and leaned back in his chair to stretch. He hated doing paperwork at home, taking over the kitchen table, but he hated doing it at the hospital more. Both Eric and Drew were home for the night, and he would rather sit in the kitchen finishing up than be at the hospital, missing the sounds of conversation and the TV. They were going to watch a movie as soon as he was done. He hoped it had explosions.

He stood up and crossed to the fridge, grabbing a couple of beers and a can of Coke for himself. He could hear Eric ask Drew something in the living room; it sounded like they were teasing each other about what show to watch next.

"No more TV," he said as he went in and handed them each a beer. "I'm done. Movie time."

He felt good. Relaxed. He was home, Drew and Eric were both there, and they could sit and vegetate for a change. All three of them.

Eric shifted in the easy chair as Scott sat on the floor by the couch. Drew was lying on it, stretched out and looking like he wasn't going to move for hours. He glanced up in surprise when Eric reached out for the remote and turned the TV off.

"I have something to tell you guys, actually," Eric said softly.

Drew sat up a little on the couch and Scott felt something uneasy settle in the back of his mind. Eric was suddenly tense and he wouldn't meet their eyes, his gaze leveled at the floor just to the right of Scott's foot.

"'Ric? Everything okay?" Drew asked, his voice low and concerned.

Eric shook his head. "Nothing like that. It's just…well, I'm going to get a new place at the beginning of September. I wanted to give you as much notice as possible, in case you need someone to move in and cover the rent."

Scott couldn't swallow and he was pretty sure that if Drew didn't say something in the next couple of seconds he was going to make a fool of himself.

"Find a nice place?" Drew asked, his voice still low, sounding cautious to Scott's ear. He glanced back and saw Drew give him a quick look that told him Drew wasn't going to let this happen easily. He felt cold, though, and wanted to crawl up on the couch with him. Or over to Eric's chair and just tell him not to leave them.

Eric was still looking at the floor. "Not yet, no."

Drew sat up all the way, swinging his legs over the side of the couch. "So, it's not so much getting a new place as it is leaving this place," he said evenly. "Why?"

Eric bit his lip. "It's not working out anymore, is all," he said, finally glancing up. But he still didn't meet their eyes.

"Why?"

"It's…fuck. It's complicated, and I really don't want to get into it." Eric stood up. "Look, I just can't stay anymore, and I'm really sorry. I gotta go—"

"Don't." Scott wasn't sure if he or Drew was more surprised when he spoke.

"Scott—"

"Just—don't. Don't go." Scott couldn't get anything else to come out. He looked at Drew, hoping that he would know what he was supposed to do.

Drew nodded, once. He put a hand on Scott's shoulder, squeezing gently as he looked up at Eric. "There's something we want to talk to you about."

Eric looked at them, his eyes flicking from one the other. "Yeah? Like what?" He sounded tired and faintly suspicious.

"Sit down, 'ric. This is gonna be a bit of a…" Drew paused and looked at Scott. "Well, shit. Just sit down. This isn't going to be easy on any of us."

Eric sat down slowly, sinking into the easy chair like he expected it to swallow him up and was half hoping that it did. "What's up?" he said finally, his face serious.

Drew shifted on the couch, moving imperceptibly closer to the easy chair, one hand still on Scott. Scott reached up and laid his hand on Drew's, letting him know he was there, that he agreed they had to do this right now.

"We don't want you to leave," Drew said.

"I gathered that, but—"

"No." Drew shook his head. "You don't understand. Let me finish. We want you to stay. With us. To be…a part of us. We want you to stay here with us. I want to be with you. Scott does, too."

Eric stared at him, eyes wide. There was silence for a few moments and then he said, "What?"

"We want you to be a part of what we are. We want you in our home, in our bed, in our relationship. To make it your own. Be with us." Drew looked at Scott. "I can't think of any other way to say it."

Scott just nodded, watching Eric.

Eric was pale and staring into space. He bit at his lip once and then rubbed the fingers of one hand over the back of the other. Eventually, he stood up. "I have to think about this. I'm going to go for a drive. No, no, I'm not. I can't drive right now. I'm going to my room. I'll be back." Then he walked down the hall and they heard his door close.

"Fuck," Drew said under his breath. "Sorry, Scott. Oh, shit, I messed that up so fucking bad." Drew groaned and lay back down on the couch.

"No, you didn't," Scott said, pushing at Drew's legs until he could join him on the couch. "Think about it for a second. Of course he needs to think, you just offered him a marriage and he didn't even know we were dating."

Drew glanced up at him and gave him a ghost of a smile. "Hope you're right, Doc, 'cause if he tries to leave, I'm going to plan B."

"What's that?"

"Hallway wrestling. Naked this time."

Scott rolled his eyes. "That'd work."

They sat on the couch for almost an hour before Eric came back out to the living room. Drew sat up again and Scott pushed away the voice that was trying to comment on how very tall six-foot three is from a seated position. A little intimidating.

Eric stood in front of them. "So, what happens the first time one of you sees me with the other one and gets upset?"

"Not gonna happen," Scott and Drew replied in unison.

Eric sighed and sat in the chair again. "What's not going to happen?"

Drew leaned forward. "The jealousy bit. Scott knows I love him. I know he loves me. And we both want you to be a part of—"

"You keep saying that, and I don't get how you could," Eric interrupted.

"Could what?" Drew countered.

Scott felt a wave of nausea pass through him. This wasn't going to work. Eric was too surprised by what Drew had offered and they'd freaked him out. He reached over and took Drew's hand.

"How you could want me in," Eric said, as if that explained everything. "What do I have to add to what you've already got?"

"You," Drew said. "We want you."

Eric shook his head again and buried his face in his hands, elbows on his knees. When he looked up it was at Scott. "Are you going to say anything? Is this what you want, too?"

Without even looking at Drew, Scott let go of his hand and stood up, crossed to Eric and dropped to his knees in front of him. "Yes," he said softly. He put one hand at the back of Eric's neck, the other lightly on one cheek and leaned in and kissed him.

It wasn't a tentative kiss, or a gentle one. It was hungry and possessive and demanding, and the scariest thing Scott had ever done. He was aware of Eric's stunned non-reaction for a couple of seconds, then he heard a low moan from Eric's throat as the big man opened his mouth to him, letting him in.

"Well, I'll be damned," Drew said behind him, his voice awed.

Scott broke the kiss to breathe and saw the look on Eric's face. He seemed about ready to apologize and Scott suddenly realized that Drew's comment would have been easy to misinterpret. "Don't worry, I'll explain later," he said, and then he kissed Eric again, before either of them could panic.

Drew pressed up against his back, arms going around him, hips pushing into his ass. "Ah shit, Scott. Let me have a turn."

Eric moaned into the kiss and Scott pulled back, letting Drew lean over his shoulder to take his place. They were kissing right beside him and if he hadn't been hard before he certainly was now. The two of them were stunning, Eric making little noises that tried to start as deep rumbles and ended up as needy moans, and Drew not letting him back away at all.

When Eric finally pulled back, breathing heavily and eyes wide, Scott smiled at him. "Stay with us?" he asked, trying not to sound like he was begging. He was on his knees as it was, literally, and he didn't want to sound completely desperate. Even if he was.

Eric blinked at him and nodded. "Yes—" He might have been trying to say something else, but they were kissing again, Scott pulling Eric off the chair so the three of them were sprawled on the floor.

Scott quickly lost track of exactly who was doing what. All he was really aware of, for a few moments, was the sound of Eric saying yes and the intensity of their kiss, the way that Eric felt on him, beside him, Drew pressed close and sharing their need.

The three of them moved together, rolling and reaching, kissing and touching. He kissed Drew and watched as Drew teased at the soft skin under Eric's ear; Drew had a hand on his ass, holding him close as their hips worked together, and he had one hand working at Eric's fly as Drew stole another kiss. He moaned softly, watching their tongues dance, as Eric's arm held him as tightly as Drew's.

Eric broke the kiss, his breathing even more ragged. "Can we—" The rest of his question faded in a gasp as Drew bit at his neck.

"Slow down?" Scott offered, rubbing at Eric's cock through his jeans and moving his hand lower to cup Eric's balls.

Eric looked at him like he was insane. "Do this naked."

"Oh, fuck, yes," Drew said with a groan. Eric's hands were busy, too. "And in our bed."

The three of them managed to untangle long enough to stand up and start down the hall. Drew and Eric both stripped off their shirts as they walked and Scott heard a strangled noise come from his own throat. God, they were sexy.

Drew grinned at him and pinned him to the wall. "Keep it together, Doc. Got more clothes to get rid of."

"Like this," Eric said, sliding his hands under Scott's sweatshirt and pushing it up and off.

Oh, yeah. Like that. Their hands glided over him and Scott shivered. "Bed," he said, trying not to squeak as a hand slid over his prick. "Now."

Drew grinned at him and stepped back. "You know where it is."

Eric moved toward his own room. "I need to get—" He gestured with one arm and seemed to retreat into himself, shoulders slumping slightly, his face beginning to flush. Couldn't have that.

Scott pushed him up against the door frame and tore Eric's jeans open, pushing them down with determination. "You aren't gonna believe how fast I get your blood work back," he said, his head going to Eric's chest. He licked and bit a trail down the man's body, tracing cut muscles with his tongue as his hands moved over hard thighs.

When he went to his knees and started to lick and suck at Eric's balls, the big man's head hit the wall with a solid thunk. Drew pushed past them into Eric's room, one hand skimming Scott's shoulders.

Scott heard them kissing, and then Drew said, "Where are they, 'ric?"

Scott took one of Eric's balls into his mouth and sucked gently. "Oh, fuck. Oh, fuck. Top drawer, left."

Scott happily kept doing what he was doing and then Drew was back, rolling a rubber on Eric's prick for him. He took Eric's cock into his mouth and set to work, tongue teasing and playing, suction light. He looked up to see Drew fuck Eric's mouth with his tongue and moaned, making Eric's eyes go wide and his hips start to thrust. Perfect.

"Want to watch," Drew said, his voice husky. He pulled away and stripped his own jeans off, leaving one last sucking kiss on Eric's broad chest before working at Scott's jeans. Drew's fingers teased at Scott's cock and then he was gone, leaning against the wall in the hallway, jacking off while he watched Scott sucking Eric's dick.

"Oh, shit," Eric moaned. "Not gonna be long." A big hand moved gently over his head, wide fingers caressing his face.

Eric's cock was long and thick and promising, hard and wanting. He sucked harder, bobbing his head faster, one hand going to his own shaft. He glanced at Drew, took in the wide, glazed eyes and had to squeeze the base of his erection. "Want you," he said before going back to Eric.

Both Drew and Eric shuddered, and then Eric was thrusting fast and hard, his breath shaky, soft moans spilling from his mouth. Drew pulled harder on his own prick, legs splayed, one hand going to his balls.

"Oh, God, now!" Eric cried, and the cock in his mouth began to pulse as Eric shot. Scott almost came, too, and Drew did, shooting onto his stomach before sliding down the wall, legs unable to keep him up.

When Eric was done, Scott pulled away and kissed his thigh before turning to Drew, one hand swiping come off his belly.

"Now," he ground out, slicking himself with Drew's spunk. Drew spread for him on the floor of their hallway and Scott pushed in, thrust hard a couple of times, and came with a roar.

When he could see again they were all laying on the floor, looking stunned and happy. "Shower?"

"God, yes."

The shower proved to be a little crowded so Scott cleaned up as best he could and left them to it, going to lock up the house for the night. He made sure the lights were out and the doors were locked, then gathered up the three pagers and the portable phone and headed to the bedroom.

Drew and Eric were already there, which was nice. He could hear them from down the hall, hear the rumbles of conversation and Drew's long groan that he knew meant they had started without him. He grinned and walked faster.

He stepped in the door and dropped the pagers and the phone on the floor, his half-hard cock suddenly harder than steel. "Oh, God," he whispered, moving to the bed.

Drew was on all fours on the middle of the bed, Eric behind him, pushing in slowly. It was the hottest thing he'd ever seen, bar none. Eric was all muscle, hard and cut and like a sculpture, smooth warm skin, a little paler than Drew. Drew was as stunning as he always was, a flush covering his body as he moved back onto Eric, his eyes wide and needy, his face radiating pleasure.

Scott sprawled on the bed, grabbing the lube. "Holy shit, you two are going to kill me," he said, kissing Drew hard and then pushing himself up to kiss Eric. They both groaned in response.

"Good?" Eric asked.

"Fuck, yes," Drew said. "Wanted this for so long, 'ric. Need you."

Scott worked his cock with a slippery hand and nodded. "We do. We need you. We want you." He moved again, touching them both, letting his hands wander over skin, kissing one and then the other, pulling at nipples and teasing Drew's prick before drawing back to watch again.

They were speeding up a little, Eric pushing deep. Drew's eyes were wild and hungry and he was starting to shake. "Harder, 'ric. Fuck me."

Eric did. He slammed into Drew again and again, eyes closed, fingers digging into Drew's hips. Drew cried out, almost sobbing. Scott almost forgot to breathe, they were so amazing. His own cock was throbbing and his hand worked tighter and faster, palm grazing the tip and making him shudder.

"Scott—" Drew moaned. "Please, need to come—"

Scott got in front of Drew, intending to push him up by the shoulders so he could suck him off while Eric rode him, but as soon as he was there Drew had his own mouth open and he pushed in, down Drew's throat.

Three. Moving and fucking and sucking and it wasn't going to last long, not this time. Drew came first, spraying onto the bed, his cry muffled.

"Oh, shit, yes!" Eric groaned, thrusting hard enough to force Drew forward, to force Scott deeper. Eric's head tipped back, his stomach muscles rolled and twitched as he came deep in Drew's ass.

"Love you," Scott whispered, his eyes rolling back in his head, fire racing down his spine and out his cock. "Fuck. Love you."

Chapter Thirty

When the phone rang, Eric's training kicked in and he sat up in bed, wide awake. Scott and Drew did, too, the three of them all looking for the phone.

"Got it," Scott said, rolling off the bed onto the floor. Eric watched him crawl the few feet to where the phone and their pagers lay on the floor, and then his brain sort of clicked into place. He was watching a naked Scott. A naked Scott who had sucked him off and slept curled around him. And he was next to an equally naked Drew whom he had fucked and slept next to, their legs tangled together.

"Oh, God," he whispered. Then he fell back on the bed and grabbed a pillow, burying his face in it.

"None of that," Drew said, snatching the pillow away and kissing him soundly, one hand snaking between his legs to stroke his balls. "You're ours now."

Eric whimpered into Drew's mouth and arched into the touch, deciding to panic later.

"Drew," Scott said. "Phone."

"Shit." Drew reached for the phone with his other hand, the one on Eric's balls moving up to tease his morning erection. "Smyth," he said into the phone.

Scott climbed back into bed, looking at Eric almost shyly. "Morning," he said.

"Morning," Eric said, trying not to moan as Drew's fingers feathered over him.

Scott looked like he didn't know what to do. Eric felt panic rising up in him.

"Damn. No one else? Fine. Give me ten." Drew tossed the phone on the bed and said, "Gotta go into work for a couple of hours." Then the hand disappeared and Eric did moan, this time at the loss rather than the touch. Drew kissed him and then leaned over, pulling Scott close enough to kiss. "Don't exhaust yourselves." When Drew got up he pulled at Scott, who pretty much just fell on top of Eric.

Eric blinked and considered what to do for about half a second. What was he supposed to do with a naked doctor draped over him? He decided to try kissing him and see what happened.

Scott gave a happy sounding whimper and kissed him back, wiggling around until he was cradled in Eric's spread thighs. "Oh. That worked," Eric said inanely.

"Oh, yeah. That," Drew said as he pulled on a pair of sweatpants. "He's easy, but you gotta make the first move. Tell you more when I get home." Then Drew was gone from the bed, pulling on a T-shirt and heading out the door. "Back soon."

Eric looked at Scott. "I do?"

"Sorta. But you just did, so we're good." Scott wiggled some more.

"Oh. Okay." Eric wiggled back. "So…?"

Scott licked his neck and looked at him with too wide eyes, swallowing hard. "Want you, 'ric. Want to be in you."

Eric's cock twitched and he thought he may have forgotten to take a breath. He didn't say anything, just kissed Scott hard, big hands wrapping around to reach Scott's ass, pulling him as close as he could.

Scott moaned into the kiss and moved against him, letting him feel how much he was wanted. Hands wandered over his chest, followed soon after by Scott's tongue. God, the man had a mouth like a wet dream. Kissed like an angel, liked to taste and lick and suck and— "Oh, shit, that feels good," he groaned as Scott nipped at the skin on his side.

He got a grin in return and then Scott was reaching for the lube and the condoms. Eric watched with mingled anticipation and wonder as Scott got ready, then cried out as he was opened. It felt so good, had been so very long.

Scott didn't waste time, didn't tease, just got him ready and filled him, looking him in the eye. It was a couple of moments before Eric realized exactly what was going on. Scott wasn't going to fuck him, wasn't going to nail him to the mattress. Scott was making love to him.

Long slow strokes that left him breathless. Kisses that seared him, designed not so much as to arouse but to let him know that he was wanted and needed. He could feel what Scott was giving him, could feel trust and desire, hunger and wanting; he could feel Scott's emotions in those kisses, could taste them, sweet and gentle.

Scott's cock skated across his prostate and he gasped. Scott did it again and again, never stopping the sweet kisses, the low sounds that Eric could barely make out.

"What?" he finally managed. "What are you saying?"

Scott leaned up and thrust deeply into him. He stared at him, eyes hazy, looking almost drugged. "Said I can't believe you're finally here. Can't believe how lucky I am. Said I love you."

Eric's back arched and a shudder ran through his body. "Oh, God."

Scott wrapped a hand around his erection and started stroking him.

"Love you, Eric. Need you. Needed you for so long—"

"Scott—" Eric came, all of his senses spinning out of control.

Scott moved in him, not stopping, a look of determination on his face. "Gonna say it until you believe me. I love you."

Eric waited until he had regained some control over his body before raising his hands to Scott's face. He traced full, swollen lips, brushed his fingers over a strong jaw in need of a shave. "I believe you," he whispered as Scott continued to love him. "I love you. Love you, love Drew, love you both."

Scott kissed him then, feeding Eric his cries as he came.

They moved to the shower, when they could, and Eric couldn't help staring.

Scott looked at him, eyes still dilated. "You're beautiful," he said in a low voice, one hand going to Eric's waist.

Eric dipped his head and kissed him. "Was just thinking the same thing about you," he said softly.

Scott chuckled into the kiss. "We have it so bad," he said lightly.

Eric grinned back at him and washed his hair for him.

Clean and awake, they moved to the living room, Scott stopping in the kitchen to grab coffee for them both. "Drew is a saint about the coffee," he remarked.

Eric nodded happily. "Don't think I've had to make a pot in the morning since I moved in."

Scott sat next to him on the couch and Eric pulled him a little closer, smiling shyly.

Scott leaned into him with a happy sigh. "You seem unfreaked," he said carefully.

"I'm totally freaked," Eric admitted.

Scott looked at him. "Yeah?"

Eric nodded. "Doesn't mean I'm changing my mind, though. Took me less than a minute last night to figure out you guys meant it. Knew you wouldn't play me, not about something like this. I know you were—are—serious about wanting us to be an us."

Scott nodded. "We are. We love you. Just didn't know how to say it, and when you said you were leaving…ran out of time to figure it out."

Eric smiled. "I get that."

"So what's got you freaked?" Scott asked. "Aside from finding out your roommates want you in their relationship and suddenly having two partners?" Scott's tone indicated that he knew that alone was enough to freak anyone out. "You were gone for a long time last night before you said yes."

"Had to figure out why you wanted me. Then I decided that it didn't matter, not right then. What mattered was there was no way I could leave. I couldn't walk out and throw away what I'd been wanting, not when it was offered to me. I was moving out because I loved you; be dumb to leave because I was wanted back."

"Yeah. You gonna be okay? It's weird, I know, and things will be strange for a bit. Don't see any of us settling down for a few days, at least. But if you need us to back off or tell you anything, just say. We're not…we don't want you to freak anymore than is natural. If that makes any sort of sense." Scott sounded flustered and looked at him with confused eyes. His expression cleared and he grinned. "This is silly."

Eric grinned back. "Yeah. But it's us being silly. We're allowed." He kissed the end of Scott's nose. "Tell me about this first move thing?"

Scott groaned into the kiss, but it wasn't the hungry groans he'd heard before. "It's stupid."

Eric shrugged. "Maybe, but I want to understand. It's part of you."

Scott sighed. "Yeah. Short version is someone I loved a lot read me the riot act about being pushy. Pretty much tore me up, and now I just can't. I get a sick feeling, and my head starts to pound, and I just get so scared that I'll get hurt again. Even when it's Drew."

Eric stared at him. "You've never come onto him? Pulled him into the bedroom or whatever?"

"Never even kissed him first. Just been able to initiate 'good bye, see you after work' kisses in the last few months."

Eric blinked. "You kissed me last night."

Scott bit his lip. "Had no choice. And if you were going to leave anyway…"

Eric sat up. "You did that for me?"

"Yeah. Couldn't let you just leave us." Scott wouldn't look at him, was staring at his knees.

"Hey," Eric said softly. "C'mere."

Scott looked up, finally, and Eric kissed him, softly. "Thank you."

They were still kissing on the couch when Drew came home.

Chapter Thirty-one

Things didn't really change so much as just relax around the house. Scott and Drew were more affectionate with each other, letting the touches and casual kisses out now, letting Eric see them love each other. They weren't shy about kissing or touching him, either, though he did have to reach out to Scott first. It took him a couple of weeks to get used to that; the need to grab Scott's hand as he walked by, the need to pay attention to what Scott's eyes and body language were telling him. It wasn't like Scott was passive at all, he just really seemed to need something solid to show him it was all right. Sometimes Eric wasn't sure if he got the signals right, but there had never been a time he reached for Scott that the man hadn't moved into his arms. Eric just had to trust Scott to let him know if he was wrong. He found the trust came pretty easily.

Loving them was easy.

***

The first time he came home after a swing shift he'd rolled in at one in the morning to find both of them asleep in the big bed and both having morning shifts. He went to sleep in his old room, not wanting to wake them by getting into bed; they needed their sleep. No one said anything, but when he got home from work the next night his bed had been taken apart and his old room was full of books and boxes. He slept in their bed, and that was it. It was his bed, too. Lesson learned.

***

About a month after they become three, Eric and Drew shared a call, a car accident that was a real mess. One of the cars went up in flames scant minutes after they had cut the last occupant out; Eric had felt the blast from the fuel tank as he was lifting the gurney into the bus, and had turned to see Drew falling to the ground. There was no time to check on him.

He'd done his job, taken the patient in, working at what he was supposed to do, and forced Drew from his mind. When he'd handed the patient off in the ER he'd grabbed an incoming EMT from the scene and asked what the hell had happened.

"It blew sky high, is what. No one hurt, but about six guys landed on their asses. If it wasn't so fucking scary it would have been funny."

Eric finished his shift and caught a lift home instead of walking from the hospital like usual. He ran into the house and met Drew and Scott in the kitchen. Scott was cutting vegetables, listening as Drew described the explosion, and merely raised an eyebrow when Eric tackled Drew, pushing him into the table and kissing him hard, hands running over his back.

"You're okay?"

"Yeah. Better while you're doing that," Drew said with a chuckle.

"Don't fucking laugh at me," Eric spat. "Scared the hell out of me, seeing you fall like that."

Drew sobered immediately. "You saw?"

Eric nodded, staring at him. "Had to go, had to work, couldn't think, didn't know…"

Understanding dawned in Drew's eyes and Scott was there, pressing into his back. Neither of them said anything, just held on, hands stroking and petting and calming.

Drew's mouth found his, kissing him deeply, pouring reassurance into him. Scott disappeared for a second and Eric could hear him moving a pot off the stove, turning things off. He came back, hands going around Eric's waist to pull his shirt free from his pants.

"Want to do this here, or you want to move to the bed?" Scott asked quietly.

Eric didn't answer, just let Drew push him back, let Scott steer them as they went down the hall. Not once did he stop kissing Drew. He didn't stop until they were on the bed, naked and moving together, need carrying them.

"I love you, 'ric," Drew said, looking in his eyes.

Eric nodded once and kissed him again. "Love you, too."

Scott had a hand on his back and another on Drew's shoulder, just there and solid and real and a part of it when they came.

***

When Eric came home covered in blood the next week, Scott was coming out of the bedroom. Eric's shift wasn't over for another three hours, but he couldn't stay. No one had really expected him

134

to, and when he signed out he'd written in where he'd pick up the hours. He needed to be home. He needed Scott.

He stopped in the middle of the hall and looked down at his uniform. Scott stood there, waiting, calm and perfectly right.

"She was sixteen. Cut herself up really good. Told me she'd just do it again, that it didn't matter how good a job I did fixin' her up, life wasn't worth it." Even to his own ears his voice sounded hollow. Sometimes he hated his job.

Scott took a step forward and laid a hand on his cheek. "It matters. And life is worth it. Come on." Scott turned and led him into the bathroom, started filling the tub before Eric was even there.

Eric didn't say anything as Scott stripped the ruined uniform off, and he didn't say anything when Scott told him to get in the tub. He just did as he was told, let Scott take care of him. Like he knew Scott would.

Scott washed him. Washed the blood off his arms, and off his neck and the backs of his hands. Scott talked, and it didn't matter, really, what he said. The tone said Scott knew what he was feeling, and that it was okay. The feeling of gentle hands on his skin told him he was safe and home and loved. The look in Scott's eyes said that he was going to be warm and held for as long as he needed, plus however long Scott needed to.

He let Scott love him with his voice and his hands and his being. And he loved him for it, loved him because he had known this was his for the asking.

Chapter Thirty-two

Eric looked out the kitchen window and shuddered. "What the hell is he doing?"

Drew laughed and came up behind him, sliding his arms around his waist and nuzzling his shoulder. "Barbequing. He swears he's going to use the grill until it's buried in snow."

Eric shook his head. "It's the end of freaking November. It's cold. There's frost on the ground."

"He wanted steak done right."

"He's a nut."

"Yeah. But he's our nut."

When their nut came in from the cold he was bearing a plate of steaks and had blue lips. Eric shook his head again and kissed Scott before taking the plate and putting it on the table. "You're freezing."

Scott shivered and moved closer, letting Eric wrap his arms around him. "Yeah. But the steaks are nice."

Drew leaned over and kissed Scott, too. "Let's eat then, and see about warming you up."

Scott grinned. "How are you gonna do that?"

Drew looked him up and down and then looked at Eric. "Well, I figure we all get naked, go to bed, and then we turn the big guy here into a smorgasbord."

Eric blinked. "Me?"

Scott purred and rubbed up against him. "Oh, yeah. You. Get you between us, make you lose the power of speech—that always warms me up."

Eric blinked again, his eyes losing focus. The last time he'd been the middle, he had, in fact, lost the power of speech. Had damn near lost consciousness, too. "How...I mean what...how..."

Scott smiled at him. "See? Working already."

Drew was leaning closer now, eyes hungry. He didn't look like he was thinking about the steaks, and his hands were most certainly not reaching for plates. "Think supper can wait," he said and started pulling them to the bedroom.

"But—" Eric said, then realized he actually had no objections to sex before supper as opposed to after. Scott laughed at him, apparently thinking that the misfiring of Eric's brain was highly amusing. Eric kissed him, just to shut him up. By the time he was done Scott was breathless, hips rocking into his.

"God, you two look good," Drew said. Then he pulled Eric onto the bed and took over the kiss.

Eric wasn't exactly sure how they managed to get undressed. It took a long time, he knew that. Someone was always wanting to touch or kiss and there were the usual distractions that happened when Drew was the one removing pants. Drew really liked to suck, and neither Eric nor Scott minded unless he stopped. This time he just managed to get them both worked up enough to start to thrust hard, pushing into his mouth, and then he'd be gone, distracting them again by kissing or touching somewhere else.

Eric was pretty sure he wasn't going last long enough to be in the middle of anything. Scott was making hungry needy noises, moving against him hard and fast, cock painting a trail along his thigh and Drew was just as bad, doing everything he knew to turn Eric inside out. A hand rubbed along his right side, gliding over the patch of skin just above his hip that always made him shiver, and a hot mouth was working at his neck, drawing his own needy noises out.

He didn't even realize Scott had moved back until he felt slippery fingers slide over his ass and down as far as his balls. "Oh, God," he whimpered. "You're really gonna—"

"Oh, yeah," Scott said in his ear. "Gonna make you feel so good, 'ric. Just wait." Then fingers were pushing into him, a knee spreading his legs a little wider. He pushed back onto Scott's hand, not able to stop, not wanting to.

He braced himself, hands on his thighs as Drew kissed his way down his chest. Last time he'd been helpless, rocking between fingers and mouth, unable to do anything but feel. He'd felt it for days. This time was going to be just as good, Drew's eyes and mouth hungry for him. Made him feel powerful and strong and needed.

Then Scott pushed him forward a bit. He wasn't expecting it and started to fall, getting his hands out in front in time to avoid landing on Drew. "What—" he started, the words breaking off as he felt the head of Scott's cock pushing at him. "Oh..."

"Yeah. Oh." Drew was smiling at him, then shifting around to lay in front of him. Eric stared at Drew grabbed the lube and slicked his fingers. "Gonna blow your mind, 'ric."

Eric gasped as Scott moved in him, hands on his hips. Long strokes that had him going deep every time.

"Fuck. Good, Scott." He let his head drop forward, eyes closing as he rode.

"Look at me, 'ric," Drew said, voice hoarse and tight.

Eric opened his eyes and saw Drew slide two fingers into his own ass. He bucked against Scott and swore, nearly coming then and there.

Drew gasped and spread his legs, fingers moving deeper. "Want you. Want you in me."

"Holy shit," Scott said, his rhythm faltering. "Oh, fuck."

Eric just stared.

Drew opened himself and finally slid forward, wrapping his legs around Eric's waist and pulling his hips up. "Fuck me, 'ric."

Eric couldn't even move. Drew leaned up and kissed him, tongue thrusting and opening his mouth wide, a hand guiding Eric's cock where he wanted it. And Eric sank into him, pushing into his heat steadily. When he was as deep as he could get all three of them froze for a moment.

"God," Scott whispered. "Oh, God."

Eric couldn't speak.

Scott pulled back and started to thrust, Drew picking up the rhythm fast. Eric stared into Drew's eyes, sensations washing over him like a wind storm, one pressure leading to the next and back again. Drew's eyes were dark, his breath coming in hitching gasps as Scott pushed Eric deeper and deeper.

Eric gathered himself as best he could and moved with them, the extra sensations he could create just by moving, just by loving with them pushing them all closer to the edge.

Scott was babbling, maybe making up for Eric's lack of words. He was swearing and saying 'oh, God' and 'yeah' and 'hot' and other stuff that sounded just right, his thrusts getting erratic before evening out again.

Drew was moaning and grunting and fisting his cock and that did it for Eric. Watching Drew's hand, feeling his lovers, seeing the look in Drew's eyes...when Drew looked right at him it was like he had a direct line to Eric's very soul.

Drew came, spilling over his hand, ass milking Eric's cock.

"Oh, God," Eric finally managed. He came with a roar, letting loose all the sounds he hadn't been able to before.

He wasn't sure exactly when Scott came; they were all in a pile, half asleep, hands touching and mouths kissing, whispers and sighs filling the room.

"Love you," Eric said as sleep stole over him.

Chapter Thirty-three

Scott was worried.

Eric was sick. What had started as a cold took less than two days to settle into his chest and his fever had escalated to the point that Scott had called him in sick at work, saying that as his doctor he was ordering Eric to bed for a week. He'd also told Drew that he was staying home with Eric instead of going for their monthly dinner with Drew's parents.

"His fever is pretty high," he said, "and I don't want to leave him alone. I want to make sure he's hydrated, and just keep an eye on him."

Drew looked faintly worried. "It's just a cold, right?"

Scott shrugged one shoulder, more than willing to downplay his fears. He didn't see any reason for both of them to be worried. "There's some fluid in his lungs, and his cough is non-productive. I just want to watch, make sure it doesn't progress to pneumonia."

Drew nodded and called his mother, canceling their plans. Then he went and sat on the bed, one hand constantly touching Eric as he slept. Scott stood in the doorway, watching Drew watch Eric.

Eric slept fitfully, tossing the blankets off as he got hot, and then shivering. Each time, Drew would tuck him in again, and Scott would check his temperature. Scott made sure that Eric had something to drink whenever he was awake enough to sit up, and listened carefully to his cough.

After a couple of hours Drew followed him into the kitchen. "It's bad?"

"Not great," Scott said carefully. "His fever isn't breaking, but he's keeping fluid down and he's lucid. If his fever gets much higher, or if he stops drinking, I'll have him admitted and put on an IV."

Drew frowned and ran a hand through his hair. "Maybe it would be best to—"

He was interrupted by a knock at the door and his mother calling out that she had food.

Drew let his mom in, helping her with the multitude of plastic containers she'd brought. "Mom, you didn't need to do this."

"Hush, now," Ellen said with a smile, handing over more food. "I had all this, you have a sick roommate—by the way, that big one is chicken soup—and it wasn't any trouble to bring it over."

Scott grinned. Ellen's cooking was a treat, and he thought it was kind of her to deliver it to them. He thought about it for a moment and realized that they had cancelled early enough that she wouldn't have started cooking yet; she'd done this especially for them.

"Thank you, Ellen," he said with a warm smile. "This is really nice."

She flushed a little and puttered for a couple of moments, getting things ready to heat up or keep warm in the oven. "You're all set," she said finally. "I'll just go powder my nose and get out of here so you can eat and take care of Eric."

She went down the hall and Scott smiled at Drew. "She's so cool."

Drew grinned. "Yeah. And she makes a mean casserole."

Scott got a bowl out and started dishing soup for Eric. "Not sure he'll eat this, but the broth will do him good anyway."

Drew nodded and hugged him. "He's gonna be fine."

"Of course he is. This will just speed that up, yeah?" Scott said lightly.

Ellen came back down the hall and stood in the doorway until they both looked at her, Drew still with one arm around Scott's waist.

"Would either of you care to tell me why Eric is sleeping in your bed? Or why he doesn't seem to actually have his own room?" She was pale, holding herself perfectly still, and Scott wondered if she was about to faint.

Drew stared. "Um. Yeah. About that..." He trailed off and looked at Scott.

Scott looked back. He had no idea what to say either.

Ellen stepped closer. "What is going on in this house?" Her voice was low and restrained, but her eyes flashed and she looked terrified.

"Eric is—well, he's...oh, damn." Drew looked something less than calm too, and Scott suddenly realized that he was going to have to say something.

"Eric is with us," he blurted.

"With you." Ellen didn't sound like she believed him, or like she believed her own ears. "He's sleeping with you?"

Scott shook his head. "Not exactly. Well, yes, he is. But we love him, and he loves us. The three of us—"

"You can't be serious." Ellen shook her head. "No, that isn't possible." She walked a few more steps into the room. "No," she said, her voice firm. "I won't accept that. Three men sharing a bed? Sharing their lives?" She looked at Drew. "Tell me what's going on, Andrew."

Drew straightened. "I'm in love with Scott, and I'm in love with Eric," he said calmly. "They both love me, and each other. We live here, together. I'm not sure what else to tell you."

"You can tell me why. Was Scott just not enough for you? Or is this his fault? Did he drag Eric home, talk you into this?" Her eyes were hard and accusing, her steps starting to falter as she neared the door.

"No! There isn't anywhere to put blame, because there isn't any. I can't help who I love." Drew's shoulders were set, his tone as definite as hers.

"You can so! As soon as you knew what was happening, as soon as you looked at that man as anything other than a roommate, you should have told him to leave. Or has this been going on since before he moved in?" She turned to Scott, furious. "This is your fault. Before you, Drew would never have—"

"Have what, Mom? Been happy? Been loved so much it makes me smile all the frigging time? Been able to come home anytime and know that there was someone here for me?" Drew's voice was getting as loud at Ellen's.

Scott bit his lip and grabbed Drew's hand. "Look, we need to calm down—"

"Calm?" Ellen yelled. "Calm? How much am I supposed to accept, you two? First Drew's gay, and yes, I dealt with that. I love my boy, I can accept that, with a bit of work. I got through that. Now you tell me there's another man in this house, another man in your bed, and I'm just supposed to welcome him? I can't do that, I can't deal with this. I won't. This isn't right, it isn't proper, and it isn't something I'm willing to think about."

Drew stared at her. "He's my partner. As much as Scott is."

"Then I hope you'll be happy. I'll tell your father why we won't be seeing you."

"You'll disown me?"

"No. But Scott and Eric will not be welcome in our home. This is wrong."

"That's the same as disowning me."

"That's your choice."

Drew reached for Scott, his legs buckling and tears standing out in his eyes. Ellen's own tears were flowing freely.

"Please," Scott whispered. "Please, can we just take a couple of days and stop saying these things for now? Take some time to think before you hurt each other too badly to be fixed?"

"Does your mother know, Scott?" Ellen asked quietly.

"No. No, she doesn't. She wouldn't understand."

"She understands," Ellen assured him. "Better than you know, I think."

Scott knew then that his mother would know by the end of the evening. Ellen was just upset enough to tell her.

"Please don't," he said.

"I think I have to. Mothers should know these things."

Drew stood up again, his hand on Scott's shoulder. He opened his mouth to speak, just as Eric walked in the kitchen, fully clothed.

Eric was pale, spots of high color on his cheeks, and he seemed to actually tremble as he walked.

"Hello," he said calmly. "Sorry to interrupt, but I have to go now."

Scott moved to him carefully. "Go where, 'ric?"

"I'm late for work. I'll just have some juice and get out of the way so you can keep visiting." He moved toward the fridge, one hand reaching for the handle and missing. "Oops."

"Eric, you should be in bed. I called you in sick, remember?"

"I'm not sick," Eric said, sounding surprised. "Just a little headache."

"Really?" Scott asked mildly. "Let me see." He reached a hand up to Eric's brow and frowned. "Sorry, 'ric. You have a fever. Go back to bed, okay?"

Eric smiled at him. "Doctor's orders?"

"Yep."

"Okay." Eric turned and walked out of the room.

Scott ignored Ellen and turned to Drew. "He's burning up and he's not thinking clearly. You pack a bag and start the car, I'll call the hospital and tell them I'm admitting him." He turned to Ellen. "I'm sorry, but we'll have to talk about this later. Our partner is very ill and we have to leave now."

She looked at him for a moment and then at Drew. She left without a word.

When Scott got back to the house in the middle of the night there was a message on the machine from his mother. He wasn't sure what she was saying, exactly; he couldn't tell through the tears. He deleted the message and went to bed.

Eric was in the hospital for a week, mostly sleeping. Scott spent as much time as he could with him, and Drew was there for as long as he could stretch the limits of the visiting hours. They didn't discuss their parents while they were at the hospital, and when Eric asked them what was wrong they told him they were worried about him, that they wanted him home.

They did want him home. The bed was too big, and the house was empty.

Scott and Drew were lying in bed on the third night before either of them spoke of it.

"Have you talked to your mother?" Drew whispered in the dark.

"No. She won't take my calls. My father told me not to call again. He said they would call when they were ready to deal with it."

"Did they seem angry or hurt?"

Scott rolled over and wrapped an arm around Drew, moving close. "I'm not sure. Confused, I think. Dad asked me why I couldn't just choose. I tried to tell him—"

"But they just don't understand."

"Yeah." Scott sighed and tried to move even closer. The bed was cold. He was used to sleeping in the middle. "How about you? Get through to either of them?"

"Dad told me I was always welcome. Mom said the same thing. But you two aren't."

There didn't really seem to be much else to say. They didn't sleep well.

Eric came home from the hospital with clear lungs and as weak as a newborn lamb. He listened when they told him what had happened and didn't say much. When they were done explaining he sat on the couch and looked at the floor for a long time.

"I can move out within the week," he said at last, his voice hollow.

Scott couldn't breathe. Drew stood up and walked to Eric, kneeling in front of him. "And why would you do that?" he asked quietly.

"You shouldn't give up your families for me," Eric replied.

"So we should give you up for them? Are you insane? There is no fucking way I'm letting you leave me, not like this. You don't love me, fine. You want out, fine. That I can talk to you about, try to understand, try to change. This? Not a chance." Drew's voice was tight, barely controlled anger sputtering in his eyes. "Eric, what do you think this is? You think you're some toy for us to play with? What the fuck do I have to do to make you see that I love you?"

Eric looked at him, eyes wide. "But if I go, you and Scott can get your families back, you'll still have each other—"

"And we won't have you. We didn't just make room for you in our relationship, 'ric. This is something else now, something the three of us have built. Sure, we'd have each other, but there would be a hole. We wouldn't be us, and it wouldn't work. We need you. We need you because we love you. You aren't some add-on, you're our partner."

Scott nodded. "He's right. You're as much my partner, my lover, as Drew is. This is us here, not me and Drew and then you. Why don't you get that?"

Eric looked from Drew to Scott, his eyes serious. "Because no one's ever loved me? Because my family was destroyed by one of its own? I just don't want you two to lose what I've already lost. It would kill me to go—"

"And it would kill us to let you. We wouldn't last without you, 'ric. The balance…shit. We're three. There isn't any other way, anymore. Me and Scott, we can't go back. More importantly, we don't want to go back. We need you, we want you, and yeah, I'd let my parents miss out on having me at the supper table once a month if that's what it takes to make them see that. But I don't know how to make you see it." Drew stood up and sighed. "Love you, Eric. Tell me how to make you see it."

Eric looked up at him, his eyes dark. Scott marveled at how a man so large could look so small and frail, misery wrapped around him like a shroud. "Just keep telling me. Keep loving me, please. Don't know what I'd do without you." He stood up and walked to Drew, reaching one hand out to touch Drew's face. "I love you. Just want you to be happy, to have everything you need."

"What I need is you and Scott, here, with me. Loving me. Letting me know what we have is good."

Eric nodded. "I can do that. I can stay and love you. But I'll keep wishing you had your parents, too."

"Hell, we all wish that," Drew said, moving into Eric's arms.

Scott watched them and smiled. He was still smiling when they both reached for him, their arms working in concert to draw him into the embrace. They were together, and it was good. Someday, maybe, their families would see that.

Chapter Thirty-four

Two in the morning and he had to be back at the hospital in six hours. Scott let himself into the house as quietly as he could and dropped his coat by the door, wondering if he should have just slept there. Didn't matter now; he was home and he was tired.

He got a drink of water in the kitchen and headed to the bedroom, hoping the others were home. Could go back and check the whiteboard calendar in the kitchen where they all posted their schedules, but the bedroom was closer, so he just kept walking. Find out soon enough if he had to sleep alone.

He opened the door to the room and let the light from the hall spill in, across the bed. They were both there, sleeping on opposite sides of the big bed, arms stretched out to the middle, fingers laced together. He grinned at them and shook his head. When it was all of them, they slept in a pile, but when it was just Eric and Drew they spread out, managing to only touch with their fingers or toes.

He stripped down and crawled up the middle of the bed, separating their hands. As soon as he lay down they both rolled into him, legs and arms wrapping around him and over him, trying to get at each other as well. This was why he didn't sleep at the hospital.

"Hey," sleepy voice number one said in his ear. "What time is it?"

"Two. Go back to sleep, 'ric."

Eric just huffed into his hair and shifted closer. "Bad day?"

"Long day. And I gotta be back there in six hours."

Sleepy voice number two chimed in. "Sucks. You tired or sleepy?" Drew was already reaching down between his legs, stroking his thighs.

"Tired."

"Got it. Take care of you." Then Drew was stroking him, and sliding on him and moving down the bed.

"Drew, you don't have to — "

Eric laughed softly in his ear. "You sick, Doc? Gonna turn down a blow job?"

Scott shrugged as Drew made his way down. "It's late. I can sleep without it. Think I might even be too tired to get it up."

"Uh, no, not having much trouble." Drew sounded highly amused by the conversation. "Shut up and let me do this, will you? Then we can all go to sleep."

Eric's long body was behind him, spooning him, and Scott just relaxed into him. Drew would take care of him. He didn't tease. It was too damn late and they were all too tired to play; this was just to take the edge off, to send Scott off into sleep.

He sighed happily as Drew took him into his mouth and started to suck softly, his tongue licking and dancing, calloused fingers playing at his balls. He felt himself get harder as Drew worked at his shaft, feeling Eric nuzzling at his neck, big hands floating over his stomach, light touches that he was always surprised could come from such a big man.

"S'good. Feels nice, Drew."

Eric hummed and kissed a path along his shoulder and up to his ear. "Rest, Doc. Just let go and float." Then he started suckling at the soft skin below his ear and Scott closed his eyes, following instructions to let it go.

Let go of the god-awful day, the stink of the hospital, the blood, the tears. Let go of traffic, bitching in the break room, and pompous doctors. Let it all go and just felt.

Strong arms holding him. Warm bed. Nice house. And a really talented mouth working on him. He started to thrust his hips lazily, letting his shaft slide between wet lips. Drew sucked harder, started to use his tongue on the head of Scott's cock, teasing at the sensitive skin. Eric's hands were tracing patterns on his stomach and drifting up to tug at his nipples.

Scott moaned and moved faster, not wanting to drag it out, just needing release and more and now and oh, God, please like that.

He turned his head and kissed Eric hard as he came for Drew, his body shuddering with the release. Eric gentled the kiss as Drew brought him down, licking and nibbling at his cock, scattering kisses on his thighs and hips. Then Drew was there, arms around them both and he moved to allow Drew into the kiss, tasting himself on the other man's lips.

"Sleepy now?"

"Yeah," Scott murmured with a small grin. He reached down to touch Eric's erection, but his hand was brushed away.

"Don't worry 'bout us, Doc. Sleep. We had our fun earlier."

Scott just sighed happily and wiggled into an embrace. They lay together in silence, almost asleep for a few minutes.

"Drew?"

"Hmm?"

"Was it a bad one?" Drew's hair smelled of smoke and oil and the sticky stuff that always clung to him after a fire.

"Nah. Well, house fire. No one home. It's okay."

"Good."

Drew held him tighter for a minute and kissed his chest. "Sleep, Doc."

Scott slept.

Chapter Thirty-five

Drew was trying to read the newspaper with very little success. Scott had taken over the kitchen table with patient charts and had his nose buried in a book, so the person flicking at the edge of the sports section in his hands had to be Eric.

"Stop it."

Flick.

"Eric. Cut it out."

Flick.

"Eric."

Nothing.

Drew folded the top of the paper down and peered at Eric. The big man was lying on the floor at Drew's feet, smiling up at him, eyes dilated and hungry.

"What's the problem? Bored?" Drew felt himself being drawn into Eric's gaze and cursed inwardly. Damn bastard only had to look at him. And he knew it, too.

"Yeah. Wanna play?" Eric was already moving to sit up, big hands on Drew's thighs, moving upward.

Drew rolled his eyes. "Like you'll stop until I give in."

Eric laughed and kneeled in front of him, reaching for his waistband.

Drew looked over his shoulder into the kitchen. "Scott. Eric's all wound up. Wanna help me out here? Lay him flat so I can actually read the paper sometime tonight?"

There was the sound of a book slamming shut and a chair scraping on the kitchen floor. Scott stood in the door, leaning on the doorframe for a moment before walking over and pushing Eric to the floor, straddling his hips. "Should let the man read his paper, Eric. If that's what he really wants."

"Hey, now!" Drew was a little upset that the hands which had been about to make him a happy man were now plastered on Scott's ass.

"You said to lay him flat. He's flat. I'm gonna lay him. You want in, get down here."

God, he could be pushy when he was horny. The man never asked for anything, but you offer him anything and he'd be all over it. Drew let a hand drift down over his cock, stroking himself lightly through his sweatpants as he watched the men in his life go at it.

They were kissing, mouths hungry, as Eric's big hands tugged Scott's university sweatshirt up and off, then went to work on his jeans. Soft and faded, they were Scott's favorite pair. They were Drew's favorites, too; they fit the man so well, sort of an off-the-rack showcase for his ass.

Scott rolled over off Eric and lifted his hips so Eric could pull the jeans off. Drew looked at them, one completely naked and hard, the other still fully clothed. That just wasn't right.

He pushed himself off the chair and landed on his knees beside Scott, on the opposite side of Eric. "Get naked, 'ric. Want to see you."

Eric's eyes flashed and he grinned before leaning over Scott to push his tongue into Drew's mouth. They kissed, long and hard, until Scott swore at them and there was a hand pulling at the front of his sweatpants. Drew just grinned into the kiss and pulled Eric's shirt up, sliding his hands over the broad chest. Fuck, he was a big man. Broad and hard and solid.

He broke the kiss long enough to get the shirt off over Eric's head and look down at Scott, who was still lying on the floor looking slightly dazed and really turned on.

"You two are so hot together," Scott finally said.

Drew grinned at him. "Not bad yourself. But you stopped." He wiggled his hips and Eric started to laugh as he stripped off his own jeans. Scott's eyes followed Drew's thick cock as it waved in front of his face, then he shook his head and sat up far enough to take Drew into his mouth.

Drew gasped at the heat and suction. "Jesus."

Eric fell silent and watched. It was a rare treat for Scott to go down on them. Drew watched Scott's head moving up and down his shaft and glanced at Eric, his eyes wide. The man had settled with his back against the chair and was pulling himself off, eyes on Scott's mouth.

Drew shuddered as the tip of Scott's tongue pressed into his slit and did his best to stay upright. Scott moved a hand to Drew's balls and tugged gently; Eric did the same to himself and moaned.

"Christ, Scott. You don't stop, I'm gonna blow."

Scott looked up at Drew and grinned around his cock, one brow raised. Then he moved faster and harder, fingers dancing where his mouth wasn't reaching, and Drew gasped.

Eric swore and moved over to them, leaning in to kiss Drew hard. Drew felt like he was floating, tight wet heat around his prick and a strong tongue fucking his mouth. Eric put a hand to the back of his head and kept him there, pouring heat and need into his mouth, muffling Drew's cry when he came.

Scott sat back and grinned at him as Drew fell to the floor in a heap. Eric reached around under the chair cursing. "Where's the damn lube?"

Drew pointed under the couch and Eric dove for it, getting it open and slicking his cock in a rush. He pushed Scott back onto the floor with one hand, settling between the man's legs. "You ready for me?"

"Anytime, 'ric," Scott said, his legs sliding over Eric's thighs, the movement easy and comfortable. Eric slid into him with one fast stroke.

"Oh, shit. So fucking hard."

Eric thrust again. "Too much for ya?"

"God, no."

Drew watched Scott's face as Eric fucked him, watched every muscle twitch and saw the spark in the man's eye. Eric moved faster, deeper, and Scott's hips moved to meet his, every one of his moans met with one of Scott's.

"Shit, you two could make a statue come. Fucking hot."

Eric tossed a grin at Drew, then looked back down at Scott. "'S good, Doc."

"Yeah, 'ric. Good."

Eric pulled Scott's ass up a little, changed the angle, and Drew watched as Scott's eyes rolled back. "Found the spot, Drew. Help me out here, will ya?"

Drew shifted from his spot on the floor. He'd had a good view, but playing was always better than watching. He crawled over and kissed Scott hard, running a finger over the head of the man's prick. He kissed Eric, too, then lay down next to them and returned Scott's favor.

He grasped Scott's shaft in one hand and angled it away from his belly as he swirled his tongue over the tip, catching the unbelievable taste of the man. When Scott moaned Eric thrust hard into his ass, making Scott buck up as he rode the hard cock in his ass. Drew had been waiting for it, and when Scott thrust up he dropped his head low, relaxing his mouth and throat.

Drew was the only one of them able to deep throat and he saved it for special occasions. He swallowed hard and felt Scott's cock flex in his mouth before he moved up with a long, sucking pull.

"Shit. You're gonna send him flying before I'm ready," Eric said, with a groan. He thrust harder and Scott swore.

"Not gonna matter, 'ric. Gonna shoot anyway if you keep that up."

Drew glanced up at Eric as best he could and they locked eyes. Right. Blow his mind. Drew sucked hard and used every trick he could think of. Eric switched to short, shallow thrusts, stroking over Scott's gland again and again.

Within moments Scott was gasping, making an unbelievable amount of noise. Drew felt Scott start to tremble, knew the split second Scott's eyes flew open and locked with his that he was going to come.

"Fuck, yes!" Scott yelled.

Drew swallowed hard, trying to keep up with Scott as he spent himself. He heard a long, deep groan and could feel the vibrations as Eric came, his shudders making Scott's body tremble with him.

Drew lifted his head out of the way as Eric came down, settling on Scott. They shared a kiss, three tongues moving together, all of them tasting Scott.

Finally, Scott nudged Eric with his hand. "You're squishing me."

Eric chuckled and shifted off, making Scott whimper for a moment. Drew curled up around him but Scott eased his arm away and stood up.

"Where're you going?" Drew asked.

"Gotta finish these charts," Scott said as he pulled his sweatshirt back on.

Eric chuckled and moved to the couch.

"And what the fuck are you doing over there?" Drew was beginning to sound a little indignant.

Eric stared at him. "It's Saturday night, man."

Oh. Right. Cops. The one hour a week that there was to be no fucking of any kind. Drew sighed and reached for his newspaper.

Chapter Thirty-six

Eric had fallen asleep alone, which was bad. But he'd also fallen asleep knowing that he was the first one home on what was going to be an amazing three-day stretch. Thing about being a single guy was that you could take vacation time in the middle of the week once in a long while and everyone loved you for not begging to have weekends off. And somehow, the three of them had managed to get the same three days off. It had a taken a month of planning and shift change requests, but in the morning, seventy-two hours of sun in the back yard, barbeque, and unlimited fucking would start.

Eric knew that Scott had come home in the middle of the night; he remembered waking up enough to wrap himself around the man and get a nice kiss before falling asleep again. And he was pretty sure that Drew had shown up, unless Scott had grown another hand. Which would be useful, but it would be nicer if Drew were home. He kept his eyes closed and tried to snuggle into Scott's heat, but he couldn't find him. He could hear him though. Could hear them both, now that he was mostly awake. Whispered conversation started to filter through the sleep barrier and he pried one eye open.

"Wake him up," Drew said, arms looped around Scott's neck, his voice made even fuzzier by the fact that he was nuzzling Scott's neck.

"No, Drew. He's real tired. Did a lot of runs yesterday. But I'm awake." Scott sounded entirely unrepentant that he was talking Drew into paying him all the attention. Eric grinned a little.

"Noticed that, Doc. Whatever shall I do with you?"

Scott laughed and rolled on top of the fireman, dragging the sheets off Eric as he went. Now that was just not fair. Eric was about to protest when Scott started moving, hips rocking into Drew's, and his mouth claimed Drew's in a deep kiss. Watching had its benefits.

Eric lay back and watched them as they moved faster, Drew's hands on Scott's ass, pulling him tight as they rubbed and slid together. They were making soft moaning noises that went straight to Eric's cock, and he moved a hand to it, pulling himself slow and steady. Drew rolled them over again and moved down, sucking at one of Scott's nipples as the man arched his back, groaning. Eric closed his eyes and just listened for a while, smelling them together, hearing them as their need built.

"Oh, yeah, Drew," Scott breathed, and Eric opened his eyes, knowing that Drew was sucking Scott off and wanting in on the action now. He rolled over onto his side and ran a hand through Drew's hair as he moved up and down on Scott, then leaned over to kiss his shoulder. Drew knew he was there; they'd say good morning later.

But Scott was ready and available now. Eric crawled up beside him and took a kiss. "Morning, Doc."

"Morning, 'ric. Sleep well?" Scott's attempt at conversation was cut off by a gasp and jerk. "Fuck, Drew! Do that again!"

Drew did, and Scott moaned, his eyes drifting shut as his hips rose and fell. "Christ. So good, Drew."

Drew hummed something and Scott fisted the sheets in his hand.

Eric watched and grinned. Drew glanced up at him and his grin grew wider. "You're blowing his mind, babe. Get him off, will you? I want my turn." He stroked his cock again, showing off for Drew, but it was Scott who gasped.

"Oh, God. Want that."

Eric looked at him and then at Drew again, who was happily playing with Scott's balls and teasing his cock with the flat of his tongue. "When did he get so selfish? Get blown and fucked? Is it his turn?"

Drew sucked at Scott once more, a good long pull on the thick shaft, and then came off it with a pop as the suction broke. "Actually, I think it is. Was me last week, and you got it about four days before that."

"No, that was him."

"Drew!" Scott was not in his happy place anymore, clearly.

"You sure?" Drew sounded skeptical.

"Fuck, yes, I was the one doing the sucking that time."

"Shit, you two." Scott was sounding a little desperate. "You figure it out, I'm getting off." Scott started pumping his cock, fast and hard, his hips snapping up to meet his fist.

Eric and Drew watched for moment and then Drew shrugged. "Want a taste?"

"Sure." Eric moved down the bed to kneel beside Scott and bent down, following Scott's fist with his mouth.

Scott didn't manage to say anything coherent, but he did moan happily. Eric cupped Scott's balls and tugged gently as he slid his tongue over the head of his cock, knew that he was real close. He teased the soft skin behind Scott's balls and sucked him in as far as he could and then swallowed, letting his throat do the work.

"Oh, God, oh, God, oh, God—" Scott came for him, tasting strong and sweet behind the bitter. Eric swallowed him down and licked at his cock and balls for a while, bringing Scott back to earth before sliding up his body to kiss him properly. Drew pressed up against them, joining the kiss, his hips pushing his own hard prick against Eric's thigh.

Eric shifted off Scott and pulled Drew onto him. "Fuck me."

"Going to."

Then slick strong fingers were in his ass and he lifted his legs up and back. Drew slid home with a sigh and Eric pulled him down for another kiss. God, he loved kissing these two. So fucking good being here with them. Nothing better than three in the bed and no rush to get out of it.

Scott moved to his side, hands roaming everywhere, He was licking at one of Eric's nipples and tugging at the other with his fingers, his body moving against Eric's. Warm hands caressed him, Scott's mouth tasted him; Scott had a gentle touch that made everything he did so fucking intense. He kissed a trail up to Eric's neck as Drew started moving in his ass, long, fast strokes that he could feel in his bones.

"Gonna fuck you through the mattress, 'ric."

"Yeah, Drew. Like that." And Christ, it felt like he would, too. He was deep, fucking driving into him with every stroke. Eric moved a hand down to pull at his cock as Scott took his mouth in a searing kiss. Scott licked a path along his jaw to his ear and sucked on his earlobe for a moment. Eric moaned and pulled his cock harder. So fucking good.

Scott's voice in his ear. "Oh, yeah, do that. I love watching you jerk off. So fucking hot, 'ric. Sexy as hell. Show me how much you need to come. Ride him hard."

Eric moaned, his hips jerking up to meet Drew's, tilting his ass to get that thick cock even deeper. "Harder, Drew. Fuck me."

"Oh, shit." Drew was starting to sweat, a bead of moisture trailing down his chest. Scott saw it, too, and after kissing Eric fast and hard he was licking it off, then biting at Drew's nipples, stroking his own hard cock fast.

Drew held Scott's head to his chest, leaning into him as his own head fell back. Eric drank in the sight of Drew's long body, from his hips up over the flat stomach to the defined pecs, past Scott's head, his tongue now licking trails all over Drew's chest, up the long line of his neck…he pulled at his cock once more and came with a groan, his hips freezing as his ass clenched at Drew's cock, still pounding into him.

"Oh, fuck!" Drew yelled, and heat filled him as Drew came. Drew pushed Scott onto the bed and Eric pulled him in to kiss him as Drew fisted Scott's shaft, making the man go over again, this time his cry muted by Eric's mouth.

Drew collapsed onto him and they all shared kisses, wet and sloppy and wonderful. Warm in their bed, nicely awake and newly fucked…was going to be a great three days. Eric started to hope it would rain and they could skip the sunshine in the backyard part of the plan.

Chapter Thirty-seven

Third Thursday in a row. Drew watched the Purolator guy walk to the door and grinned. This was becoming fun.

The first time he was puzzled. He wasn't expecting anything, certainly not porn. But the tape was kind of funny—gay firemen, fucking in the station. He'd stuck it on top of the TV without watching it and had gone to work, wondering who'd sent it. He sort of figured it was Eric, but Scott had a weird sense of humor, so it could have been either of them.

They either didn't see the DVD or just didn't say anything about it, and it wasn't until he looked closer at the shipping invoice that he realized it had been charged to his own card. Funny. One of the two was playing a game, and Drew decided to wait before saying anything—this was going to take planning.

He still hadn't said anything by the next Thursday, when another box arrived. He stared at the leather straps for almost three minutes before figuring out which part went where, and then he blushed. Good thing no one was home, 'cause just the idea gave him a boner and he jacked off just holding it.

And again, he'd paid for it. His Visa card was having fits.

That time he'd taken the DVD and the strappy thing and stuck them in a drawer, a plan finally taking shape. It was all in the timing.

He hadn't been counting on a third delivery, but when the truck pulled up he found himself grinning and getting hard at the same time. More fun, and hopefully something he could incorporate into the plan.

Drew signed for the box and tossed it on the coffee table as he made some preparations. First, notes on the doors. His men would be home in less than an hour and he didn't want them bringing company with them. The notes just said that if they weren't alone to ring the bell and he'd unlock the door for them. With any luck that would keep them from just wandering in.

Doors all locked, curtains drawn, the video and the leather taken out. And lube. Needed lube. Good thing they had lots.

He set everything on the coffee table next to the box and checked the time again. Scott and Eric were supposed to be home just after four, and it was almost twenty past three. Tricky. He'd have to take his time or start later, and he wasn't really sure he wanted to wait. Just getting ready was getting him hot.

He stuck the disc into the player and let it run past the piracy shit, then paused it just at the opening credits. He hoped it wasn't really cheesy bad porn—sort of disrupted the plan if the porn was a turn off. He looked at the leather and smirked. Actually, getting turned off didn't seem to be much of a danger.

When he started to unwrap the box he realized he was holding his breath and gave himself a mental shake. God, there was such a thing as being too into this.

Whoever was sending him this stuff didn't disappoint.

"Good God," he said, then blushed. Talking out loud in an empty house was just another sign that he was more than ready to play with his new toys. With this new toy.

Fat and long, the dildo was almost intimidating. Shiny. Flexible. Silicone. Fire Engine Red.

Drew held it, just looking at it for a long moment. He'd never used one before and the images flashing through his mind were quickening his breath. He set it down and quickly stripped off his sweatpants, staring at it.

Settled on the couch he pressed play on the remote and dropped the leather straps onto his belly, still looking at the dildo. The music from the video filled the room, some funky beat that had a lot of bass behind it thudding with his pulse. Drew reached for the red monster, and without really thinking about it raised it to his mouth and licked it, sucking the head into his mouth.

Yep, bigger than his boys. He shuddered when he realized what he was doing, one hand going to his balls, the other putting the dildo on the couch next to him. He watched the movie, playing with the leather straps on his belly, the hand on his balls moving up to stroke his cock.

The porn wasn't bad. He'd probably seen better, but this one had firemen, or at least fire trucks. He refused to think about what it meant that fire trucks turned him on. Maybe he was just so worked up that everything was making him hard.

On the screen one guy was sitting on the back of the truck, another guy bent over sucking his cock. Nice. Then a third 'fireman' turned up and stripped off, starting to finger fuck the guy with a dick in his mouth. Even better.

Drew twisted one of the leather bits around his fingers, wondering if he should put it on yet. The straps were soft, the snaps cool to the touch. He'd just mostly convinced himself to do it when the three guys on the TV were joined by three more.

Drew watched as an impossible combination of sucking, jacking, and fucking took shape, the six men all bending and grunting and working on whatever body part presented itself. At one point there was a guy sucking cock, getting sucked and fucked, and his hands were working one of the others. It was weird and strangely horrific. Drew couldn't stop watching.

By the time the last guy had shot his load all over the belly of a very worn-out 'fireman', Drew was a stunned mess. And his erection had faded to half-mast, which just wouldn't do, not if he was going to make his boys pay for their gifts.

He started stroking his cock again as the scene shifted, looking at the time on the stereo display. His men were due home in about ten minutes. He fervently hoped the next bit was more to his liking.

He cupped his balls in one hand, rolling them gently as the other hand worked his cock. He knew what he liked, and he'd started to firm up again when the lone man on screen was joined by another. He grinned to himself when he realized the director hadn't bothered with some lame set up—they were heading right into the action.

Part of his mind was scoffing at the idea of a firehouse having communal showers, but his cock liked the idea. Steam and water, naked men…what could be better?

The actors exchanged a few words that Drew didn't bother listening to and got right to it, the one with thick blond hair shoving the brunet into the wall and taking a hungry kiss with lots of tongue. The brunet wasn't the type to play hard to get, apparently, his hand going to the blond's prick and starting a nice rhythm.

Drew's hand matched him, a long slow glide that made him moan softly. Felt good. Looked good, too. The guys in the shower were still kissing, hands smoothing over wet skin, tweaking nipples and stroking flesh. It looked like they were enjoying it.

The blond's hips started moving and he dropped his head to bite and lick at the other guy's neck, panting and moaning. "Suck me," he said, and it wasn't an order, didn't even sound like a line, just sounded like he wanted it.

Fucking hot.

Drew rubbed his cock when the brunet dropped to his knees and didn't even mind the editing that made a condom appear magically already on the blond. He watched the dark head start to bob, watched him taking that nice hard prick in all the way, and groaned.

Fuck, he was gonna come, his cock was leaking all over his belly, and it wasn't fucking time yet. Quickly, Drew grabbed for the leather and snapped the ring into place around the base of his shaft, fiddling with the leather straps until his balls were bound, apart and away from his body.

He hips were mimicking the blond's. God, he wanted to come. Drew swiped his fingers over the head of his dick and gasped. So fucking sensitive, so perfect. He was almost ready to fly.

The blond came with a shout, the condom off, the brunet jerking him off and catching the ribbons of spunk on his chest. Then they were both on their feet again, kissing, grabbing, panting...it was like real sex. It was hotter than hell and Drew wanted to watch them fuck.

The blond faced the wall and spread his legs, getting kisses all along his shoulders and the other man held and touched him. A big hand coasting over his ass and the blond shuddered, begging for it.

Drew reached for the lube.

When the blond took two fingers so did Drew, though Drew's gasp was louder. His cock was aching, hard and hot, and when he reached deep, twisted his fingers just right, he almost bucked right off the couch.

"Jesus Christ," he panted, not worried about talking to an empty room. The TV was almost forgotten, he needed so bad. He grabbed the dildo in one hand and fucked himself with the other, waiting until his legs were trembling before sliding his fingers out and slicking the toy with lube.

He watched the TV again, one leg over the back of the couch, the other on the floor, wholly open. The toy was pressing at his hole, and he was just about ready to take it, almost ready to fly.

The guys on the screen were almost ready too, still kissing and moaning, the magic condom in place, and...

"What the fuck?"

"Oh, my God!"

Drew blinked and tried to focus on Scott and Eric. Scott looked stunned, completely unprepared and so not even close to having his dick catch up with what his eyes were seeing. Eric looked like he was going to pass out, but he was grinning.

"Eric owes me two hundred and twenty three dollars," Drew said calmly, then he rocked his hips and pushed hard, impaling himself on the toy. "Oh, Jesus fucking Christ."

"Drew?" Scott seemed to have developed a squeak.

"Like the toys?" Eric asked, already stripping off his clothes.

"Yeah." Drew slid the dildo out a bit and then back in, searching for the right spot. "Scott? You okay, love?"

"Huh?"

Eric laughed. "Scott. You gonna stand there, or are you gonna play?"

"Huh?"

Drew arched his back, the TV forgotten as he watched his men. Eric was naked and hard, his cock curving up to his belly. Scott stared at the toy as Drew moved it in and out. "Feels good, Scott," he said.

Scott moved closer, still staring. He sank to his knees next to the couch and watched as Drew kept the toy moving, finally finding the right angle to hit his prostate on every thrust.

"Oh, fuck," Drew groaned, moving the toy faster. Harder.

Eric started taking Scott's clothes off, and Drew was vaguely aware that they were breathing faster, but it was outside of him, outside of the waves rolling through his body. He'd wanted to do this and watch his men fucking but it wasn't going to be like that. Not at all.

Hands on him, but he wasn't sure whose. It didn't really matter, it was them. Drew's eyes closed and he moved faster, hips rocking up, his hand moving faster, fucking himself harder and deeper and faster and God he needed to come. His cock was so hard it hurt, his balls were throbbing.

A head between his thighs, heat and wet and a tongue tracing his hole, lapping around the toy. He heard a scream, figured it was himself.

Wet heat around his cock and fingers, smart fingers, fingers that worked, unsnapping the cock ring and he was coming, cock jerking as he shot pulse after pulse of spunk into someone's mouth. The edges of the world grayed out.

When he came to, or at least became sensible again, the toy was gone, tossed onto a towel, and the leather was on the coffee table. Scott was kissing him, and Eric was panting down near his thigh.

"Mmurgh?"

162

"Yeah, that sounds about right," Scott said. "Good?"

"Jesus. Should have had a physical before I did that. You?"

"Came all over the couch. Eric at least managed to come on you, so there's not a whole lot of mess to clean up."

Drew nodded, one hand reaching down to find Eric's hair. "You owe me money," he said sleepily.

Eric kissed his hand. "That mean you don't want to know what's coming next week?"

Part Four
Chapter Thirty-eight

Scott woke up in the early afternoon, alone in the big bed. He'd worked all night and had to be back at the hospital by four, but right then what he really wanted was breakfast and some time with his partners. He climbed out of bed and pulled on a pair of boxer shorts, listening for voices. He couldn't remember if either of them was going to be home. He wandered into the kitchen and got a glass of juice, yawning and stretching all the way. It wasn't until he put the empty glass in the sink that he heard Eric's low groan from the living room.

"What are you doing?" he called playfully.

Drew's happy chuckle came to him as he crossed the kitchen. "Admiring the view."

They were standing in front of the window, Drew behind Eric, arms around his waist and both hands down the front of Eric's shorts. Eric was leaning back into Drew, hips moving languidly as Drew stroked him off.

Scott went into the living room, his smile growing. "Well, it is pretty nice. Can I watch, too?"

"No, really," Drew insisted. "Eric found a new summer sport for us. Watching lawns being mowed and trucks being washed. Check it out." He kissed Eric's shoulder and pointed Scott to the window with a look.

Scott moved closer, one hand trailing down Drew's back. He paused to take a kiss from Eric, who just moaned softly in response as Drew's hand teased him, and looked out the window.

"New neighbors?" Scott asked. The house across the street had been on the market for almost a month and now there was a sold sticker up and a pickup truck full of boxes in the drive.

"Just the one, so far," Drew said. "In the house right now—oh, there he is." He did something that made Eric gasp and chuckled again. "You are so fucking easy," he murmured.

Scott watched as a man came out of the house and climbed onto the back of the truck to haul down a box. He was wearing jeans and sneakers, going shirtless in the late spring air, and even from across the street Scott could see the hints of red in his hair. He was about thirty or so, Scott guessed; it was hard to tell through glass and distance. But even the two yards and the street between them didn't hide the man's finer features.

"New guy is hot," he said, still watching.

"Eric noticed that almost right away, didn't you, 'ric?" Drew said, his voice full of laughter.

Scott turned and grinned. They looked so happy together, Drew teasing Eric with words and hands, Eric flushed from arousal and embarrassment. They kissed each other hard for a moment and Eric groaned softly.

"Not him who has me so worked up," Eric protested.

Drew just grinned and winked at Scott. Then he pulled at Eric's cock again.

"You're telling me that when Drew put his hand down your pants he found a soft prick?" Scott asked, moving closer. He licked Eric's neck, smiling when the big man shuddered.

"Well, no, not exactly..." Eric said hoarsely. His breath hitched in his chest.

Scott glanced out the window again. "I think perhaps that nice man over there could use a hand moving in. I think that would be a very neighborly thing to do, don't you?"

Drew's answering grin was positively wicked. "Why, Scott, I do think you have a particularly gracious suggestion. 'ric? What do you think?"

Eric groaned. "I think there's no fucking way I'm going anywhere like this."

"Mmm. Good point. Very. Scott? Any ideas?"

Scott pretended to consider the situation. "You could keep doing what you're doing, I suppose. Or you could go down on him."

"Could. Or I could fuck you while you suck him off," Drew countered.

"Or you could fuck him while I suck him off."

"Or he could fuck you while—"

Eric whimpered and bucked into Drew's hand, the smell of his come filling the air. Drew and Scott both showered him with kisses and led him to the bathroom to clean up, laughing as they went.

Fifteen minutes later they headed across the street, dressed for moving boxes and shifting furniture.

"Need a hand or six?" Drew said to their new neighbor as they walked up his driveway.

The man stared at them for a moment before he grinned and nodded. "Not going to turn an offer like that down," he said, his voice deep and rough. He moved forward, hand extended. "James Mouzouris."

"Drew Smyth," Drew said, returning the handshake. "This is Scott Campbell, and that's Eric St Laurent."

Scott and Eric nodded, their arms already full of boxes.

"Right this way, then," James said, passing a box to Drew and grabbing one for himself. As he led the way into the house he asked, "You all share the place across the street?"

"Yeah," Eric said, setting his box down against a wall in the entry. "You by yourself?"

"So far. New to the city and all," James said. "Not much stuff to fill the place with," he remarked, gesturing to the near empty home. "One of the small benefits of moving often is keeping the collection of crap down to nothing. If I want to keep something it has to fit in the truck."

Scott laughed and led the way back to the truck.

"You move a lot, huh?" Drew said. "Must be hard on your family."

James shook his head. "Nah. We're not that close. There's a lot of us; it's sort of hard to keep track of everyone. As long as I call home once in a while and make sure they know where I am, everyone's happy."

Scott could almost feel the wave of sadness come off Drew. Neither of them had really spoken to their parents in almost five months. Scott still called every couple of weeks and talked to his father; every time, he was told that they weren't ready to discuss Eric's place in Scott's relationship yet. For Drew's part, he talked to both of his parents, but they were still insisting that he was making a mistake and it was made clear that Scott and Eric were not welcome.

Scott brushed away the gloomy family thoughts and went back to moving boxes, admiring the way that Drew and Eric grilled James. It amazed him how much information they could get just by trading friendly banter as they shifted boxes from the truck to the house.

Drew started listing all the local pizza places, complete with phone numbers, which had Eric rolling his eyes.

"Don't care much for pizza," James said, the tone clearly designed to tease.

"Oh, my God! A heathen! What sort of man are you?" Drew challenged with a laugh.

166

"Down, boy," Scott said mildly, passing him a box.

"That's my line," Drew said as he walked by him. He leered a little, too, making Scott grin.

Eric snickered and started bombarding James with more questions. No, he'd never lived in Ottawa before, although he'd spent a good part of the past four months there. He was from the mid-west United States, and yes, he moved often for work, usually every three years or so. The worst place he'd lived was six months in Buffalo, New York; the best was a year in Oregon. He bought the house because he knew he'd be in Ottawa for at least two years and the market was good. He was thirty, never married, he actually did like pizza but would sell body parts for a good cheesecake. Yes, his last name was Greek, and no, he'd never been there. Yes, the heavy boxes they were taking to the basement were books, yes, he read a lot, but he also liked to run and play basketball.

Eric was just starting to tell him about the paths he ran on along the canal when Drew's pager went off.

"Shit, gotta go," he said, looking at the display. "See you around, James," he added, turning to dash across the street.

"Be careful!" Scott and Eric yelled after him. We love you.

"Always," he called back. I love you both.

James threw them a questioning look.

"Fireman," Eric said, picking up one of the last boxes. He set it down again as his own pager went off. "Hell. Looks like I'm up, too," he said. "See you later."

"Watch yourself," Scott said as Eric started down the drive. I love you.

"Of course." Love you, too.

James watched Eric run across the street and stop Drew as he pulled out of their drive. Eric got in Drew's car and they drove off at only slightly more than the speed limit.

"Fireman, too?" he asked Scott.

"EMT."

"Oh. Do they always go on calls together?"

"Nope. They run into each other sometimes, though." Scott looked around the yard. "The only other time I remember them both getting called was for a hell of a car wreck. Whatever it is, it's bad."

James nodded and they were quiet for a moment in the late May sun.

Scott shook himself. "Anyway, they'll do their jobs. They're both damn good at what they do; I'd make myself sick if I worried about them every time they went to work, you know?" He didn't wait for a reply, just picked up another box and smiled at James. "Let's get this done for you before I have to go to work, too, yeah?"

James grinned back at him. "This is damn kind of you. All of you, I mean." He followed Scott in with the last box and directed him to his office.

Scott brushed the thanks off and took a second to glance over the computer system James had partially set up. "What do you do, anyway?"

"Writer. Well, reporter, I guess. Sort of on extended assignment, doing research and writing a long series for a magazine." James looked at him with a grin. "So, fireman, EMT and ... cop?"

Scott laughed. "Nope. Doctor."

"ER?"

"Sometimes. Not really, though—I'm in cardio. Haven't spent much time in the ER since I finished my residency. Only get called down for—well, for emergencies."

James chuckled. "Still, though. An emergency team living across the street. That's cool."

"Hope you never need us," Scott said. He checked his watch and said his good byes, inviting James over for a barbeque the next weekend. He thought James seemed like a nice guy; he hoped first impressions were true, in this case.

Chapter Thirty-nine

It was bad.

Drew looked around the room, what little he could see through the thick, roiling smoke. Even with the oxygen tank and face mask it was getting harder to breathe, though he knew it was only his imagination. He spotted his team, all four of them, and followed as they moved through the big office space, making sure there was no one left. Finally, Blake raised his arm and pointed to the door. The room was clear; time to get out and let the outside crew do their job.

They made their way as a single unit toward where they knew the exit was, going carefully. The smoke was thicker now. Part of Drew's mind noted that the building, most likely all ten stories, was a loss. The fire had started in the basement, but even here, on the fourth floor, they could feel the heat. If the lower floors went, the entire structure would destabilize and the building would need extensive work if it were to be used again.

They were almost at the doorway when he heard the creak and groan, felt the building tremble. They all froze for a split second, then rushed to the doorway. Nick Zerr pushed Drew hard to the left as the building shuddered, the floor rising up to meet them, and Drew's world went black.

***

It was bad.

Eric and his partner arrived at the scene along with the second wave of fire engines, four ambulances already there. They immediately set to work tending those who needed on-site first aid, letting others transport more serious cases to the hospital. There were people everywhere behind the line of firefighters; EMTs and paramedics treating cuts and burns, giving oxygen, wrapping strains and sprains. One man had a heart attack in the midst of it all and was rushed away; another tried to go back into the building to rescue his personal papers and had to be restrained.

Eric worked methodically, going where he was told and assessing needs, treating quickly and efficiently. He didn't flinch when he heard the warnings about the building's stability; he had his job to do.

When the building fell there was no stunned silence. Everyone worked, the rescue teams already in motion, those treating the injured going on as they were, preparing for the more serious cases they were about to receive. They worked as they were trained to do, pushing the fear and the horror away until they were done. Eric was thinking, not reacting. He did his job. He bandaged the last burn and rechecked his supplies before moving forward to await the firemen bearing the latest casualties.

When they came, they passed over body after body before turning to go back into the blaze. Ambulances arrived and left, Eric now taking burn victims to the hospital as well, the patients now coming to him unconscious and suffering from smoke inhalation.

By the third time he arrived at the scene, news reporters were in full force, already announcing two deaths and speculating on the slim chance of survival for the firefighters still inside. Eric tuned it out, as he was trained to do. His focus was always on the patient he was working on, the noise and sirens falling away.

Their worst case came to them on a backboard; set onto the stretcher and right into the ambulance, Eric last in. He started cataloguing injuries, his partner monitoring vital statistics and trying to stabilize the man's life signs. He listed broken bones, the possible back injury, the expected internal damage, each fragment of speech interspersed with Stevenson calling out the fluctuating blood pressure, thready and slowing pulse, fixed and dilated pupils.

He knew this man, knew most of the firefighters. "Who is it?" he asked. If he was about to lose a friend he wanted to know who.

"Smyth."

***

It was bad.

Scott had been doing his rounds in the cardio unit when he was paged to the ER. By the time he got there, organized chaos reigned. He was told where he was needed in triage and he started treating the first of the bad cases.

Voices floated around him, people calling out orders, others crying out in pain. They were told the building was down, or at least down enough that they were going to be swamped with more critical care patients.

Elective surgeries were cancelled, operating rooms prepared. Scott was doing a fast check on a crash cart when he looked up and saw Eric leaning on the wall, staring at him. He was gray.

"Eric?" he said, walking to him. "What is it?"

Eric just stared at him, tears making a shiny trail down his cheeks.

Scott grabbed a passing nurse. "The firemen?"

"Just in—three of them, so far. The worst is in with Dr. Wells."

Scott ran.

A team surrounded the gurney, Dr. Wells issuing orders, a nurse cutting off the last of Drew's clothes. He was intubated, already on a ventilator; charred and broken and so very damaged.

"Doctor!" Wells barked. "Are you going to stand there or are you going to help save this man's life?"

Scott couldn't move, couldn't speak.

"Doctor!" Wells barked again.

One of the nurses said something softly.

"Then get him the hell out of here," Wells ordered, "and don't let him back in. I'll talk to him after the surgery."

Scott let himself be led to the waiting room. Eric was still leaning on the wall in the hallway, but came with him when Scott touched his arm.

"I'm sorry, Dr. Campbell," the nurse said. "We're doing all we can."

"Tell me."

"Dr. Wells will, in a little bit. Right now, I need to help him." She turned to go.

"Tell me he'll live."

She looked back at him. "We're doing our best."

Scott and Eric sat, not looking at each other. They twisted their fingers together and waited.

"Scott?"

"Yes."

"Are we losing him?"

"No."

"Are you sure?"

Scott didn't answer.

Chapter Forty

"I have to call his parents." Scott didn't know how long they had been sitting there; it could have been ten minutes, it could have been half an hour.

Eric didn't say anything, just squeezed his hand gently before letting go. Scott went to the nurse's station and picked up the phone, dialing automatically. He had no idea what to say.

It was picked up halfway through the first ring.

"Hello?" Drew's father.

"Kenneth, it's Scott." His voice sounded hollow, even to his own ears. There was a pause and Scott suddenly realized that Kenneth could hear the hustle and noise of the ER; he should have gone to the break room.

"You're at the hospital. That building on TV—"

"He's hurt pretty badly, you better come."

Kenneth took a deep breath, the exhalation loud over the phone. "But he's alive?" Scott could hear Ellen in the background, asking what was going on. "Hold on, Scott." Quieter voices, muffled by a hand, as Drew's father told Ellen their son was hurt. "We're on our way."

"Yes, sir." Scott hung up the phone and went back to Eric.

Eric looked at him, eyes sad and scared. "They're coming? Should I go?"

"Fuck, no. I need you here. You need me. Screw them, if they want to fight now." The very thought made Scott angrier than it should have; rage was starting to build, the need to do something, anything. He paced and got coffee and paced some more. Finally, he saw Ellen coming through the ER doors and went to stand by Eric.

"How is he?" Kenneth said when they got close enough to be heard.

"We don't know anything right now. He's still in surgery," Scott said, wishing he had something to offer them. They looked at one another for a long moment, then Ellen sank into a chair and started to weep. She didn't cry long, just a few seconds, but the tears seemed to release something in each of them and they started to talk.

"He's still alive," Kenneth said, and Scott wondered who exactly he was trying to reassure. He decided it didn't matter.

"Did you see him at all?" Kenneth asked Scott.

"Yeah. And Eric—" Belatedly he realized that Eric and Kenneth had never met, that this was the first time the two men had laid eyes on one another.

Kenneth eyed Eric for a moment. "So, you're Eric." He suddenly sighed and sat next to Ellen. "I…damn. I didn't want to meet you like this. Can we just not deal with the…relationship right now?"

Scott and Eric sat down, tangling their fingers once more. "We don't want to fight. We can't—not right now," Eric said.

The four of them sat in near silence for almost six hours. Every once in a while one of them would go get coffee or something to eat, the food being something to do while they were waiting, a way to keep their hands busy for a few short moments.

Scott saw Dr. Wells before the rest of them did and he stood up.

"Dr. Campbell," Wells said as he came up to them. "Do you want to talk here?"

Scott nodded and sat back down. "This is Kenneth and Ellen Smyth, his parents." He turned to Eric but Wells broke in.

"Aren't you the EMT who brought him in?"

Eric nodded and Ellen gasped.

"Good work." Wells looked at the chart in his hands. "Mr. Smyth has Dr. Campbell listed as his emergency contact and an Eric St Laurent listed as his next of kin." He looked at Eric again, the question in his eyes.

"I'm his partner," Eric said clearly.

Dr. Wells nodded and then blinked, looking at Scott. "I thought you—"

"It's complicated," Scott said mildly. "Point is, how is he?"

Dr. Wells blinked again and shook his head, more to himself, Scott thought, than anything else. He sat down and told them.

"He's still unconscious, but that's not unusual; I wouldn't expect him to be awake for another few hours because of the anesthesia. It appears that when the building fell he landed on his chest and something fell on top of him; his oxygen tank took most of the force, which essentially saved his life. That and the rescue team getting him out of the fire itself.

"He does not have a back injury. He docs, however, have several broken bones—the right femur broke just above the knee, five ribs, the left clavicle—and there was some internal damage due to the ribs. His large intestine was punctured, his right kidney and his bladder were both torn. That was all repaired in surgery, and I don't expect any unusual complications." He paused and Scott nodded, looking at Eric. Eric seemed to be settling into himself; it was easier to deal with when they knew what was going on. Hours of sitting and not knowing, only having images of Drew as he was before he'd gotten help had played hell on all their nerves.

Wells turned to Drew's parents. "There are some minor burns; his clothing was designed to protect him, and in that respect he got off relatively lightly. The left side of his face got superficial burns—treated promptly and correctly, I doubt he'll even have scars. There is a worse patch on his right arm, just above his wrist, where his jacket sleeve was torn; that may require a skin graft—I'm not sure, it's not my area, but I'll have a specialist look at it.

"There's always concern about the lungs in these situations. Smoke can do a great deal of damage, and it may be a few days before we have a clear picture of any damage. He's still on the ventilator, and I won't have him taken off until he's awake. We were worried that the ribs may have punctured a lung, but that wasn't the case, and there's no blood in his lungs, which gives me hope that there is minimal damage from the smoke."

He paused again, then said, "I know this is a lot of information to take in, I'm almost done. You can see him soon."

Ellen shuddered, then sat straighter in her chair. "Go on," she said, her voice shaking only slightly.

"There is some swelling around his brain. Chances are that when he fell, he sustained a concussion, but this is an area we watch very closely. Most likely the swelling will subside on its own as his body rests and starts to heal, but you should be aware that the longer there is pressure on the brain the more likely the chances are that he'll sustain some brain damage. I can't offer you anything more than that right now—it's still very early in the game, and we hope that it will clear up on its own, quickly. If it doesn't, we can talk again."

He stood up, not giving any of them a chance to react. "He's in ICU. You can see him, one at a time, for a few minutes each, but then he'll need to be left for a while. I'll be checking him frequently, and if you have any questions after you've seen him and talked to each other, you can have me paged, or ask Dr. Campbell to hunt me down. If you'll come this way?" He turned on his heel and they all stood, walking behind him.

Kenneth and Ellen held hands. So did Scott and Eric.

Scott and Eric waited in the hall as Drew's parents went in together, breaking Dr. Wells' admonition to only go one at a time. Scott was just as happy. They were only with Drew for about five minutes, and when they came out Ellen was weeping, Kenneth looking as gray as Eric had earlier.

"He's on so many machines," he said quietly.

Scott reached a hand out and gently squeezed the man's arm. Kenneth looked faintly surprised, but he laid his hand on Scott's and squeezed back.

"Go on, 'ric," Scott said. "Go see him."

Eric gave him a look full of love and thanks and went into the hospital room. The others were quiet in the hall, Kenneth's arm around his wife, whispering comfort into her ear. Scott leaned his head back on the wall and closed his eyes.

Eric touched his cheek and Scott opened his eyes to look into his lover's. Blue eyes soft and shiny, more tired than he had ever seen them. But there was hope there, too. "Your turn, Doc."

Scott smiled at him and went in. He knew what to expect, could picture it all just from Wells' words. He wasn't fazed by the monitors or the tubes, the sound of the ventilator breathing for Drew. He didn't mind the way the light played over Drew's damaged skin. What cut him to his heart was the sight of Drew lying straight in the bed, head resting so perfectly on the pillow, the sheets tucked in under his arms.

Drew slept in a sprawl, or draped over him. Never in three years had Scott seen his lover sleeping like this. He sighed and sat down, his fingers tracing Drew's.

"I love you. Need you. Come back to me, Drew."

He sat for his five minutes, listening to the ventilator. When it was time for him to go he said it again. "I love you. Come back, Drew."

None of them wanted to leave; Dr. Wells checked on Drew regularly, giving them updates which consisted mostly of 'no change' or 'he's doing as well as we had expected'. Kenneth and Ellen went to get something to eat after Scott made sure they had his cell phone and he'd promised to call if anything happened while they were gone.

They came back and he sent Eric to get something from the cafeteria. They were allowed periodic visits with Drew, and they each took their turn, coming out looking more and more tired.

Finally, Ellen agreed to go home and sleep for a few hours; Eric had already fallen asleep on a chair.

They had been gone for forty-five minutes when Wells came out of Drew's room and smiled. He said a few words to Scott and walked away, his step light.

Scott grinned. He walked over to Eric and shook him gently. "Hey, you. Wake up."

Eric sat bolt upright. "Is he okay?"

"He will be," Scott said. "Wells says the swelling is down and he should wake up soon."

Eric didn't say anything, just reached up and grabbed Scott, pulling him into his lap and kissing him hard.

Scott kissed him back, hungry and needing the touch of this man, the comfort only a lover could give. They shared their pain and their fear, let all the anxiety bleed out; they shared their love for Drew, and each other, their need for contact and solace. Scott was getting breathless and part of his mind noted that it was a good thing they were sitting down. The intensity would have knocked him off his feet.

"What the fuck?"

Scott pulled away from Eric and looked up into Dave's baffled face.

"Dave," he said. "What—"

"Came to see Drew. He's in there completely fucked up and you two are out here making out? Jesus Christ, Scott. What the fuck is going on? Drew would freak if he knew—"

"No, Dave—"

"Cheating right outside his—"

"Not cheating—"

"And you! Eric—"

"We're all together!" Scott finally shouted. "God!"

Dave stared. "You're what now?"

"The three of us are together. And when the hell did you figure out me and Drew, anyway?"

Dave shook his head. "About three days after you moved in. You two are so not subtle. But, Eric? What the hell is that all about?"

Eric shifted and Scott suddenly realized he was still in his lap. He stood up. "Eric and Drew and I have a three-way relationship. We all love each other."

176

Dave sat down. "Oh." He thought for a moment. "Oh. Since when?"

"Nine months or so," Eric said. "But only 'cause we were all stupid for about five months."

Dave didn't say anything. "So. Drew. He's okay? I'm assuming you were celebrating something. Making out in the hall like that. And please, don't ever let me see any of you do that again. Vicky Lynn wouldn't like it if I came home damaged."

Scott almost laughed. Eric grinned and reached out a hand. They could touch each other in front of Dave now. Or at least hold hands.

"He's going to be okay. He's not awake yet, but he's going to be okay."

Chapter Forty-one

Eric pulled in the driveway and stopped, utterly exhausted. Scott had convinced him that he should go home for a few hours and get some sleep, so he'd taken Scott's car; he still thought he should be at the hospital, but Scott pointed out that they were only five minutes away and he'd been up for almost thirty hours.

Drew hadn't woken up.

Eric sat in the car looking at the house and sighed. The door seemed so far away. He made his way into the house and debated a shower, then sat on the couch and stared at the wall. He ached. His arms, his legs, his back…every part of his body was screaming for rest, but he knew he couldn't sleep yet. Drew was sleeping for them.

Eric noticed the polite knocking on the door just as it became less than polite banging. He stumbled through the kitchen and shook his head; he'd spaced.

"James," he said when he pulled the door open. "Sorry, didn't hear you."

James nodded. "I saw you sitting on the couch through the window, or I would have just turned around—thought you were sleeping or something." He held out a rectangular pan. "Here. Lasagna."

Eric blinked. "What? Why?"

James shrugged. "Mom always told me that when people are going through a hard time they forget to eat because it's too hard to cook. So I cooked."

Eric stared. "Uh, come in?" he said, backing up. His brain started to work again as James stepped into the kitchen. "You didn't have to—I mean, this is really nice of you. Thanks." He took the pan and put it on the counter. "How did you know? About Drew, I mean?"

James leaned on the counter. "Was on the news. When y'all didn't come home I made some calls."

Eric gave him a blank look. "Calls?"

"Oh. Yeah, I guess you and Scott have had a lot on your minds." He flashed Eric a grin. "Not much chance of sharing gossip about the new neighbor. I'm a reporter; I have some contacts at the Citizen. They have contacts at the hospital. Once I knew he wasn't one of the firefighters who were killed, I waited. You still didn't come home, so I assumed he was one of the ones on the critical list."

Eric nodded. "I haven't seen any coverage. How many died?" A flash of pain went through him. He knew firefighters. He didn't want to lose anyone.

"Two firefighters, one office worker." James bit his lip. "Names haven't been released yet, but I know them. If you want."

Eric nodded slowly. "Yeah. I wanna know."

"Joshua Blake and Nicolas Zerr." James was looking at him carefully.

Eric didn't know Joshua Blake well, only that he liked to use his last name exclusively and seemed nice enough. Young. Married a couple of years. Nick, though. Nick had played poker with them once or twice. Lost to Scott. Nick had family, three kids under twelve.

"Shit," Eric said mildly. He didn't really feel anything. "I'm too tired to process, you know?"

James nodded. "How's Drew?"

"Not good. He's out of surgery, but he's still unconscious." Eric tried very hard not to picture Drew in his hospital bed. "He should be awake by now," he whispered.

James looked sympathetic, but remained silent.

"He's just so...still. Drew's never still, he's always going, always talking or teasing or moving. It's just not right, you know? Makes it almost creepy. And I know it was an accident, that he was in there doing his job, that he was helping people—but it makes me mad, too. That someone's mistake, somewhere along the line, could have killed him. That it did kill people. For the first time, I'm pissed off about an accident, and I don't know who to be angry at." He looked up at the ceiling. "I'm just so fucking tired. Scott's still there, I couldn't make him come home, but he could make me. And that pisses me off too."

"At Scott?" James asked quietly.

"No. Yes. Hell. I don't know. I should be at the hospital. I want to be there when he wakes up."

"So go back. Or at least get some sleep. Look, Drew's got someone there when he wakes up, yeah? Scott's gonna need to crash, too, you can take over for him. What about his family?" James's voice was low and soothing.

Eric sat down at the table. "His mom and dad are there and gone and there again. It's rough on them—doesn't help that there's some tension, either. He hasn't really talked to them in months and now he's out of it and they're…worried sick. Which they should be." He paused and bit his lip. "But they've been hurting him since January, and part of me wants to tell them to just back off and we'll call them when he wakes up." He looked up at James and winced. "Fuck, that's twisted, isn't it? I mean, they could have been so upset that they didn't even show—they love him, they just let something that doesn't involve them get in the way, and now they're scared they'll lose him. I should be happy they're there for him now."

"But sometimes it doesn't work that way," James said. "Family is tricky. Mine's a minefield of power plays. I have this one brother you wouldn't believe."

Eric smiled without humor. "Yeah, I bet I would."

James shifted. "Maybe you would at that," he said softly. "Anyway, I'll get out of your way and let you sleep." He moved toward the door. "Let me know how Drew is when you think of it, yeah?"

"Sure," Eric said, standing up. "And thanks. For the food, and for coming by." He shrugged, feeling a little self-conscious. "Maybe when he's awake and I've gotten some sleep I can show you the running paths by the canal. If you want."

James smiled and ducked his head. "Yeah. That'd be great. Call me." He closed the door gently behind himself and Eric stood in the kitchen wondering what exactly had just happened.

He put the pan in the fridge and wrote a note so he wouldn't forget to tell Scott it was there and went to bed. The phone woke him three hours later.

"He's awake, love. Come and see."

Chapter Forty-two

It was dark.

Drew tried to open his eyes but his body rebelled, refusing to do what it was told. He tried to touch his eyelids, but his arms didn't move. It was confusing and vaguely scary. Drew decided he was dreaming and that everything would make sense in the morning.

The next thing he was aware of was pain. His breath hitched, and then air was forced into his lungs and sucked out again. He was cold and alone in the dark. He retreated in foggy confusion, his mind moving back further into the darkness.

A touch on his hand told him he was real.

Drew tried to touch back; wasn't sure if he did or not. Warm fingers on his, gentle, but solid and real. He couldn't feel anything else, couldn't tell if he was naked or dressed or if he was lying down or not. Disorientation made it hard to think. It was easier to sleep.

Light.

Voices. Quiet and soothing, almost like sounds underwater, garbled words came to him. He told his eyes to open and, impossibly, they did.

His mother was looking at him, her eyes sad and tired but going suddenly wide. "Drew? Baby?" Her hand was on his, not the touch he'd felt before. Her skin was too soft, too gentle.

He tried to speak and couldn't, his lungs forced in their rhythm again. He was being killed. Pain, dull and aching in his chest, sharper in his leg and shoulder, throbbing in his head, and still his lungs worked, air pushing in and out.

Darkness slid around him, welcomed him back. Painlessly.

He came back once more, knew that time had passed. The voices were still there, but clear, different.

"You said he was awake." Eric. Tired and sad and scared. Oh, love…

"He was. He will be. The ventilator is out, he's breathing well. He'll wake up soon." Scott. Even more tired. Taking care of 'ric, telling him sweet lies. Lover…

"He was. Really. He saw me, Eric. He'll be back with us, I promise." His mother? Talking to Eric?

Drew opened his eyes, tested his lungs. Both were working, surprisingly. It appeared that he was going to get his body back one part at a time. He hoped his back came to him last—it really hurt.

"Boys?" he whispered. "Mom?"

They were there. Really there. And his father was as well, standing at his mother's shoulder, and no one was fighting, no one was being mean.

"I'm hurt really bad, aren't I?" he asked, his voice rasping in his throat.

"Don't talk," Scott said, fingers playing over his hand. That was the touch he'd felt. His love, with him in the dark. Scott looked him in the eye, his own eyes shining. "God, I love you."

"Love you—" he started, then Eric's fingers were on his lips.

"Don't talk. Bad for your throat. Wait a bit, drink first."

He looked at Eric and stared, tried to tell him with his eyes how much he loved him, how scared all of this was making him. He needed to know what the hell was happening.

Eric's eyes softened. "Love you, too," he whispered. He paused, worry returning to his eyes. "Do you remember what happened?"

Drew tried. Everything was jumbled together, moving someone's boxes and driving to work, playing basketball in the drive, and playing with Eric's...he felt his cheek heat and moved past that, quickly. There was smoke and heat everywhere, and his pager was going off. Nothing made sense. He shook his head.

"Do you remember—?"

"Let's just leave that for now, if we can," a voice interrupted from the door. A doctor came in, looking cool and efficient. "Mr. Smyth, I'm Dr. Wells. I'm going to ask your parents and partner to leave us for a few moments so I can see how you're doing, tell you what's going on with your injuries." The doctor looked at Scott, faintly puzzled, but then continued. "Frankly, I doubt you'll remember much of what I have to say, but I'd like to tell you what you can expect in the next few days."

Drew decided that the doctor seemed nice enough, and that he had an easy smile. His parents stood up, his mom leaning down to kiss his cheek before she moved to the door. Eric kissed him, too, lips gentle and soft, pressing on his for an all too short time. Eric stepped back, Scott was leaning over to kiss him, and Drew could see the doctor's eyebrows climb into his hairline. He could also see his father's smile.

Scott's kiss was familiar and full of love; perfect and warm. He tasted like relief and the crumbled edges of fear. "Love you."

Scott stood up and brushed at his eyes with the back of his hand. "Be in the hall. Not leaving for long."

Eric's hand on his. "We'll be right back. Promise."

They left and the doctor started checking his eyes, his temperature, asking about his level of pain. Then he listed the injuries to his body, the broken bones, the ripped and damaged organs, the stresses the surgery had put on him. They talked about pain, how long it would hurt, when it would fade, and what he could take to make it manageable.

"When can I go home?" Drew asked.

Dr. Wells stood up. "Not until we know for sure that your kidney and bladder are working, and that the risk of infection has passed. We'll be taking out the catheter in a couple of days. For now, though, you just have to rest. And, when you wake up tomorrow and the medication has made this entire conversation fuzzy, we'll talk about it all again." He moved to the door and smiled. "I'll send your family in. Let them be the first to sign your casts before I kick them all out so you—and they—can get some sleep."

He did just that, standing at the door until everyone was back in and issuing orders for everyone to get some sleep. He gave Scott a pointed look, and Drew wondered just how long his lover had been awake. Then he held out a pen and smiled. "So, who's going to sign first? Parents?"

Drew's father reached for the pen and handed it to Scott. "One of the partners, I think."

There was utter silence in the room. Scott took the pen and whispered, "Thank you," before signing the cast on Drew's leg. He passed the pen back, and within moments there were four lines on his thigh. Scott. Dad. Eric. Mom.

He looked at his parents and ignored the doctor, still standing at the door. "This gonna last?" he asked, his voice rasping in his throat.

"Almost lost you by accident. Not going to lose you by choice," his father said. "Can't say I understand it, though. But I do know they love you, and that's enough."

He looked at his mother, pale and tired and looking so old. She looked so sad. "I'm sorry," she said. "I'm just so sorry."

Drew nodded. "And tired. Maybe we can talk about it when we're not so freaked and tired and scared." Drew thought he might be starting to slur his words a little, or maybe his hearing was being messed up. He thought about it for a couple of moments and then remembered to blink.

"Gotta sleep," he said, everyone made motions to touch him again before they left. His mom. His dad. His lovers, who kissed him so well. Then he was alone and could sleep without being cold.

When he woke up it was dark outside the window. He counted it a minor victory that he knew there was a window this time. Dave was there, sitting in a chair, talking quietly to Eric.

Together they told him more about the fire, about Nick and Blake, and who was hurt and who was fine. Dave looked beaten up, like he'd just had the worst day of his life. Eric looked better, like he'd had some sleep.

"Where's Scott?" Drew asked when Dave left.

"Sleeping. And then he has orders to eat. He'll be here soon, though, and then I'll have to go. I have to work midnight tomorrow and I'm still pretty tired. I tried to get more time off, but now that you're out of danger I could only get two days."

Drew nodded. "S'okay, love. You gonna hang out here when you're not working?"

"Couldn't keep me away."

"Gonna smuggle me real food?"

"Already got some really good lasagna all ready to go," Eric said with a grin.

Chapter Forty-three

Eric woke up when Scott came into the bedroom, still damp from his shower. He grinned as Scott crawled up the middle of the bed and slid under the covers; he still made a point of sleeping in the middle, still got into bed the same way. Drew would be home soon, and Scott refused to get used to the empty spot on the mattress.

Eric curled around him, waiting until Scott was pressed along his belly, warm from the heat of his shower. "How's Drew?" He'd go to the hospital himself soon, stay for the evening visiting hours and then as late as he could before the nurses insisted he leave.

"Bored. Horny. Cranky."

"He's...oh." Eric hadn't even thought about sex since the fire, other than in the 'hey it's morning and look what I have to deal with' way. They'd been working or at the hospital, and it just wasn't important. Except now Drew was thinking about it. And Eric was reacting, and Eric had a nice warm Scott right there with him. "How did this...come up in conversation?" He knew he was blushing.

Scott laughed and wiggled, twisting around so they were facing each other. Eric stroked Scott's thigh and kissed him before letting him answer.

"He was asleep when I got there this morning so I went to get a cup of coffee. When I got back to his room he was awake and furious. I asked him what was wrong and he threw the sheets off, said he couldn't even jerk off right with his arm bound up like it is."

"Oh," Eric gasped, the image stark and sharp in his mind. "He can—"

"Oh, yeah. Of course he can. But you know he likes to use both hands. So he was pissed."

"What did you do?"

"Pulled the curtain around the bed and sucked him off."

Eric didn't even say anything, just rolled on top of Scott, their hips grinding, cocks hot and hard together. The sounds of their groans and gasps filled his ears, words of need and hunger; Scott was swearing and clutching him, he was kissing Scott hard, his hips liquid as they moved, desperate for release and each other. He had to touch and squeeze, but as soon as he managed to force a hand between them Scott screamed and came. Eric thrust back, Scott's mouth finding his and carrying him to the edge and pushing him over; he roared and shot and they were messy and perfect and warm and they needed Drew back so very badly.

**

"No." Drew would have had his arms crossed over his chest, Eric thought, but one of them was still strapped up. He was trying to sink into the couch and was the very model of petulance.

"Drew, really—" Scott was using his doctor voice. Not good. Eric eased back another step, closer to the kitchen. Ellen and Kenneth had already fled once they'd seen their boy safely home and had taken in the change of his mood.

"No," Drew repeated. "No fucking way, Scott."

Eric winced. He hated it when they fought, hated the tone of voice, hated his own inner nervous reaction.

Scott tried again. "You need to rest and you need to keep still. I really think the bedroom—"

"I said no. I've been in a bed for damn near two weeks; I'm sick of it. I'll be fine on the couch, and I'll go to bed at night, just like a normal person."

That sounded reasonable to Eric, and when Scott turned pleading blue eyes on him he held up his hands. "Don't drag me into this. I don't want either of you pissed at me, and I'm out of it."

Scott frowned at him. "Major surgery, 'ric. Casts. Taped ribs. Bed."

That sounded reasonable, too. Eric was glad he wasn't fighting.

"Bed is dull," Drew said succinctly.

"We'll put the TV in there," Scott said quickly, then bit his lip. He'd just lost and he knew it. "Damn."

Eric looked at Drew, wondering how he was going to play out the victory. He had a gleam in his eye and Eric sighed softly.

"We've discussed that before, haven't we?" Drew asked. Not waiting for a reply he pushed on. "And why don't we have a TV in the bedroom, Scott?"

Scott mumbled a reply and threw himself into the armchair.

"What was that?" Drew actually sounded gleeful as he settled himself ever further into the couch.

Scott sighed. "Because we all work shifts and the bedroom is for sleeping or sex."

"And I'm not so much with the sex, at the moment, and I can't sleep twenty-four hours a day." Drew was matter-of-fact. "What is the living room for?"

"Living. TV. Sex."

"Now, it has just been proven beyond doubt, by several doctors, that I am indeed alive. So, I'll stay here, thanks. Where I can watch TV, talk to people who come by, give stage directions for the actual sex; in general, live. Besides, it's closer to the kitchen and therefore less of a walk for you all when you have to fetch and carry for me."

Scott looked at Eric, one eyebrow raised. "Fetch and carry? Did you agree to that?"

Eric blushed and looked at the floor. "There might have been some mention of role playing, yeah."

Scott stared. "Role playing?"

Eric blushed harder.

Drew cleared his throat. "Eric loves me," he declared. "He's gonna be my much favored slave boy. There's an opening for a houseboy, if you're interested. I need a body servant, too. I kinda like the idea of sponge baths."

Scott sputtered, but Eric knew it was an act. That was confirmed when Scott finally stood up and asked, "What are the fringe benefits of being your slave, oh master?"

"Well, you get to please me, as often as you like. And you get kisses, and I'll let you fraternize with your fellow slave, whenever you want. Right in front of me would be nice, as long as one of you stays awake long enough to make me a very happy master when you're done. That would earn you extra kisses. And when I get these casts off I'll fuck you through the floor, or the nearest wall, or whatever."

Scott grinned and shook his head. "How come being your slave sounds so much like being your partner?"

"Maybe 'cause you've been my slave for years." Drew's eyes had gone soft, and Eric couldn't stop the smile trying to cross his face. He loved it when they got all gooey and romantic.

Scott crossed the few feet separating them and kissed Drew gently. "Your slave, Master," he said softly. When he reached a hand out behind him Eric took it, easy and natural and right.

Eric joined their kiss, mindful of Drew's shoulder, one hand on Scott's back.

"You both know I'm your slave, too, right?" Drew said, his words starting to slur a little as the pain medication kicked in.

"Yeah," Eric said. "We just don't lord it over you; we're nice that way."

"Idiot," Drew teased, kissing him again. "Now, what shall my first orders be?"

"To let you rest," Scott said firmly.

Drew looked disappointed.

Eric leaned in again. "Have a nap and I'll see what I can do about that sponge bath when you wake up," he offered.

Drew grinned fuzzily at him. "Most favored. Right now, anyway. Love you."

"Love you, too. Sleep."

Drew slept.

Chapter Forty-four

Drew slept a lot, those first couple of weeks, and Eric—in his totally honest moments—was glad. It was good that he was healing, it was good he was resting. And every moment he was asleep was a moment he wasn't utterly miserable.

Dew was not suited to forced inactivity. He was also not suited to being dependant on anyone for anything, let alone basics like getting up, or food and drink. The game of master and slave had soon palled for him and he was most reluctant to actually ask one of them for anything, no matter how much he wanted a glass of juice so he could swallow his pills, or how good one more pillow would feel.

That wasn't to say he was grouchy all the time, or he didn't actually ask for those things; it just grated on him that he had to ask. He was occasionally snappish, almost always withdrawn, and he rarely smiled without making it an effort. If he was in a good mood, just after he woke up or for the twenty lucid moments he had after his meds, he would sometimes play up the master and slave game, which Eric always went along with. It made Drew happy.

Eric discovered that the mood in the house could sometimes be swayed by the judicious application of kisses, space, and the offer of a sponge bath. Usually that would work. If Drew was really in a mood, however, he would accuse Eric of being patronizing, resulting in Eric's retreat to the driveway to shoot hoops or to the phone to see if James wanted to go for a run. When he came back, Drew would always apologize, honestly sorry and upset.

"You don't need to be sorry. It's okay to be upset," Eric said the second time it happened.

Drew shook his head. "I can be upset and resentful of the damn casts, but I don't need to be a prick. It's not okay to hurt you like that, 'ric."

Eric kissed him and let the subject drop. He casually checked the pitcher of juice on the end table, making sure it was at least half-full so Drew wouldn't have to ask for more. When he kissed Drew again, he could feel his smile against his mouth.

"What?"

"Sponge bath?" Drew asked hopefully.

Eric grinned and went to get a cloth and a bowl of hot water.

Drew loved sponge baths. Well, he hated that they were the only way he could get clean, but he certainly loved the way his men gave them. Hot water, soft cloth, naked skin, and to finish off, a hot mouth around him after several minutes of torture by strong teasing fingers and the soft cloth.

Sponge baths were sex. Sponge baths were loving and connecting, and being with his men.

Because of the restrictions of the casts Drew was observing more than he was participating, and he was learning. He was picking up on patterns in their sex lives he hadn't seen before, and he was storing all kinds of information away for later use.

Scott, for all that he was good at it and had a magic mouth, had never really been one for giving blow jobs all that often. He did it, and he liked it, but it was clearly not his favorite thing. Drew had long known that, but now he knew that if Eric was there, and willing, Scott's blow jobs were more enthusiastic if he knew he'd get to fuck Eric hard after Drew had gotten off. Once he'd realized that, Drew would get hard again, fast; anticipation of watching was almost as hot as Scott's mouth on him.

Eric was even more of a bottom than he'd thought. He was happiest if Scott was in him, or Drew was coming down his throat, and he got off on the master/slave play. He'd come hardest sucking Drew off and jerking off, if they were alone. When Scott was there, too, Drew would get Scott's mouth, Scott would get Eric's ass, and Eric would happily swallow him a second time.

Drew also learned that he liked sex a lot more when he could move. Blow jobs were nice, and watching was nice, but he was going to go nuts if he didn't get a chance to move soon.

***

Dave came to visit. He passed on cards and gifts and well wishes, and told Drew about the funerals, and what was being done for Nick Zerr's family. They talked about how long Drew would be off work, and how long workman's compensation would last before he had to go on a disability leave.

"I have three months. The casts come off in two, then physio starts up full force. If I can get the upper body strength back I don't see why I can't go back before the comp runs out," Drew said.

Dave nodded. "That'd be great. You'll have to pass the physical and all, but I'm sure the physio will help." Dave was looking at him oddly, had been since he'd gotten there.

The timer on the end table went off and Drew reached for the pain meds.

"What are you on now?" Dave asked.

"Finished the stuff to keep infection away, so now I'm just on stuff for pain. Tylenol three in the day time, mostly, and Percocet at night."

"Is the pain still bad?"

Drew shrugged. "Yeah. Well, not so much the bones, they were fine after a couple of days. The incisions are sore, but don't get too bad unless I move too much. My back, though...fucking hurts. Scott says it's added stress on the muscles 'cause my gut's all messed up. All I know is that I stayed awake all night when I tried the Tylenol instead of the Percocet—which pissed Scott off beyond belief. You think your doctor lectures you? Try living with one. I'll try again in a day or so, see how it goes."

Dave looked vaguely uncomfortably again.

"What's up?" Drew asked.

"Nothing, really. I just—that is, I know—are you...shit." Dave sighed and leaned back. "Damn it all. I saw Scott and Eric, when you were in the hospital, just before you woke up. They were...well, they were kissing."

Drew stared. "Oh. And what did you do?"

"Cursed Scott out until he shut me up by saying all three of you are together." Dave looked him in the eye. "Are you?"

Drew stared. "You knew about me and Scott?"

"Well, yeah. Just figured that since you never said anything it wasn't any of my business. Figured Scott wasn't out or something."

"He's not, really. I mean, he is, but not at work. Eric, though. He's not. Like, at all. We know, our parents do—though that was an accident—and yeah, we're all together." Drew stopped himself from asking if that was going to be a problem for Dave; he was too tired to fight about it, too tired to care.

"Okay," Dave said, standing up to leave. "I wasn't about to go telling anyone anyway—never said a word about you and Scott and that's been going on for three years. Won't say anything about Eric. Well, except to Vicky Lynn; woman gets damn pissy if I don't fill her on these things. She cares about you guys." He headed toward the door. "That reminds me, she's been cooking up a storm. I'll be bringing a shitload of food by in a couple of days."

Then he was gone and Drew was asleep.

Chapter Forty-five

Drew had always had nightmares. He didn't think you could do the work he did and not have them. When he was in the casts it was hardest, because he couldn't move, couldn't fight his way out, and when he woke up he was in a world of pain.

Before the fire, Scott would be there to calm him, to love him, and Eric would be there to hold him and tell him where he was and that everything was okay. Now they were still there, but when they told him he was okay it was a lie.

He wasn't okay. He was scared and worried and terrified of the next fire and terrified that he wouldn't have another fire to fight. He couldn't go back to work for the fear, and he couldn't not go back because what else would he do?

He loved his job; it was his identity. He fought the heat and smoke and he pulled the people out of wrecked cars and he got the kittens from the trees. He was the adrenaline king. He needed the rush.

The rush had tried to kill him. Maybe next time it would; it certainly would if he kept thinking about it.

He sat in the living room in the middle of the night and tried to brush off the dreams, as if they were smoke. Maybe they were smoke. Maybe it was the dreams that would kill him, like the smoke had tried.

Maybe he thought too much and needed to go back to bed, back to warm bodies that would treat him right and love him. Maybe the dreams weren't strong enough to stand up to that. But maybe they were.

The dreams were getting worse. The ache in his back was getting worse. He could barely stand, for the pain. He reached for the meds and cursed them thoroughly under his breath. They made him sleepy and dozy and stupid, but they let his back rest, let his mind sleep without dreams.

He drank his juice and watched the dawn come in the living room windows. Another night lost to the fire. Another battle lost.

***

Eric turned the steak over on the grill and smiled at Scott, accepting the cold beer bottle. "Thanks."

"Not a problem. How're they coming?" Scott had been hovering for almost two whole minutes before asking, which was a record of some kind. He didn't give up the grilling to anyone very often.

"They're fine. Swear I won't burn 'em," Eric said with a grin and a wink. He looked at James and rolled his eyes. "Can you distract him while when I dump barbeque sauce on them?"

James laughed at the look on Scott's face and said seriously, "Sure. How? Football? Basketball? The recipe for my mom's Apple Crisp?"

Scott glared at them both. "Don't need a distraction, 'cause there is no way in hell that anyone is putting goop on the meat." He looked thoughtful for a moment, then added, "She use cinnamon? In the crisp, I mean?"

Eric threw back his head and laughed.

He felt good. It was a sunny afternoon, the food was good, the beer cold, and they were all relaxed and having a good time. Well, they would be when Drew finally made it outside. He'd slept most of the day away and was in the shower trying to wake up.

As if sensing the direction of his thoughts James moved next to him and asked quietly, "How's Drew?"

Eric watched Scott walk across the yard to toss a soccer ball back to the kids next door. "He's fine," he said. He looked at James and shrugged. "He's…tired a lot. Sleeps all the time, and doesn't talk much. So, I guess he's not so good. But the casts come off tomorrow, and I expect once he can move again he'll feel better."

James nodded. "Not one for sitting still much, is he?"

"Nope," Eric agreed, checking Scott's steak. If any of them was going to get exactly what they wanted it better be Scott. "He really isn't. He's…I think he's frustrated. He can't work, he can't get any exercise, he's bored. It's hard, you know?"

James nodded. "Understandable. You'd be a mess, too, if you couldn't get out and run, yeah? Same thing."

"Yep." Eric turned the steak he'd decided was Drew's. "But, like I said, the casts are off tomorrow and then he's got physio and shit. He'll be happier, I think."

"Anything is better than this," Drew's voice came. "Hey, James."

Eric looked up and smiled as Drew made his way over, hair wet from the shower, one crutch making his walk awkward and ungainly. But at least he was moving.

194

"Drew," James said in greeting. "Tomorrow, huh?"

"Can't get here soon enough," Drew said. "Scott, stop fussing. Lord."

Scott blushed a little and backed off, letting Drew lower himself into a lawn chair. "Sorry."

Drew smiled at him fondly. "Don't be. I shouldn't bitch." He glanced at Eric and grinned. "You gonna feed us today, or you making us wait?"

Eric gave him a threatening look and made sure he got his steak last before they settled down to eat and drink and pass the evening away. July was just getting geared up, warm, but not too hot to sit out, and they stayed out well past dark talking about nothing at all.

James finally stood up, a little wobbly from the beer, and asked Eric if they were going for a run in the morning.

"Sorry, taking Drew in to get the casts off. How about Saturday?"

"Friday's better. Going to be away most weekends this summer—got a friend who has some land in the Valley, doing some camping."

"Cool. I'll call you, then." One of the nice things about running with James was that he worked from home and could pretty much head out when Eric wanted to, fitting it in around his shifts. James nodded and said goodnight to the three of them before heading across the street.

When they went in the house, Drew settled himself on the couch and looked at them hopefully. "Last night like this, boys. Sponge bath?"

Eric laughed and went to get the bowl while Scott took care of the getting naked part. They all wanted the casts gone, but one more sponge bath wasn't necessarily a bad thing.

Chapter Forty-six

Drew rolled over, thankful he could. He'd taken Eric to bed after they'd gotten home from the hospital and hadn't let him leave, not even when Scott got home. The three of them had played and slept and made love again, and now he was awake and pleasantly sore.

Except for where the pain wasn't so pleasant.

He waited in the dark, listening to the sounds of his men sleeping. Their breathing, Eric's soft snores, the little breathy moan Scott made when Eric shifted against him. He could smell smoke and knew it wasn't real. He could hear the snap and pop of wood bursting, and he could feel heat along his skin where the cast had been.

His leg was weak, though they said it would be at full strength before he knew it. His arms hurt from the brief physio workout; or maybe it was from holding himself up above Scott's back, watching as he made love to his partners for the first time in a month and a half.

He was willing to bet his back would be killing him in the morning—Scott had told him to just lie back and relax, but no. He had to do the doing, had to move, had to push too far. He couldn't just lie still anymore; he thought he would rather just sit on the couch and wind up watching again than be passive about it. He felt like he would lose himself if he didn't move.

So he'd moved and loved and made sure they felt as much as he did.

But now they were asleep and he was alone again, time creeping in the dark.

***

He wasn't getting better. A month of physio and moving and getting out of the house and he was still tired, still aching, still withdrawn. A month of doctors poking his bones and checking his scars, a month of X-rays on his back that had shown nothing wrong. A month of forced cheerfulness and bouts of anger that left Drew shaking and Scott retreating, Eric quiet and sad.

"We gotta do something," Scott said when Drew went out to the driveway to shoot baskets. They'd just had a minor blow up over nothing, Scott saying something in the wrong tone of voice, or Drew zoning out of the conversation again—Scott wasn't sure which.

Eric sighed and nodded. "Like what? He's just going to get pissy if we try to get him to do something he doesn't want."

"So we do something he likes. Something stupid and fun, something that can't get misunderstood or taken wrong." Scott suddenly grinned, an idea forming. "Just need one night where it's all about fun."

Eric grinned back. "We got enough popcorn? Enough to eat and throw?"

"Yup. Go get the idiot in. We'll relax him if it kills us."

Scott suspected that if this didn't work he really would have to start planning something more drastic. Drew was slipping out of their reach.

It was surprisingly easy to get Drew in the house; Scott figured shooting baskets was just plain dull on his own and Drew was feeling sheepish enough to be led in and fed, then plied with a hot shower and the promise of all the popcorn he wanted. By nine o'clock they were in the living room, tape in the VCR and roles assigned.

Scott was a little confused. "How can I be both Buttercup and Inigo? Don't they have conversations and stuff?"

"Because Drew can't be Wesley and Inigo. The whole fight at the top of the Cliffs of Insanity? And no one can be Buttercup and Wesley, 'cause that's just masturbation," Eric explained.

"But you're all the bad guys and Fezzik…that's not gonna work."

"Sure it will. Just go with it."

Scott just rolled his eyes and settled back, shrieking when he was supposed to and kissing Wesley for all he was worth whenever he got the chance. The fight at the top of the Cliffs was impressive and Wesley's wresting match with Fezzik was a little more pornographic than Rob Reiner had envisioned, but all in all it was a good time.

It wasn't until Buttercup threw the Man in Black down the hill and Wesley missed his cue that things got weird.

Scott nudged Drew with his knee. "Hey. Wesley. Let Buttercup know it's you, man. Can't have our big reunion scene if I don't know."

"What?" Drew asked, his voice fuzzy. "Oh, right. Sorry. 'As you wish'."

Scott looked at him, taking in the glassy eyes and the way he was sitting, favoring his shoulder a little. "You okay?"

Drew blinked at him and then looked at Eric, biting his lip. "I'm fine. Really. Just tired, I think. Maybe I should go to bed." He stood up and then leaned down again to kiss Scott. "Love you, Doc."

"Love you, too," Scott said. "You sure you're okay?"

"Yeah, just had a bad day. Gonna sleep. You guys watch the movie and maybe move the big orgy into the bedroom later." He offered Scott a leer that was maybe half the strength of his usual, and then kissed Eric goodnight before heading down the hall.

Eric turned off the TV and they looked at each other for a long moment. Scott felt slightly sick, and he desperately needed Eric to tell him he was wrong. Instead Eric opened the drawer in the table next to him and took out the Tylenol bottle.

"No," Scott said. "Not going to."

"Have to," Eric said quietly.

Scott stood up and went to the kitchen, telling himself he wanted a glass of water. He picked up another bottle of Tylenol on the way back though, and handed it to Eric.

Eric set it next to the first one and looked at Scott, his eyes sad. "Where else?" he asked.

Scott didn't say anything for a moment. "Tell me I'm wrong, 'ric," he whispered.

"Sure. You're wrong. I'm wrong. How many more bottles are there?" Eric stood up and started walking through the house. He went to the bathroom and came back with two prescription bottles and another Tylenol bottle. Scott went to the garage and got two more, Eric found another in the kitchen and one in the other table in the living room; the ones that were a surprise were in the spare rooms and the basement.

By the time they had gathered up all the Tylenol they could find, they had fourteen bottles on the coffee table.

Scott picked up the prescription bottles. One was a ten-pill refill for Percocet he had prescribed in the second week after the fire. There were thirteen pills in the bottle. The other was a fifteen-pill prescription; it had eight. The large bottle of Tylenol from the bathroom had Tylenol in it. The other eleven didn't.

Scott counted and separated pills while Eric opened bottles. Fifty-three Percocet, twenty-two Tylenol with codeine and eighteen Percodan.

He looked at Eric and then at the pills, all lined up on the table, neat and tidy. "Fuck," he said mildly. Eric held out his arms, let him fall forward to him.

They sat on the floor, crying.

Chapter Forty-seven

Drew's head felt like it was wrapped in cotton. He kept his breathing as regular as he could as he woke up; he needed a few moments to take stock before he let the guys know he was awake. He wasn't exactly sure when he'd started doing that, but he knew he hadn't when he was in the hospital, or even in the first few weeks home.

His head was better than it had been on some days. He'd occasionally woken up feeling like the cotton had been replaced with wet flannel, his brain foggy and heavy, every motion like he was working through honey. One morning he'd lain there, pretending to be asleep, listening to his lovers whisper and move and make love, unable to react in any way. He hadn't even gotten hard, which scared him more than the cloudy mind fog. He'd backed off on the medication then, waited until his body ached and screamed for it. Twenty-two hours and forty-five minutes.

His head felt okay. Close enough to 'just waking up fog' that Drew could move on. His heartbeat felt regular and strong, not the too fast rhythm he'd had the night before when he'd gone to bed. Drew stretched and groaned softly, ready to let his lovers know that he was awake, one hand reaching down to scratch his belly before drifting lower to his morning erection.

He was happier about the morning wood than his head or his heartbeat, regardless of whether it just meant he had to piss or not. It meant he was still there, and despite the pain and the fear, Drew knew he wanted to live.

He rolled over, looking for Scott and Eric, looking for warm bodies and sleepy kisses. He opened his eyes when his hands met cool sheets.

The other side of the bed was still tucked in, the covers smooth. His men hadn't come to bed at all. He looked at the window to confirm it was actually morning, that he hadn't just napped; the sun was bright, the angle putting the time around eight in the morning.

Drew grabbed a pair of sweatpants and went into the bathroom needing to see himself in the mirror before he went to find his partners. He relieved himself, brushed his teeth, and had the pants on before he realized they were Eric's. He tried to ignore the tight, hard feeling in his stomach. They had never stayed up all night without him before. Even when he was a mess of plaster they'd shared the bed.

He walked down the hall toward the living room. "Guys? Are you okay? What's going on?" He stepped into the living room, the final word almost not making it past his lips. He froze, taking in everything at once, his instincts screaming at him to run, to hide, to deny, deny, deny.

Eric was sitting in the middle of the couch, knees drawn up to his chest, red-rimmed and bloodshot eyes looking up at him, his mouth soft and gentle, but not opening to greet him.

Scott stood at the window, back to the room, hands clasped behind him. His shoulders were square and set, and he didn't turn around.

On the coffee table was a drinking glass holding familiar pills—so many pills. A line of empty Tylenol bottles, each one upside down, taunted him.

A tiny, uninvolved part of Drew's mind noted that if someone had asked him, and if he'd been honest, how many pills he had—if someone had just said, 'Hey Drew, how many Percocet you got kicking around?' he would have said maybe a couple dozen. There had to be close to a hundred pills in the glass. He counted the bottles. They'd missed two—most likely the one in the dresser and the one in his car. Add on another dozen pills then.

No one said anything. Scott turned around.

"It's not—" Drew started to say, fear and fear's bastard child denial kicking into gear. He caught the look in Scott's face and stopped. Resignation, sadness, love. He tried again, even as his body created little aches that would mutate into searing, pill-needing pain.

"I'm not sure what to do," he said, his legs suddenly unable to support his weight. He sat on the floor, looking at the glass of pills.

"It's up to you, Drew. It's your choice. All the choices here are for you to make." Scott sounded calm. Tired, utterly wrung out, but calm. He wasn't demanding truth or apologies for the lies, wasn't yelling or giving Drew any grounds for the anger welling up in him.

"Choices?" he asked. "I don't have choices here. If I had choices I wouldn't be in this..." It was weak and he knew it, but it was a place to start, somewhere to spark a spot of rage so he could let it out. He rubbed a hand over his face and glared at Scott.

Scott gave him a mild look and stood there, not moving at all. Not coming closer. "You can choose to stop," he said. "You can choose to keep going until you move onto something else when these don't work anymore. You can choose to keep using until you die." His voice was still low, but it had a hollow sound to it, an edge that Drew had never heard before.

"Will you leave me?" Drew didn't know the question was there until he'd asked it.

"No," Eric said. He didn't move from the couch, but at least he looked at Drew. "Can't be without you. I don't know how to live without you anymore."

Drew looked at him and saw only the earnest honesty in his face. Eric would stay, no matter what. "Scott?"

There was silence until he looked up, looked right at his lover, his partner of more than three years, the centre of his world.

"I won't watch you destroy yourself."

Drew couldn't breathe. Shards of glass picked at his skin, showing him his world shattering around him, everything splintering in his mind.

Eric said it. "You'd leave us?" His voice was stunned, the look of pain on his face cutting Drew as deeply as anything could.

Scott shook his head. "Not willingly, and not until I've done everything possible to help. But, yes. I'd leave you both rather than stay and watch Drew self-destruct."

Drew's mind shut down. He didn't want to listen to them fight, didn't want to hear Eric trying to make Scott stop threatening them; he didn't want to watch his life explode. He didn't want to see what he'd done to them.

Choices. He'd been trying to avoid choices. He couldn't decide if he wanted juice or water and Scott was trying to make him choose between…what? He had a physical in two weeks for the department. What would he do if they said he couldn't work? He didn't know how to be anything else. What were his choices then?

Not that they were going to let him go back to work with the painkiller cocktail he was on swimming in his blood work. Too many things going on—couldn't work for the pain, couldn't work for the pain killers, and couldn't not work.

Scott was going to leave him.

Drew barely made it to the bathroom before throwing up. He was dimly aware of water running in the tub and arms around his waist, then hot tears on his back. He closed his eyes and started to sob, his body shaking and heaving. He was lifted, held close and surrounded by both of them as they all got in the tub, hot water pounding down on them.

Drew clung to Scott, refusing to give him up even when the water ran cold. Eric finally turned the water off and stripped all three of them of their sodden clothes, speaking softly the entire time, calming. Naked and shivering, Drew allowed them to towel him off and lead him, pliant and drained, to the bed.

He wrapped himself around Scott, wanting Eric to hold him as well but not knowing how to ask. He didn't have to. Eric settled behind him, covering the three of them in blankets before wrapping an arm around Drew's waist and holding Scott's hip.

For now they were still three.

"Will you sleep?" Scott whispered.

"No," Drew said as honestly as he could. "Too scared. I need to know what my options are." He thought for a moment and added, "Medically, I mean." He didn't know if the distinction was needed or not.

There was a pause. "Depends on what you want," Scott said.

Anger flowed again, fed by defensiveness and the shame he'd carried for weeks. "Shit, Scott. You want the whole NA bit? 'Hi, my name's Drew and I'm an addict. My drug of choice is Percocet, but in a pinch I'll take Percodan or anything with codeine.' You need me to say that?"

"No," Scott said softy. "But I think you did. I was referring to how you want to detoxify."

There was a long silence. Drew thought up half a dozen things to say—mean and angry, sad and desperate—and dismissed them. "What do you mean?" he asked, suddenly tired.

"Well, you can do it here at home, which would be rough, or at a hospital," Scott explained. "You can go cold turkey, go on methadone—which you'll then have to come off later, so I don't really advise it—or you can do a rapid detox."

Drew waited.

Scott took a breath and went on, speaking slowly and carefully. "If you do cold turkey here at home, we'll stay with you. At the hospital you can have nurses and monitors." Scott's hands were rubbing Drew's arms, fingers tracing and squeezing.

"You'll be here? To make sure I don't cheat?" Drew pushed a feeling very much like resentment away. They were trying to help, not accuse him of being weak.

"No, to clean you up," Scott said flatly. "Make sure you don't choke when you vomit, wash you, tell you when you're hallucinating..."

Eric flinched behind him, his arm twitching.

"Oh."

"That could last a few hours or a couple of days. Then the cravings will hit; you'll need to see a counselor for a few months, too, to help you deal with the cravings and to get at any underlying issues if there are any."

Drew decided to ignore that for the moment.

"What's rapid detox?" he asked, hoping it was better than puking, sweating and seeing things.

"It's a treatment that's done by putting the patient under general anesthesia and administering an agent that cleans the body of the toxin in a couple of hours. Your body goes through the entire detoxification while you're out—you're on machines and monitors that make sure you're safe when your body rids itself of the drugs. The puking and shit? You still do that, but you're unconscious.

"When you wake up you're clean and you don't get the physical cravings. The whole thing takes less than a day—you go home at the end of the day, actually. The detox is done fast and safe." Scott looked at him seriously. "It's done at a private clinic. There's one out west and one in Toronto—I can make some calls and see where the closest one is, see if there is one here in the city."

Drew blinked. "You're serious? That sounds way better than the other." He waited for the catch.

"It is. You'll still need drug counseling for four to six months after, though."

Drew was starting to see that counseling was a big part of what Scott wanted.

"This isn't covered by Medicare is it?" he asked.

Scott shook his head. "Nope. But don't worry about it—you want to get clean that way we've got it covered. It's less than six thousand dollars, I think. We can swing it."

No, they couldn't.

"You hiding cash on me?" he asked, only half joking.

"No," Eric said. "I am."

Drew turned his head. "'Scuse me?"

Eric blushed. "Well, not really. Paid off my student loan last December and I've been sticking the payment into an account I've had since I was twelve. Never took a dime out, thinking I'd take us

204

all on vacation in the winter, you know? Mexico or something. But I'd rather get you healthy."

Drew started to protest but Eric stopped him with a look.

"You're my partner, Drew. Don't piss me off. What's mine is ours and all that shit, right? If I can pay for this I will, and I don't want to hear anything about it."

Drew just nodded, unable to speak in the face of determination, faith, and love.

"Besides, we have almost enough in savings anyway," Scott put in. "Just have a lean Christmas is all."

"I'll let you two figure out how to pay for it then," he said. Scott's look was serious, his eyes searching, and Drew said, "Bring me back, Scott. Help me feel something."

"I'll make the calls," Scott said. "See how soon we can get you in."

"How do I get through today?" Drew whispered.

Scott's eyes got sad again. "I guess you stay in bed and take a pill."

Drew felt tears well up in his eyes. Scott kissed each eyelid and cleared his throat a couple of times. "Gonna bring you back, lover. We'll make you better, I swear."

"Don't let me get lost," Drew begged, tears flowing freely.

"We won't. Need you too much."

Drew could feel Eric's tears splash on his shoulders.

"Love you so much, Drew."

They curled together, three, and wept.

Chapter Forty-eight

Eric thought there was a good chance he would actually crawl out of his skin. Scott and Drew had been gone for a little less than two hours and he had already vacuumed, cleaned the bathroom, done the dishes, started the laundry, and dusted the living room. He looked around the garage and sighed, not sure where to start. The problem, he decided, was that the garage was tidy. There wasn't any puttering to be done.

He turned on the radio and put the volume as loud as he dared, considering it was only half past eight in the morning, and popped the hood on his car. He stared at the engine and tried to force himself to think about what the next step was. He sighed again and slammed the hood back down. Maybe he should just clean the interior.

He sat in the car for a few minutes and realized he was about to cry again. "Fuck this," he said under his breath. "Just fuck it all to hell and back."

He closed the garage and looked across the street. One of the easiest things about being friends with James was that, working from home, he was pretty flexible about when they could go for a run. Just the thought of moving, the rhythm of going at a steady pace, was enough to send Eric across the road.

"I need to run," he said when James opened the door, dressed in loose slacks and a T-shirt.

James looked at him carefully and Eric wondered if his eyes were still bloodshot, if he looked as bad as he felt.

"Can you run?" James asked.

"Yeah. Need to. Just don't think I can drive."

James nodded and stepped back, inviting him in. "I'll get changed."

They didn't talk on the way to the canal, just drove, and then stretched. Neither of them ran for speed, just distance, but usually James would pull ahead, lost in his own head and going at his own pace. James was just naturally faster, and he would often wind up a few meters ahead, then drop back to meet Eric. Eric had told him once that he didn't mind, that James should just go at his own speed and they'd meet up at the car, but James had shaken his head and kept going the same way, so they ran in a weird stop and start motion that Eric was sure would drive him mad if he were James.

This time James stuck right by him, never going any more than a foot away.

They ran for almost an hour, looping around the paths until Eric slowed to his cool down pace and finally stopped by a picnic table to stretch again. James didn't ask any questions until they were done and sitting.

"You okay?"

Eric shook his head and looked at the ground in front of him. "Not really. Things are…really bad right now." He glanced at James, who was giving him a steady look, just sitting still and quiet. "You ever feel like your life is something you're just observing? Like everyone else is doing the doing and you're just reacting?"

"Used to," James said after a pause. "Used to know what I had to do because it was just the way things were supposed to be. Not so much now."

"I never knew what was supposed to happen. Never really know now. Stuff just…happens to me, and half the time I don't get it unless it's all spelled out for me. Don't know what I even feel unless I sit and think about it." He looked at the ground again and took a breath. "How much have you figured out about the way things are at our house?" he asked quietly.

"Some," James said. "Know that Scott and Drew are together, know you fit in there somewhere, too. I've seen the way you all look at each other, but you don't flirt with them the way they do with each other. Just figured that meant you were shyer than them, or that you weren't in their bed yet."

Eric started and looked at him, feeling his cheeks heat. "Guess we really aren't as discreet as we thought; seems like half the world knows. Yeah, we're together. I'm just not as out as they are. Hell, no one is as out as Drew, unless they're into drag." The thought of Drew cut into him like a knife. "You're not freaked," he observed.

James looked startled for a moment, then smiled a little. "Not going to get upset when I see people happy. It works for you." The smile faded. "Or isn't it? That why you're upset?"

Eric shook his head. "No. Maybe. I don't know. Fuck. It's not really my tale to tell, you know?"

"Isn't it?" James asked. "It's your relationship." He ran a hand through his hair. "Eric, you look like shit, you couldn't even drive yourself here, and now you're talking in circles. Tell me what's got you so twisted. Can't help if I don't know what's wrong."

Eric looked at him and sighed. "Just being here is a help," he said honestly. He sat a little straighter and looked around the park before speaking again. "Drew's gone to Toronto, to a clinic Scott got him into." He met James's eyes. "He's going into detox."

Something very close to anger flared in James's eyes and disappeared again before Eric could figure out exactly what it was and was replaced with sadness and sympathy. "Shit. It's good he's getting help, though. Must be real tough on you and Scott."

Eric nodded. "I'm not so much upset about that—well, yeah, I am. It's this big fucking thing, you know? Drew getting hurt, getting addicted to the pain medication, not being here with us. Him not being able to see that we were there, him not letting us help. It's…like I thought I fit, that I'd found my place, and then he didn't let me do what I was supposed to, he didn't let me help him."

"Maybe he thought it was his job to take care of you. Like he was trying to keep it from hurting you." James looked at him seriously. "And maybe he just didn't know how to ask."

Eric shrugged. "I didn't know. I should have known, I'm trained to see when someone's high. Scott—he's a mess. He was making calls all over the place getting people to look at Drew's back, and all these doctors were just giving 'scripts for more meds."

James just nodded and sat there, letting Eric spill it all out. The sun was warm on his back and Eric looked at the trees, not really noticing them.

"So now he's got this detox thing which means he'll be clean when they get home tomorrow, and then he's got to figure out if he can go back to work now or not. He wasn't sure if he could while he's in drug counseling, and he doesn't want to call Dave and find out. He's ashamed.

"Plus, he has to start dealing with the accident now, has to face what happened. That's where me and Scott messed up, you know? So fucking happy he was alive and home we didn't ever talk about it, didn't try to get him to remember. It's this big monster we just ignore."

Eric sighed and looked at James again. "I'm sorry. I just needed…something."

"You needed to talk to someone who isn't living it," James said. "You and Scott are going through the same shit, and you have to support each other. Me? You can tell me you're pissed and it doesn't matter the way it would if you told them."

"I'm not pissed off," Eric said with surprise.

"Aren't you?"

"Why would I be?" Eric countered.

"Because you feel like Drew didn't trust you enough to lean on you. Because Scott's the doctor and he should have clued in faster. Because you didn't force Drew to talk. Because—"

"Please stop."

James fell silent.

Eric looked at the ground again. "I'm angry because I'm not sure where I stand anymore." He bit his lip for a moment and added, "Scott was going to leave us if Drew didn't get help."

James nodded. "And you were going to stay."

"Can't live without them. Thought Scott needed us. Thought Drew needed us. Now it looks like I'm the only one who needs."

James shook his head. "I think they need, too. But I think they are also really secure in knowing how much you need them. You might have to tell them that you're not as sure about them anymore. 'Cause if you keep thinking like they don't need you the way you have to have them? Won't get any easier."

Eric smiled grimly. "And when do I do that, exactly? Before or after Drew starts dealing with all the other shit? No. They don't need my panic on top of all that."

"Now you're the one not leaning, not trusting," James said softly. "Tell Scott. First chance you get, tell him it really hurt to know he'd leave you. Then listen to what he says." James stood up and stretched his calves again. "This is going to take some talking, Eric. You just gotta start it."

Chapter Forty-nine

"Eric? Are you out here?"

Eric looked up from the workbench as Scott entered the garage and offered him a small smile. "Hey."

"Hey, love." Scott was looking at him carefully, blue eyes searching. Eric tried to make the smile brighter.

Scott didn't seem to buy it, and his voice was hesitant. "Just wondered if you wanted something special for supper. Maybe order Chinese?"

Eric shrugged. "Sure, whatever you want. Is Drew going to be home?"

Scott shook his head. "He's going to his folks again. Just easier, you know?"

Eric nodded as Scott walked toward him. Drew's therapy appointments ended at five and the office was close to his parents' so he often went there before coming home. They had all gone the first few times, but it seemed to be stressful for Drew, who wanted to talk to them about how the appointment had gone but not in front of his parents. The three of them were still a little uncomfortable being at his parents' house and the added stress of the appointments made it more difficult than it had to be.

Scott touched his face and looked into his eyes, smiling a little when Eric nuzzled into his hand. "What's wrong?" Scott asked quietly.

Eric raised an eyebrow.

"I know," Scott said. "What's right? But it's more with you. Something's been eating you for days now. Talk to me."

Eric sighed and stood up. "Let's go in."

Scott followed him into the house and waited until they were sitting in the living room, curled up on the couch. "Eric? What is it?"

Eric looked at him and touched his arm, let his fingers trace Scott's wrist. God, he loved this man so much it scared him sometimes. "I don't know how to talk about it. Really. If I could find the right words I'd be happy to tell you, I just don't know what to say that won't make me look like an insecure idiot."

"Just say it, then. I'll listen and try to hear what you mean— doesn't matter if you don't get it exactly right." Scott's eyes were dark and serious, his forehead drawn and tight. He captured Eric's fingers in his own. "I love you. You can tell me anything."

"Can I? That's just it, Scott," Eric said before he could chicken out. Scott's eyes were already wide and hurt and Eric just wanted to take it all back but he had to keep going. "I thought there was nothing we could do to make you leave. I thought we were...strong and good and right and together. But now—"

"That hasn't changed, Eric," Scott said forcefully. "That's all true. I love you."

Eric shook his head and forced himself to keep going. "I know you love me. But now I know that there are things you won't stand for and I don't know what they are. Suddenly, I know there are things that could make you leave, and what if I do something by mistake that makes you go?" He knew he was starting to sound panicked and desperate, but he couldn't keep the note of near hysteria out of his voice. "How do I know what will do it? How can I stop—?"

"Eric," Scott said, his voice loud enough to overpower Eric's. "Listen to me. There is nothing you can do that will make me—"

"Drew did. Drew. And if he could shake you, I could."

Scott shook his head again and squeezed Eric's hand a little tighter. "I wasn't going to leave Drew because of the pills. I wasn't going to leave him because of his addiction. The only thing that could have made me go would have been his outright refusal to fight for his life. You know he hasn't been himself since the accident, and if he was going to give up and not live...I'm not strong enough to stay."

"But you would have left me, too. Because I would have had to stay. I can't leave him, Scott. Not ever. And I won't ever leave you. If you'd have left...it would have broken me."

"Oh, love," Scott breathed. "I never meant to hurt you."

"I know that. I do. But it scares me, and I don't know how to make it stop," Eric said, his voice hollow in his own ears. "What if I do something—?"

"There isn't anything you can do, Eric. Nothing about you will make me go." Scott shifted his weight on the couch so he was facing Eric. "Drew—he would never have chosen what he was doing, wouldn't have chosen that half-life. It isn't a part of who he is. He wound up in circumstances that made it hard for him, and he needed something to pull him back. I think us finding all those pills woke him up, not me. He asked what I would do, Eric, I didn't threaten him. I just didn't lie."

"But—"

"Hush, I'm not done. There is nothing about your personality that will let you do the things that would drive me away. It isn't in you to be abusive, it isn't in you to hurt with your words or your hands. It isn't in you to lie to me, or to steal, or to kill, or to drink too much all the time, or to gamble all our money away. You're a good man, and all I can do is love you. Can't ever leave you, I promise."

Eric looked at Scott and tried to see into his head, into his heart. Blue eyes met his, tense and worried, but still full of love, a warm hand in his. Scott's legs twisted around one of his own. He wanted so badly to believe him and just let go of the fear.

Scott moved closer to him, pushing up against him. "Eric, I love you."

Eric wrapped his arms around him and pulled him even closer. "You're trembling," he whispered. "Why?"

"I'm scared, too. Scared I hurt you. Scared you won't..." Scott tilted his head and looked at him again. "Let me...let me make love to you?"

"Oh," Eric gasped. "Oh, God. Yes."

Scott kissed him, his mouth soft and sweet, melting away tension with just a touch. Hands caressing his face, his neck, fingers tracing his cheekbones and pushing through his hair. "Love you," Scott whispered. "Love your skin, the way you taste." Scott kissed a path to his neck and up to his ear. "I love the way you listen to me after a long day."

"Oh..." Words were gone, all Eric could do was put himself in Scott's hands, let him do as he wanted.

Hands pushed his shirt up and off, Scott's weight easing him back onto the couch. Eric couldn't catch his breath, lost already in the feeling of his lover's heat on his skin. Scott's mouth on his chest, tongue teasing at his nipples, hands pushing his arms up over his head.

"Love the way you move. Love your strength, love how you work to look this beautiful. Love the way you feel against me at night."

Scott moved back up him and took a kiss, long and slow, stealing Eric's breath and the helpless sounds he couldn't help making. Scott felt solid and real on him, soft sweatshirt teasing his skin, faded jeans rubbing on Eric's bare legs below his cutoffs. He could feel Scott's erection pressing along his hip and he might have growled.

"Love your hunger," Scott whispered into his mouth. "Love your touch, love your kisses, love your hands."

Eric pushed up with his hips.

Scott shifted, pulling off his own shirt. "Love the way you feel around me. Love the way I can count on you for anything. Love the way you can stand to be in the kitchen with me when I'm cooking."

Scott pulled Eric's shorts down and off and stood up, popping the buttons on his own jeans.

"Love the way you watch movies. Love the way you read the paper."

The words never stopped. Not when Scott was kissing him, not when he was stretching him, slick fingers making Eric moan and twist, making him arch his back and feel so good. Not when he was pushing into Eric's body and thrusting deep, one hand on Eric's shaft, stroking slowly.

"Love the way you work on your car. Love that you are the gentlest man I know, and I love the way you touch me. Never knew what gentle was until I felt your hands on me for the first time."

Scott held his eyes, made love to him with his words and his expressions, and drove Eric higher and further than ever before. He couldn't breath, couldn't look away. "I love you, Eric. And I always will."

Scott thrust deeper and kissed him, tongue and cock and hand pushing Eric closer and closer to orgasm, making his toes tingle and his back arch as he tried to get more, tried to have it all and not let any of it stop.

Scott's mouth slid from his own, down his neck to his shoulder. Teeth scraped at the skin and Scott groaned into his neck. "Eric. Need you. With me, with us, in my soul. Mine."

Eric froze, everything growing dim as he came, hands pulling Scott even further into him, a sharp cry echoing in the room. Scott pushed into him again and again as he came before shuddering in his arms and collapsing on top of him, spent.

"Oh, God," Scott gasped. "Oh, sweet mother of…Shit, I love you."

"I know," Eric whispered. "I believe you."

They were quiet for a few moments while they tried to get their breath back.

"Scott?"

"Hmm?"

"Think maybe we can make love to Drew when he gets home?"

Scott laughed and kissed him and Eric could see nothing but love and happiness in his eyes. "Yeah, I think we can do that. But I think we need a shower first, and Chinese food, and if he's taking a long time to get home maybe we can start without him, yeah?"

Eric grinned at him. "Yeah." He grew serious again and kissed Scott gently. "I love you. No one's ever said those things to me before. Thank you."

"They're all true. I'm glad I told you, and I'll tell you again. And again. And again." Scott's smile was warm, his eyes gentle. "Not ever going to leave you."

"Good. 'Cause I won't let you go."

Chapter Fifty

Drew was getting frustrated with counseling. They had talked about why he'd started taking the pills, which was obvious enough, and they'd talked about why he didn't stop. He'd managed to focus on the physical reasons, and had a sneaking suspicion that he'd be delving past that before long. He didn't really want to, but it was sort of the point, wasn't it?

Weeks after he'd done the detox, and all he'd really gotten out of the therapy were a few tips on how to calm himself when he started to feel like reaching for the bottle of pills that wasn't there anymore.

They had agreed on all the obvious things about him: he was an adrenaline junkie; he loved his job; he was naturally inclined to do something that others could see as dangerous if the rewards were great enough.

"What is your reward as a firefighter?" she asked.

Drew thought about it. "Aside from helping people? That's why I do it, I want to help. I pull people out, I save their homes, I go to car accidents and places where I'm needed, and I do what has to be done to help."

"But what is the immediate reward for you? How do you feel when the wrecked car is towed away and the victim is fine? How do you feel when you leave a fire scene and the people are alive and the building is intact? How do you feel when you're in a burning building, trying to save it?"

"I don't feel," Drew said. "Well, I do, of course, but it's...it's like I'm on autopilot when I'm in a fire. Everything is training and instinct. When we're done and I go home I'm either flat out exhausted or so full of energy my lover runs away in fear."

That got him a slight smile. "Can you see yourself doing something else connected to fires? If you can't go back to work, can you see yourself maybe investigating fires? Or working to train others?"

Drew shook his head slowly, trying to honestly consider the question. "No," he said finally. "I don't think I could. I need something in the thick of it. I need to be doing. I need the...well, frankly, the high. There's nothing like it."

She simply nodded.

***

She was sitting at her desk when he went in, but stood and moved to a chair near his when he sat down.

"Drew, I think we should talk about the fire."

He shrugged. "Sure. Not much to say about it, though, I can't remember what happened."

She nodded and waited. She did that a lot.

"The doctor's said that when I was knocked out the moments just before never made it into my short-term memory, and therefore aren't in my long-term memory. Even under hypnosis there wouldn't be anything—it's just not there."

"Okay. Tell me what you do remember and we'll go from there."

Drew closed his eyes for a moment, letting the heat and the smoke come to him. "I remember going in, I remember checking a large room for people. I know we got the room cleared and were told to get out. That's all."

"Have you talked to the others about it? Asked them what they remember?"

"Fuck, no." Drew couldn't even fathom the idea. "Look, two men died in there with us. Me and Talbot and McKinnley wound up unconscious and in the hospital. No one remembers anything."

She seemed unfazed. "What should have happened? Is there a procedure or something?"

Drew settled back, a little rattled. He would never talk to the others about it. The very thought of making any of them talk about it hurt too much. "Um, yeah," he said finally. "We should have been together, walking out as a unit. Same places, same faces. Sometimes, if the smoke was really thick, we'd actually be tied together so no one could get lost."

She leaned forward in her chair. "What was the formation?"

"McKinnley and Blake in front, then Talbot behind McKinnley, me, and Nick on my right."

"So the two men who died were on your right, one beside you, one just in front?"

"Yeah."

"What do you think about that?"

Drew stared at her. "What? I feel like—"

"No. Just picture it. What do you think?"

Drew's stomach knotted. He didn't want to think about it. She looked at him calmly and waited. "I don't—"

"Drew, there's something there. If you were all in proper formation..." She waited.

"I should have saved him," Drew finally whispered. "It was right next to me and I didn't save Nicky."

There was silence for a long moment.

"What if I do it again?" he asked, staring at the floor. "Or don't do it? What if, for whatever reason, I didn't see it coming and three kids lost their dad because of me?"

"Maybe he saw it coming and saved you."

"He shouldn't have. I mean, look at it. A married father of three, and me. Those kids need their father and I'm here, so fucked up I'm in drug counseling."

"You think his life was worth more than yours?"

"No. Not really." Drew sighed. "It's just not fair, you know? I got...I've got two men who would have been devastated if I'd died. But they would still have each other, still be able to go on. Nick, he had three babies. Kids that lost their daddy because I fucked up."

"Do you really think it's your fault?"

"Maybe. I don't know, I don't remember. For all I know, Nick and Blake never had a chance. But the point is, I don't know. How am I supposed to go back to work and trust that I won't get someone else killed? How do I know I can trust my instincts again?"

"You're taking too much onto yourself with too little information," she said gently. "It's possible that you missed something, yes. But it is just as likely that you saw something that saved yourself and the other two survivors. Or perhaps one of the men who died saw something that saved three men, even though he himself died." She sat straighter in her chair. "You all had the same training. You were all prepared for certain things. You know accidents happen. If you weren't in that building, if you had been outside, would you blame any of the survivors for the deaths of those two men?"

Drew shook his head. "But I was. And if I clear the physical, I will be again. What if I fuck up and more people die? Can I risk that?"

"Do you really think that's likely?"

Drew didn't answer.

"Drew, your training is a part of you, yes? Have you ever weighed the value of your life against someone else's? Have you ever had to choose between saving one person over another, or not tried to save someone instead of yourself?"

"No," Drew whispered. "I can't do that. I go in, I get people."

"And so do your co-workers. If Nick or Blake did something that saved you three they did it because they had to. And you didn't not do something to save yourself over them. It isn't fair that they died, no. But it happens. If you could have done something, you would have." She paused, waiting for him to meet her eye. "Therefore, there was nothing you could have done. It was an accident."

Drew looked at her and nodded slowly. "Maybe."

Chapter Fifty-one

"So, when are you coming back?" Dave asked.

"Soon." They were walking in the backyard, the grass more brown than green in the late summer heat.

"Need to know, Drew. I got new guys on the team, paperwork to fill out. Your leave ended, you took vacation time; if you're not careful you'll be using your sick days soon."

Drew stopped walking and turned to face him. "I need some information."

"About what?"

Drew took a breath. "What's the department policy on treatment for substance abuse?"

Dave stared. "Shit, man. Do you have any idea how many guys are in AA? Is that what's been keeping you out?"

Drew shook his head. "Not booze. Painkillers. And no, not really. The therapy…fuck. Made me think about a lot of shit. About the accident, about whether I can do the job." He started walking again, one hand slapping against his thigh. "It's just so screwed up. I got hurt, I took the pills. My back hurt, I took the pills. I had nightmares, I took the pills. Next thing I know Scott's taking me to Toronto and I come home clean, my back doesn't hurt, and the nightmares are unbelievably bad.

"Then I go to drug counseling, which is so not fun. Boring as fuck until she starts me talking about the fire. Then suddenly I'm thinking I can't do it anymore. I can't risk anyone else dying."

Dave looked at him, confused. "So, you're not coming back?"

"No, I am. Just took me some time to work it through."

"But you're cool now? I mean, you're not carrying around a load of guilt?"

"Not anymore. Regret. Fear. Worry. But the guilt is back to its proper proportion, I think."

"How'd you manage that?" Dave sounded curious and more than a little relieved.

"My boys. Talking and crying and fucking—sorry—and more talking. Listening. They were determined to make me see things right." They had been, too. Long nights spent in bed, talking until he was hoarse and letting Eric and Scott talk to him. Letting them tell him how they felt, letting him know what was okay to feel and when he was holding too tightly to the guilt. The three of them in tears, talking about how scared they were of what had happened, of what was going to happen. Long nights loving and reassuring.

He looked at Dave carefully. "Not sure how cool you are about us, and I'm not gonna fight about it. But I can tell you that those two are the most stubborn men on the planet and they made sure I got my head back on straight. You want me back on the job, I need two more weeks. Gotta take them out of here, get out of the house, the city. Then I'll be back."

"Two weeks?"

"Two weeks."

"See you then."

***

Smoke.

There was smoke everywhere. Thick and dark, and he couldn't breathe. Where was his mask? Dave tapped him on the shoulder and handed him an axe. "Get the door."

He walked to the door, smoke parting around him, light from the fire filtering through. The red Exit sign was flickering, and he raised his axe to break the door open. "It'll let the fire in," he said to Nick. "Can't do it."

"Have to, man. Gotta let it burn itself out. Purify."

Drew looked at him, tears streaking his cheeks. "Sorry."

Blake looked back at him and shook his head. "Just get out of here. Get out of hell while you can."

Drew raised the axe again, noting it had become a shovel, and started to dig. The ground was soft and he dug for a long time, the smoke filling the hole. When the hole was full of smoke he buried it and opened the door, walking out into the fire station. Dave and Mallory were sitting at a table playing poker, betting to win the new guy.

He walked over to the new guy and kissed him hard, fucking that perfect mouth with his tongue. He got hard and Eric's hand was on him, pulling him off, then Scott's mouth sucked him in and he thrust wildly, shooting down his throat.

He woke up with sticky sheets, his pillow wet from his tears.

Drew stripped the bed and threw the sheets in the laundry before checking the whiteboard in the kitchen. Scott would be off in less than an hour after working all night, and Eric was due home in two, for which he was extremely grateful. He knew he wouldn't get back to sleep.

The nightmares were happening much less frequently as time went on, but even now, months after the fire, he was getting them a few times a month. Usually he could push the aftereffects of the dreams away by curling up with a warm body next to him. Scott would hold him and brush the hair off his forehead, whispering comfort, and Eric would cradle him against that long body and pet his skin until he was relaxed and calm.

But this time he was alone in the house and he didn't want to think about the dream. He didn't want to smell the smoke, or see Nick and Blake; he did pause long enough to wonder what the hell the bit with the new guy—Bill? Will?—was, but that led him to thinking about Eric and Scott and they weren't home. He looked around the kitchen and wondered how he was going to keep himself too busy to think until his men were home.

He needed a challenge. He needed something that would test him, something complicated.

He needed to cook.

Yeah, that was it. When his boys got home they'd find the perfect breakfast waiting for them, something a little more complex than takeout coffee and doughnuts.

Drew got out the coffee beans and the new grinder. Start small. He'd tried grinding the beans earlier in the week and it hadn't gone well. He'd taken that as a personal affront—he was the coffee guy, and no damn machine was going to defeat him. He got the coffee going, pretty sure he had the water to grounds ratio right this time, and set the timer on the coffee maker. Sure that the coffee was taken care of, he pulled open the fridge door to see what he had to work with.

Eggs, cheese, tomatoes, mushrooms, onions, leftover potatoes. Good, he could manage with that. Omelets and hash browns. What could go wrong?

He was just scraping burned goop made up of mushrooms and onions into the garbage when the coffee maker turned on, about an hour and a half early. He snarled at the machine as he stopped it— he damn well knew how to set it, so the fault had to be in the wiring—and finished trashing whatever it was he was attempting to cook. He filled the sink with soap and hot water, needing to do dishes already.

The second attempt at omelets turned into scrambled eggs, but he could live with that; at least they were interesting eggs, with mushrooms and fresh tomatoes. He added some parsley and real parmesan cheese and the phone rang. He let the voice mail take the call as he watched the parsley sizzle and turn black.

When the pan was clean he started the coffee maker again. He needed it.

Mug in hand, he checked the message; Scott had been held up and would come home with Eric. Thank God.

The hash browns were perfect. Onion, non-burned parsley, and potatoes, fried without a singe; onto a plate and into the oven to keep warm.

He had another cup of coffee while he contemplated the eggs again and started toast. He added golden, lightly buttered toast to the stack in the oven, slice by slice, until there was about half a loaf of the stuff. Toast he could do.

He thought that maybe the boys wouldn't want caffeine just before going to sleep so he poured the rest of the pot into a carafe and ground decaf beans and started the coffee maker again. They could choose. He was such a good partner.

Even if eggs did defeat him.

He chopped mushrooms and decided against the parsley. He looked closely at the bulb of garlic in the fridge, and figured that not enough wasn't worth the effort of smushing it, and too much was entirely possible. He passed it over and cut up more tomato, then sautéed the mushrooms. Added eggs. Stirred. When the eggs were almost all the way cooked he added tomatoes and checked the coffee pot. Good. Things were good.

He glanced at the clock as he finished the eggs and tossed on some cheese. Where the hell had the time gone? He looked at the sink and blinked. Oh, yeah. There.

He put the eggs in the oven and set the table, then started laying out the food when he heard the garage door open. Perfect. Just fucking perfect. He patted himself on the back and muttered, "I rock. I really, really do."

The kitchen door opened and Scott came in, talking over his shoulder to Eric. "...but not like that, you know? Then it was just done."

"Yeah, I saw—holy shit." Eric froze, paper cup of take-out coffee halfway to his mouth, box of doughnuts in hand. "What the hell happened to Drew and who are you?"

Drew beamed.

Scott whistled and took Eric's coffee from him, setting it in the sink. "You've been busy," he said, pulling out a chair.

"It's nothing," Drew said.

Eric just snorted and kissed him. "You rock."

"I was just telling myself that. Eat, before it gets cold. Decaf or regular?"

Scott looked up at him. "You didn't…grind the beans, did you?"

"Well, yeah." He tried not to sound offended. "And I drank some. It's fine."

"Okay," Scott looked at him carefully. "Regular?" He didn't sound too sure, but he was heaping his plate with food, which meant he had some faith. Or he was really hungry.

Eric kissed him again. Eric was quickly becoming his favorite partner.

Scott tried the coffee and smiled at him. "Good. Really good. And the eggs are wonderful."

"You're inching your way back up to co-favorite," Drew allowed. "But if Eric keeps kissing me you'll have to pull out the big guns."

Scott leered. "I can do that."

Drew told himself that the weak feeling in his knees was because he was hungry and sat down.

Breakfast passed in a very short time considering how long it took to cook. Drew wondered how Scott stood that, seeing hours of work disappear in a few minutes. It was easier to order out. But then, takeout never got happy satisfied smiles like the ones his boys were giving him now.

Scott leaned back in his chair and stretched. "That was great, Drew, thank you. How long have you been up?" The question was casual, easy, but Drew had decided long ago to stop hiding shit from them.

"Couple hours," he said, gathering up the dishes and taking them to the sink. "Had a nightmare."

They didn't say anything, but before he could turn around Eric was behind him, hard body pressed into his back and strong arms around him. He sometimes forgot how big Eric was, the gentleness of the man making it easy to dismiss his size. Not now, though. Tall and broad and hard, huge biceps around him, making him feel safe. Warm.

Scott was standing in front of him, a little shorter, blue eyes full of concern. Drew got a flash of a mental image, the three of them lined up like steps, and it seemed so silly. Then Scott was kissing him, mouth sweet and gentle, hands on his waist.

Eric made a soft noise almost like a purr. "Love it when you do that, Doc," he whispered, his mouth next to Drew's ear.

"Do what?" Scott asked into Drew's mouth, the words slightly garbled by the kiss.

"Start. Kiss first. Anything. Gets me hot," Eric said, his voice getting husky. Drew had to agree. He also had to agree that it made Eric hot; he could feel the evidence of that in the small of his back.

Scott pulled away and raised an eyebrow. "Really?"

Drew grinned. "Oh, yeah." He slid a hand around Scott's waist and tugged him closer so he could rub on him. "See?"

Scott flushed a little and bit his lip. Drew waited, watching him think.

"Okay," Scott said decisively, a little tremor in his voice, but not much of one. "Bed. I wanna watch Eric fuck you." Then he turned around and walked down the hall, pulling his shirt off.

"Oh, Jesus." Drew wasn't sure which of them said it, but the reaction was the same. His hips jerked and he felt Eric pushing into him, the big arms tightening.

They headed down the hall as fast as they could and ploughed into Scott who had stopped inside the bedroom door.

"Where's the sheets?" Scott asked, sounding a little breathless and a lot confused.

Drew undid Scott's pants. "Washing machine. Had to change 'em, from the dream."

Eric's hands were busy too as the big man stripped and went to work on Drew's clothes. "From a nightmare?"

"It ended on a happy note, sort of," Drew said, then Eric's hand was stroking him. He leaned back into him and added, "Sort of like this, actually."

Scott finished stripping them both and pressed into him. "Yeah? What else?"

Eric's fingers were making lightning race up and down his spine, making his balls tight; making it hard to think. "Your mouth," he managed, not sure if the words were clear between the gasp and the moan. Fuck, but Eric was good at this. Then there was heat and wet and he guessed the words were clear enough because

Scott was going down on him like it really was his favorite thing to do, even though it wasn't.

But maybe making Drew happy was.

Drew soared, coming fast and loud, spilling into Scott's mouth and throat and riding Eric's fingers, not sure when they'd even slid into his ass.

Scott gave him just enough time to come down a little and then he was up, kissing him hard, sharing the salt and bitter flavor of his own passion. Drew's knees were weak, Eric's arm around his waist the only thing keeping him standing, and then that disappeared, shoving him down so he was bent at the waist, hands braced on the foot of the bed.

"One of these days," Scott whispered into his ear, "I'm gonna tie you there."

Drew swore, fingers gripping the edge of the mattress. Scott was getting the hang of surprising him.

Eric moaned behind him and he listened to the soft sucking noises. Scott was really on, hot and horny and not too afraid to show it, and Eric was loving it. Scott shifted and appeared in front of him, kneeling on the bed. "Couldn't find the lube," he said. "But I didn't really look either. Do him, 'ric."

"Oh, God." Eric was stretching him, pushing in, filling him, Scott's spit the only thing keeping him from being fucked dry. A long slow push, smooth and deep and fucking perfect.

Scott's eyes were glazed, his hand on his own cock, pulling slowly as Eric fucked him, fingers gripping his hips. He could hear Eric, words so soft they were lost, but the tone and warmth and love rolling over him in waves. He looked at Scott, saw love and need and the start of desperation.

And there was a beautiful cock being jacked right in front of him.

"Doc—" He opened his mouth and Scott groaned, long and low, and moved closer.

Drew sucked him in, nice and deep. He couldn't remember the last time he'd felt so alive, so full. Eric was pounding into him, nailing his gland on every third stroke or so, Scott's moans filling his ears as he tasted him, drew the sharp earthy flavor of him out.

Perfect.

Right.

Eric's thrusts grew ragged. "Gonna come, Doc," he said roughly. "Soon, Scott—oh, fuck, soon."

That was all Scott needed, and the cock in his mouth went as deep as the one in his ass, both of them working together, driving him, Eric's hand wrapped around him, pulling hard and Scott shifted, leaning up to kiss 'ric.

Drew groaned, sending vibrations along Scott's prick. Scott groaned into his kiss with Eric. Eric groaned and thrust again, then froze, cock twitching as he shot.

"Oh, shit, yeah—" Scott came too, right after Eric, both of them filling him with their seed.

Drew flew, shudders wracking his body. Eric had to hold him up again as his knees gave out.

Scott pulled him onto the bed, then Eric settled behind him, the three of them all riding aftershocks together, gasping and trying to catch their breath.

Nightmares be damned. This was the stuff dreams were made of.

End.

Printed in the United States
88106LV00005B/87/A